Ma'tao

"Rise Of A Chieftain"

Book 2

"Maga'lahi"

by

Myk Steel

ISBN: 978-1-7334956-8-4

Dedication

I dedicate this to the two who gave me life, my dad and mom. Michael and Betty.

For both your endearing love and support to make this all possible. I would not have it any other way! Love you both.

Introduction

The tides are changing! In this beautiful, mysterious, and at times unforgiving area of the world. The mysterious Pacific ocean may separate this island nation, yet it draws them together as a people! Too many generations have passed with the hopes of one day uniting the islands, the Islands of the Chamoru people.

One man! One man who stepped into his destiny! From Ulitao to Maga'lahi. Now a proud Chamoru Chieftain. Has the opportunity at hand to do just that! His name, his name is Ma'tao with his ever so loyal band of warriors. Consisting of Atdao, once bitter rivals now turned allies, with extraordinary navigational abilities. His twin sister Atani, Ma'tao's love, is one of the most fierce warriors in this part of the world. Aligao, Ma'tao's childhood best friend, is practically tied to the hip as soon as they first met. Da'on, a bold, audacious leader warrior in his own right. Ina, Atdao's love, and headstrong warrior herself.

Along with Pulonon, though still in Anatahan is a wise voice of reason, mentor, and compatriot. Together they bring hope and a new beginning to Guahan, their islands, and all its people!

By battling and exposing the dark forces of evil, and their leader Asuli, who will not stop at anything to keep Ma'tao and his band of warriors from achieving their goal!

So as we pick up after the battle with Haluu and acquiring his Ka'lang I Man Metgot. Ma'tao gathers his warriors as they agree to head back to Guahan, destination the village of Chochogo' to claim his birthright. But first, a quick stopover at the great village of Fu'a to meet up with Maga-'lahi Dadau. To share a calling to get more answers!

What does his destiny as Maga'lahi have in store for him? Will he be a blessing to all his people? Will all the powers that he now possesses be able to triumph over all the forces of Asuli and his evil ways? One could only hope! As the stakes have now risen. Ma'tao instantly has more directly placed on his shoulders. For once an Ulitao, to now a Maga'lahi. Only time will tell as the adventure awaits!

Table Of Contents

Chapter 1 "Arrival Of A Maga'lahi!!"……..1

Chapter 2 "An Unexpected Encounter!"….47

Chapter 3 "New Face New Lead!"………..83

Chapter 4 "Onward to Chochogo'!"…….103

Chapter 5 "Insights of Truths!"…………123

Chapter 6 "The Homecoming!"…………149

Chapter 7 "A Long Awaited Reunion!"….187

Chapter 8 "Man and Beast!"…………….209

Chapter 9 "Onward to the Swamp!"…….229

Chapter 10 "An Informed Visitation!"…..249

Chapter 11 "The Forbidden Swamp!"…277

Chapter 12 "Peace Amidst the Chaos!"..307

Chapter 13 "To the Heart!"………… 353

Chapter 14 "Through the Heart!"…… 399

Chapter 15 "Tomhom!"………………465

Chapter 16 "To the Lair!"…………… 505

Chapter 17 "Itak!"……………………525

Chapter 18 "The Reveal!"…………… 577

Chapter 1

"Arrival Of A Maga'lahi!"

Ma'tao and his warriors, who are now heading towards Guahan, find the cool early morning breeze on the ocean still mesmerizing. It is something that he knows could never get old. In those early morning hours, he realizes that he could center himself and get deep in his thoughts to find the answers to those difficult questions. And this is one of those days.

As he closes his eyes and focuses on his breaths, he feels the Sakman gliding effortlessly through the water. He thinks to himself, *With this Ka'lang, will my grandfather accept and understand what I had to do? Will he be proud to know that I did it for Ati, Guahan, and all our people? Will my father's family welcome me with open arms as their Maga'lahi?*

As he ponders on those thoughts, Atani sneaks up behind him and tickles the sides of his belly. He surprisingly opens his eyes as she asks, "What is it that you're thinking? What's on your mind now?"

Ma'tao points over the horizon towards the hazy gray image of Guahan in the distance and says, "We should be passing Ati right about now. With all that we have accomplished and been through so far, I wonder, with everything that we heard going on, will my grandfather accept what I had to do?"

Atani looks out to Ati and sincerely says, "Honestly, I want so much to tell you that he'll understand. But I don't know for sure, and I wouldn't want you to be disappointed if he didn't. One thing you can count on is that I and everyone on this Sakman do understand what you did, along with why you did it! And I will gladly do it again."

Atani grabs Ma'tao closer to her saying, "Besides, you promised me a better life alongside you In Chochogo' and I'm holding you to that promise!" They both chuckled, then Atani continues saying, "Trust me, I know how you exactly feel. I also hope that we could reach my grandfather in time. Because if he is still wearing that pendant from Asuli, the longer he has it on, the darker his soul becomes."

Ma'tao looks back out over the ocean towards Guahan and says, with a sense of urgency, "I hear you. The more Maga'lahi that Asuli gets under his control, the closer we will be to all-out war! I promise you, my love, that I will do everything in my power to keep that from happening! He couldn't stop me from receiving my Ka'lang, and he's not going to stop me on my second quest! We just need to get a clearer idea of what it is!"

At that moment, Atdao yells, "We're just about there! Wake up, you sleepy heads! Let's all prepare to go ashore."

Da'on, who is so anxious to be home finally and did not even sleep a wink, stands firmly on the bow of the Sakman as he blows one loud burst of the Ku'lo to announce their arrival. After about a minute or two, they hear a response of three short Ku'lo shots, so they proceed. All of Fu'a has gathered on the shore along with Maga'lahi Dadau to welcome them.

Da'on, so happy to see his family jumps out of the Sakman, greets Maga'lahi Dadau, then runs up to them. Aligao, just as excited to be back on his island, says to Ma'tao, "Do you think they'll welcome us back in Ati like this?" Ma'tao soaks it in and replies, "We could only hope!"

As they all step onto the shoreline and secure the Sakman, Maga'lahi Dadau, alongside Kakhana Sihek, is the first to welcome them back. Maga'lahi Dadau can not contain his excitement as he says, "I'm so overrun with joy now that you're back after receiving your Ka'lang

I Man Metgot! Now the hope that we as a people so longed for is now coming into fruition. With you and your warriors standing in front of me today!" He embraces Atdao and delightedly says, "It seems like the Sakman proved her worth! How do you like the way she handles?"

Atdao does not skip a beat and says, "She handles like a champ! She lived up to my expectations and a whole lot more!" Maga'lahi Dadau then embraces Ma'tao, and with so much excitement in his voice, says, "You also have to tell me! Without leaving anything out. Tell me how you defeated Haluu to retrieve your Ka'lang!"

Ma'tao, with just as excitement, responds, saying, "Of course! I intend to. I also want to share with you something special that happened to me. I received a vision in my sleep, a calling. I feel it to be my second quest!" Kakhana Sihek, who is standing right next to Maga'lahi Dadau, asks, "With your calling, did you receive it after you received your Ka'lang? Because I too would like to help decipher and inquire from our ancestors, what is it that you need to do!"

Ma'tao quickly agrees, saying, "Yes, I did receive it after acquiring my Ka'lang, and with your help to set us down the right path would be appreciated! That's what brought us back here first in the first place. Because from what we heard with all the tensions going on right now. We don't have any time to waste!"

Maga'lahi Dadau looks at Ma'tao and says, "My words exactly! But first, we eat! We all think better on a filled belly! Come."

Maga'lahi Dadau then calls out to his warriors to take care of and secure the Sakman. While he calls out to his villagers to prepare the feast as they all head back to his hut.

The women of the village prepare a sumptuous feast before them. As they have all eaten to their heart's content, Ma'tao tells Maga'lahi Dadau about their journey to the Apuya' Tasi.

And details regarding the battle with Haluu along with everything else that ensued after with Asuli.

Maga'lahi Dadau, in total shock, says, "That was a great battle! One that will go down in legends, I, for one, will see to that. But after everything that I thought I knew about Haluu, I never would've imagined him becoming an ally. You indeed are blessed!"

Maga'lahi Dadau places both hands on the shoulder's of Ma'tao, and says, "By the grace of Puntan along with Fu'una, we do have the makings of the actual Maga'lahi I Mantatkilu in front of us today! I knew it from the first day we met!"

Kakhana Sihek agrees then says, "We're also so blessed to have you on our side. For the forces of darkness led by Asuli are growing stronger as we speak!"

Maga'lahi Dadau then turns to look at Atdao, Atani, then back to Ma'tao and says, "Yes! Considering tensions surmounting between both of your grandfathers and their villages down south, it's only a matter of time. Only a matter of time for war if we don't step in to prevent it. The villages of central and northern Guahan will soon choose sides. Once they do, I fear that the great war once prophesied will come to pass!"

Ma'tao, in all understanding, says, "With what I now know about Asuli, he is very capable of doing just that, but I promise you! I will do everything in my power to stop that from happening to our islands and our people!"

Ma'tao then continues saying, "One thing we know for sure is that he is using pendants! Pendants of his own that contain dark magic! These pendants allow him to control the thoughts of whoever is wearing them. That is one of the powers of his Ka'lang. The Ka'lang I Manganiti!"

Atdao, with a problematic voice, says, "My grandfather! It's to my understanding that he might be under Asuli's influence! We received word about it when we were on Anatahan. Maga'lahi Dadau, when you last met with him, did you happen to notice if he was wearing a suspicious-looking pendant?"

Maga'lahi Dadau thinks then replies, "It was the first thing I noticed when I went to talk to him about peace talks with Ati! He was also more aggravated than usual and didn't want to hear anything about Ati's peace or have anything to do with Maga'lahi Sinahi. He blames you, Ma'-tao! He went as far as saying that you took Atani against her own free will, and Atdao is under some dark magic spell! How ironic! I tried to explain what we all discussed and agreed upon before leaving for the Apuya' Tasi. He wasn't having any of it! And told me I was wasting his time and that I better go before he makes an enemy out of Fu'a as well! Honestly, I don't know who that was. Because he is nowhere near the Ahgao that I remember."

Atdao, now feeling more pain about the situation, replies, "That's because he's not. That is all Asuli, and his evil is doing!"

Ina holds Atdao's hand to calm him down deeper while saying to him, "That's why we need to stay calm. I know it hurts, feel it, but don't stay there! Embrace it, and let's move forward. Getting worked up will cloud your judgment and thinking. We need you!"

Da'on looks at Aligao and says, "And we all witnessed it with Aligao on Anatahan."

Aligao, after hearing his name, immediately says, "Are we talking about that again, Da'on? If memory serves me right, you were with me when that first all went down. You just don't know when to let that go! By the way, remember the Manganiti Man Nanu? How's that working out for you so far?"

Ma'tao and the rest of the warriors laugh at the bickering between the two as Atani interrupts, saying, "That's enough, you two!" Ma'tao then turns to Maga'lahi Dadau, saying, "We now all know that Asuli is using those pendants to control the minds of whoever wears it! And with all the tensions arising recently, we all have a strong sense that he's behind all of it!" Ma'tao then adds, "From what we gather so far is that he plans on controlling as many Maga'lahi that he can, to use them and their resources to further his evil plans!"

Kakhana Sihek turns to Ma'tao and says, "About your calling. Tell us about it!"

Ma'tao confidently says, "There are elements of it that I was able to make myself out clearly. Pulonon was also helpful in helping to make sense of some details as well. One thing that I do know for sure, from deep within my heart. That it's a calling leading me towards my second quest."

Maga'lahi Dadau clears the hut with everyone except for Ma'tao, his warriors, himself, and Kakhana Sihek! He then says to Ma'tao, "Now, my son. Tell us of your calling and don't leave out any details."

So Ma'tao proceeds, "A bright flash of yellowish gold lightning! A woman's face. I looked deep into her eyes, which instantly pulls me in! I am now falling! I'm falling so fast from the heavens, spiraling down towards the earth! I'm now falling into an area of Guahan that I distinctly remember; I've been there before. I've been there before, but I can't remember when! Another bright lightning flash. I see her again! But who is she? I'm drawn deeper into those deep dark blacks of her eyes. I'm falling again! I'm falling into this place. It's a village! A village near and dear to my heart, but it's not Ati! I then hear it. A god awful scream! A scream from some large shadowy winged creature. I listen to it flying overhead. I see her, but this time she is running! But what is she running from, and who is she?! Another bright flash! I'm in a cave. The rain outside is pouring so hard that the water percolating down from the limestone rocks finds its way inside and puddles right under the entrance. I walk towards it. I see hands; it's bloodied! I bend down over the pool to catch a glimpse of who it might be. Is it me? As I focus on the reflection and I'm about to make it out, but I can't! Because this person's face is also so bloodied up, but then I see it! I see something! The Ka'lang I Man Metgot in one hand and the Gapot Ulu I Saina in the other! The bloodied hands of this person holding them smash both together, and they explode into thousands of pieces! Then I hear her! She screams! I see her as we both look up to see that evil, sinister, shadowy figure flying overhead once again! Another bright flash! Then from the heavens, something falls! Like a meteor followed by glowing red streaks of fire! The most perfectly carved sling stone launched with perfection! Again I hear her. I listen to her scream loud, and it's coming from directly behind me! I reluctantly turn, but I have to! I need to! I slowly do at first, then I felt a presence! I then turn completely, coming face to face with this lady as she says, "It's Time!"

Ma'tao looks down, takes a deep breath, and looks into the eyes of Maga'lahi Dadau then to Kakhana Sihek and quietly says, "And after she said that, I suddenly awoke."

Kakhana Sihek, even now more interested, says, "The village you described could most likely be Chochogo' since you said it wasn't Ati, but it felt so near to your heart! The giant beast of a bird is Itak! With all the tensions of war brewing, I'm not surprised that Itak is making more of its presence known. For it feeds off that negative energy of fear and hatred. The sling stone is one of legend! The Diyuk Paton Chaifi, you probably already know, was created by Chaifi (god of the underworld) to destroy the human soul that stole fire from him and brought it to our people to jumpstart civilization as we know it today."

Ma'tao then asks, "Any idea of the woman? What is her significance? How are she and I connected to all of this?"

Kakhana Sihek responds, "Now, with that, I feel that Chochogo' may have the answers you are searching for!"

Maga'lahi Dadau, after hearing that says, "Now I don't know any better way for you to experience becoming a Maga'lahi, but immersing yourself with your people! The people of

Chochogo'! A step towards becoming the Maga-'lahi I Mantatkilu! You have to show them that you're a provider and protector. You have to win their hearts and trust! For if you do, like your warriors, they will follow you to hell and back!"

Ma'tao looks at Maga'lahi Dadau and takes in everything he just said. He then looks to his warriors and says, "So like I originally thought, Chochogo' it is! Who's ready to head with me there?"

He looks at his love Atani as she says, "You already know my answer." He looks to Atdao and Ina, who both respond, "We're In!"

He looks to Da'on and says, "You're home now, my brother. You can sit this one out."

Da'on immediately responds, saying, "As you said. You're my brother, we're family now, and I'm not letting you all have all the fun! I'm in!"

Ma'tao then looks to Aligao, who is looking down, and asks, "So what Aleegs? Are you with us?" Aligao pauses for a moment. He looks back to Ma'tao, and in a slow, drawn-out voice, says, "Considering that you asked me last and we knew each other the longest. I now know that things change, people change, and we must adjust to that change to grow ourselves. So I've decided that for me it's time. Time for me to…"

Ma'tao looks at his lifelong best friend with a shocked look as he waits to hear what he thinks he's about to say. Aligao finishes his sentence by saying, "Time for me to follow you all to Cho-chogo' and partake in this quest!"

Ma'tao instantly slaps Aligao in the shoulders while laughing and says, "You know you had me there!"

Aligao then looks back at all of them, then Da'on saying, "As Da'on said! We're family now! Plus, if the Manganiti Man Nanu decide to make their appearance, someone has got to look out for Da'on!"

Da'on, after hearing that looks a bit weary, but once he is aware of it, he suddenly gets composed and shows a fist to Aligao, uttering, "Dude, now when are you ever going to let that go?!" Aligao chuckles while responding, "Not until we face them, and you conquer that fear! I'm just saying!"

Now Ina says, "Enough, you two!" Maga'lahi Dadau just laughs and says, "I love it! All families bicker, but when it matters the most, they pull together and take care of business! You all have a special chemistry together. And as I mentioned before, there's nothing you can't accomplish together!"

Ma'tao then asks, "Have you seen my grandfather?" Maga'lahi Dadau, again with a look of disappointment on his face, replies, "Yes, I did. I went to Ati right after Humatak. It didn't go any better. I didn't notice any necklace or any unusual stone other than the Ka'lang around Maga'lahi Sinahi's neck. He is still very bitter towards Maga'lahi Ahgao and Humatak. It is so evident among him and the people of Ati. More so than ever! I didn't want to tell you this, but I would rather you hear it from me than just any random person. He mentioned that if you continue with Atani or proceed on your quest with Atdao, he will consider you a traitor to him, Ati, and your people!"

Ma'tao tries to conceal the pain by those words from Maga'lahi Dadau. But all inside the hut could instantly see and feel it bother him. Ma'tao, instantaneously lost in thought, looks down while saying to his warriors in a soft voice, "Let's get our things ready and together tonight. For we leave for Chochogo' at first light."

He then exits out of the hut and slowly makes his way towards the ocean. Atani runs after him, grabs his hand, and asks, "Are you alright? I'm here for you! You know that."

Ma'tao looks back at her and softly says, "I know. It's not you. I just need some time alone to think things through. Get some rest. Because we're going to need it, on where we're going."

He then lets her hand go and proceeds towards the shoreline. Once there, he hears, "Halla! Halla! Halla Kumu Hatcha Hit !"Which translates to "Pull! Pull! Pull As One!"He heads over to see what is all the commotion.

He sees a group of Matua men (High Ranking Caste) pulling a lagua' pula (pull net) onto the shore. He turns, looking to the group of men to the right, rushing to control the net as a flurry of fish causes the net to rip as they escape. He very discreetly focuses on the torn net, opens his eyes, which are now the brilliance of yellowish gold. Then being very inconspicuous holds out his hand in front while channeling the Ka' lang I Man Metgot towards that direction. He makes repairs to the net as it loops around the fleeing school of fish! All the fishermen gawk in amazement as they look around to see who is responsible for this marvelous blessing. Though they were not aware that it was Ma'tao, they still showed gestures towards the heavens; they are thankful!

Ma'tao then pulls the power back into his Ka' lang as he hears, "Just as I mentioned earlier, prove to them in what I already know!"

While turning, he sees Maga'lahi Dadau, who just witnessed what he had done for the fishermen. Ma'tao smiles, saying, "I know that the answers we search for are in Chochogo'! I need to become Maga'lahi to create lasting change in our islands!. But it's been so long since I was last in Chochogo'! How am I supposed to lead this village that I barely even know? It doesn't make things any more comfortable knowing that my grandfather and the village I'm so fond of practicality brand me a traitor. In all that I have accomplished so far, I owe it all to Atani and my warriors!"

Maga'lahi Dadau embraces Ma'tao while saying, "And always know that! For it's the people that we love and fight for that always bring out the best in us."

Ma'tao then asks, "When you first became Maga'lahi of Fu'a, how did you earn respect and trust from the rest of the Matua?" He, in return, smirks then replies, "That my son was no easy task. Especially in Fu'a!" Upon finishing his sentence, one of the Matua men presents Maga'lahi Dadau, a gua'gua (woven basket) of the freshly caught fish, saying, "Maga'lahi, chule' ini para hagu." Which translates to "Leader, take this for you."

Maga'lahi Dadau happily accepts it turns back to Ma'tao, saying, "The same way you gained the trust and respect from your warriors, especially Atdao! It's already in you, and you'll know what to do when the time arises. And as for your grandfather, I have not lost hope in him! I've set up peace talks with him and the northern village of Gog'na, whom he allied with Ati! Gog'na could be very instrumental in quelling the tensions in the north part of the island. I'll be heading over to Gog'na at first light."

At that very moment, two ulitao run towards their direction full speed, screaming, "They're Coming! They're Coming! Warriors from Sumai!" Ma'tao and Maga'lahi Dadau immediately get the two ulitao behind them and prepares for a fight!

The Matua men, all thirteen of them, strip the stone sinkers from their net and prepare to use them as sling stones while forming a protective circle around Maga'lahi Dadau! As they complete the formation, out from the jungle spring, fifteen warriors from the village of Sumai, each one is sporting an atupat (sling) and fudfudganom (javelin spear).

Ma'tao is now feeling that tingling sensation running through his body. The heat of battle is only seconds away; he turns to Maga'lahi Dadau, asking, "Should we reason with them?" In return, he chuckles heartily, saying, "They're from Sumai! There's no reasoning! Let this go down as our first battle together!" Ma'tao snickers while saying, "It'll be an honor!"

Without hesitation or any warning, two of the Sumai warriors break from the charging group and hurl their fudfudganom towards their direction as two of the Fu'a men run towards the advancing spears shouting, "Protect Our Maga'lahi!" With so much grace and speed, they stop their flight in mid-air! The rest of the Fu'a men follow that up with a shower of sling stones! The amount of stones thrown with such accuracy quickly slows the advancing Sumai warriors! They then split into three groups. Their leader, a warrior by the name of Tayigi, leads the charge running full force towards them, shouting, "You from Fu'a! Try us if you dare!"

Ma'tao looks at Maga'lahi Dadau then to his warriors and yells, "Protect the Maga'lahi Dadau! I got this!"

Ma'tao immediately runs to meet the charging warriors! He focuses his thoughts while pacing his breaths. His eyes are now burning with a brilliance of yellowish gold! He channels the power of his Ka' lang I Man Metgot through both his palms as he directs the beams of energy to the two groups running alongside Tayigi! A loud thunderous Boom rings throughout! While the energy blast lifts each of the warriors from both groups ten feet in the air! The intense explosion knocks the wind out of all of them as they hit the ground! His demonstration of power instantly thwarts Tayigi and the rest of his warriors' attack. Without even a second thought, they all turn around and run back into the jungle towards their village, but not before one of them shouts out, "Mafac! We'll get you yet!"

Maga'lahi Dadau stands in amazement as he shouts to Ma'tao, "Wow! I knew you came into powers, but that was a sight to behold!" He then turns towards both teenage boys and yells, "Mafac! Hafa bida' da mu pa'gu?" Which translates to "Mafac! Now, what did you do today?" But all are quiet as they were still in shock at what just happened! Atdao, Atani, along with the rest of their warriors, now join them on the beach while Aligao shouts, "Sorry we're late! Who were those guys?" Da'on responds, saying, "Sumai warriors! It looks like Tayigi is up to no good again! When is he ever going to learn?"

Atdao laughs while saying, "After their brush with Ma'tao and the power of the Ka' lang I Man Metgot, maybe they'll give it a second thought when crossing over their territory!"

Mafac then interrupts and says, "I apologize, Maga'lahi Dadau, for causing this problem on our shores. Gofchegi, Amta, Ogogta, and I were just on our way back from bartering goods with Opagat village when we found that someone had sabotaged our panga (canoe). We decided even though it was risky to return home inland, we would make the journey. We didn't disrespect them or their village in any way, and we honored the pathways between villages as we always do! They must've been following us for quite some time, but they didn't make their move until we got closer to the Mapupun Valley! That's when they surrounded us! Tayigi approached us laughing while saying, "You! Your Maga'lahi, and all the people from Fu'a are finally going to be taken down and exposed for what you are! Your days of living the high life with other villages bowing down to you will soon come to an end!"

Gofchegi then adds, "He also mentioned that with Humatak on their side, it's only a matter of time!"

Mafac picks up the conversation while angered, saying, "I tried reasoning with him, but he pushed Amta! Ogogta then punched and took out one of his warriors! We all started to scrap! Everything after was a blur! I took out two more warriors, but as I looked around, Amta and Ogogta had disappeared! We must've split up in the heat of battle, and Tayigi had them taken as prisoners! That's when Gofchegi and I decided to make a run for it, to get help!"

Atdao, in disbelief, says, "I find it hard to believe that Humatak is a part of this! We have never allied ourselves with Sumai! There's more going on than we're seeing!"

Ma'tao turns to Atdao while trying to calm him down, saying, "We know there is, and we will get to the bottom of it! Believe me, if anyone understands how you feel, I do. But we need to help locate and recover Ogogta and Amta! Before heading to Chochogo'! Fu'a, along with Maga'lahi Dadau, are also crucial in getting our grandfathers to hear reason before this whole affair escalates into something we want to avoid!"

Atani holds Atdao's hand and looks him in the eyes. Immediately her brother understood that what Ma'tao speaks is the truth and gestures in acknowledgment. Ma'tao then continues saying,

"Mafac! Gofchegi! You both will lead us to where the battle with the Sumai warriors occurred!" Maga'lahi Dadau looks to both ulitao and says, "You two follow Ma'tao! You're both under his charge now!"

He then turns to Ma'tao while pleading, "We don't have any time to waste! Please locate and recover the other two. If anything was to happen to them, I feel my warriors will retaliate. Sparking up a war between our villages!"

Da'on instantly agrees, saying, "We need to head out now! Without a moment to spare."

Ma'tao fired up reinsures Maga'lahi Dadau by saying, "Keep the people calm. We'll be back with Ogogta and Amta!" Turning to his warriors, he asks, "Are we all in on this?"Aligao, not wasting any time, blurts out while smiling, "Since you couldn't wait for me to toss them few around, consider me glue by your side. Because I ain't missing out on this action!"

Atdao and Ina both look at each other, then to Ma'tao and nod in agreement. Da'on looks to Maga'lahi Dadau, who says back to him, "By fighting alongside Ma'tao, your fighting for me and all of Fu'a!"

Da'on then looks back at Ma'tao, signaling that he is with them.

Ma'tao then turns to Atani, who jokingly adds, "Really?! You're going to ask me?" They all chuckle as Ma'tao gestures them to follow as they all make haste towards the Mapupun Valley!

Chapter 2

"An Unexpected Encounter!"

Ma'tao, along with his warriors, covers the ground so quickly without any time to waste. He then signals Mafac and Gofchegi to join him up front as they approach the Mapupun Valley (Valley Of The Chipped Spear). Up along the crest of the valley resides Mapupun Village. Mafac, quietly and cautiously says to Ma'tao, "That's where they ambushed us!! Over the next ridge. Even though it happened around that area, I'm not sure if any of those warriors were from Mapupun Village." Ma'tao, with Mafac, Gofchegi, and his warriors alongside stealthily, make their way within the ridge pathway's tree line.

The wind is at a deadening standstill. This area we're in is quiet, a little too quiet., Ma'tao thinks to himself. They get closer to the crest of the ridge.

Mafac taps Ma'tao and quietly says, "The area where the conflict took place is just below us a few yards away." Ma'tao then gestures to the rest of the group to halt! He then turns to Mafac and Gofchegi while asking, "Did you happen to pass by the village at any time?"

Mafac looks around, then back to Ma'tao, saying, "No. We wanted to, but decided to take the path we were on instead." Ma'tao looks around then whispers to his warriors, saying, "I feel we should get up closer to the village and see if the other two are there!" They all agree and follow Ma'tao.

The brilliantly red-orange sun starts to set as they make their way across the ridge and down towards the valley. Ma'tao suddenly gets an uneasy feeling. He turns around while saying to them, "You all stay here and out of sight! It'll be getting dark soon. Da'on will follow me, and we'll get in closer to the village and do some re-connaissance!" They all agree as Ma'tao looks to Da'on and signals for him to follow, but not too closely.

They both come to an area at the base of the mountain. Ma'tao spots a trail that leads to the village's backside and signals to Da'on that they will follow, but walk alongside it.

The sun has completely set by now, but they just continue in the dark of night and avoid being seen. The wind blows, chilling them to the bone, but both men carefully make their way through the valley. Then up towards the mountain path as they make their way towards the village.

Ma'tao suddenly turns towards Da'on and whispers, "Stop! Did you hear that?" Da'on immediately responds, "If you heard that very faint breaking of branches and leaves? Then yes! It sounds like it's coming from fifty feet from the left of us."

They both crouch down, and while staying very still, they listen intently! Ma'tao turns to Da'on and whispers, "I don't want whoever it is out there to try and outflank us! You stay here while I backtrack and outflank them first!"

Da'on pauses for a moment then replies,

"I'll give you a couple of minutes to scout it out. Make sure to get back here or signal by whistling within ten to fifteen minutes! If you don't, I'm immediately following your tracks."

Ma'tao agrees and stealthily heads back around the direction they heard the noises to outflank whatever or whoever is within the vicinity!

As Ma'tao gracefully maneuvers each step, he heightens all his senses, not to be ambushed or caught off guard. It is a new moon, and it makes for a very dark night.

But Ma'tao thinks to himself; *I wonder if my Dark Sight goggles, which were so successful in helping me see in the dark depths of the Apuya' Tasi, I wonder if they'll help me here?* His curiosity gets the best of him, so he stops to reach into his pouch.

But just before he barely moves his hands, he immediately hears a loud thud directly behind him! He attempts to turn, but to no avail, because whoever made that noise completely caught Ma'tao by surprise and instantly placed him in a chokehold! This person is no amateur, and his chokehold on Ma'tao is wrenching even tighter! Ma'tao is restrained and can barely breathe, but he thinks to himself, *What the...? The nerve of this guy? One of my favorite forms of ambush! I must say, whoever this is, they do have one pretty firm grip! But could this be...? Nah! It couldn't be?!*

He then rapidly stands up with this person on his back! Focuses! He takes both his hands while grabbing onto this person's arm directly around his neck. And with great thrusts and speed, he powerfully takes three steps back and slams this person's back incredibly hard against the nearest tree! It simultaneously knocks all the wind out of his attacker!

Ma'tao does not stop there! He then crouches down on one knee while still firmly gripping that arm! And together with such perfect timing, he bends forward, causing his assailant's body to completely flip over him while getting slammed violently to the ground! And onto the rocks right in front of him! Whatever oxygen the tree did not expel, the rocks indeed did! His attacker, now flat on the back, raises both hands in the air!

As Ma'tao stares at him dead straight into his eyes, he yells, "Sanglo!" Sanglo is his mother's eldest brother from Ati. He was very instrumental in the upbringing of Ma'tao. From teaching Ma'tao to sail his first canoe to fighting skills on the battlefield. And every survival skill a warrior should know!

Sanglo, who is just as surprised, excitingly responds, "Ma'tao?! What are you doing here?" He instantly jumps back onto his feet and embraces his nephew while curiously asking, "How have you been? The last thing I heard about you is that you were heading off with Maga'lahi Ahgao's granddaughter!"

Ma'tao looks deep into his uncle's eyes and, with a serious voice, says, "Saina' hu, there is so much more to all of this than what you have heard!"

Immediately Sanglo's attention is drawn towards the chest of Ma'tao and, with so much thrill in his voice, asks, "Is that what I think it is?!" Ma'tao, in just as much excitement, replies, "What do you think?"

Sanglo, with much more enthusiasm, says, "It is a Ka'lang I Man Metgot! But one I have never seen! You are no longer my nephew, the ulitao." Sanglo places both hands on the shoulders of Ma'tao, and continues saying very sincerely, "It's my honor to call you Maga'lahi! I trained you well. I just wish I could've been there when you received your vision!"

Ma'tao replies graciously, saying, "I understand, and yes, you also played an intricate role in my success. I also remember grandfather sending you on a critical mission to strengthen alliances with villages in Luta! By the way, how is grandfather?"

With that question posed, Sanglo, saddened, says, "I'm not going to lie. Things have been terrible back home after word came that you left! It's not why you left; it's that you left with someone from that village! My father was infuriated! For he made it known that he always expected you to honor his leadership! And involving yourself with anything having to do with Humatak, especially after you received your vision, he felt deeply betrayed!"

Ma'tao right that second put an end to that conversation saying, "Saina hu, I mean no disrespect, but now is not the time and place to discuss this matter! As I said, I have my reasons! And I have to attend to more important issues right now! Lives depend on it!"

Sanglo does not even press the situation anymore and says, "I wholeheartedly understand! Hopefully, we could revisit it later to find a solution. On another note, some of our warriors went missing around here! Do you remember Taiasi?" Ma'tao smirks while saying, "Don't I ever! Of course, I remember him. More so, I don't think Aligao will never forget him!"

Sanglo then continues and says, "He led a group of four ulitao and sailed this way to barter some goods with our allies of Agofan Village a couple of weeks back. But they haven't returned home since! With all that has been going on lately, Maga'lahi Sinahi tasked me to locate their whereabouts. The people of Agofan said that they bartered with them, but they decided to go inland to make some trades with Opagat Village! That's where the trail goes cold! We haven't always been on the best of terms with Opagat. I decided to gain some information from my contacts in the area. My informants in Agofan also mentioned that as he was heading back home three nights ago, he passed this way and witnessed Maga'lahi Ahgao escorted by nine Humatak warriors heading towards Mapupun Village!"

Ma'tao interjects, saying, "In just hearing that! It sounds like Sumai and Mapupun villages may have allied themselves with Humatak!"

Sanglo says, "If what you speak is the truth and they bring Opagat into their fold, Agofan, who has always been strong allies with Ati, might be facing dangerous circumstances! We need to hurry!"

Ma'tao agrees and adds, "Yes, we do!" Ma'tao then whistles as a signal for Da'on to advance towards his position. Without fail, Da'on appears in a heartbeat. Da'on immediately notices Sanglo and says, "By the look of things, it seems you know each other? Is he the cause of all that commotion?"

Sanglo smirks and says, "You young ones! You seem to think to know it all! And still have so much to learn!" Ma'tao just laughs and says, "Yet, you thought you could get the drop on me!" Sanglo slaps him on the shoulder and says, "You're right! I'll give you that! But you are from Ati, and I had a hand in your upbringing!"

He then turns to Da'on and asks, "Your face is so familiar! Are you the son of Nahagua of Fu'a Village?" Da'on, with a shocked look on his face, slightly nods and says, "Yes. I'm Da'on! Did you know of my father?" Sanglo looks into Da'on's eye and replies, "Yes. He was a nobleman, a great warrior! It was an honor to fight by his side in the battle to protect Fu'a!"

Ma'tao, with a confused look, asks, "Battle to protect Fu'a?" Sanglo solemnly says, "Yes, it was almost twenty years ago to this day! A battle that prevented dark forces from entering into the physical realm through Fu'a rock!"

Da'on turns to Ma'tao and adds, "Yes, it's a battle not spoken about in my village. But all the Guardians know of it because of all who sacrificed their lives to protect humanity. My father is also Maga'lahi Dadau's younger brother and who's life was taken in that battle." He then turns to Sanglo and says, "If you know of my father and of that battle, that means.." Before Da'on could even finish his sentence, Sanglo says, "Yes. I was once a Guardian of Guahan."

Ma'tao, with a shocked expression, asks, "Why is it that I never knew you were?!" Sanglo responds, saying, "Because after I returned to

Ati after that fateful ordeal, it took me quite some time to find myself again. From that day on. Father vowed that no one from our village would ever have to be put through any of that, ever also. So no one from Ati ever joined the ranks of the Guardians of Guahan since that day on. That is why you do not know of it."

Ma'tao looks at Sanglo, and while nodding, says, "Understood, and we can relate." He then places his forehead against Sanglo's to show respect, and as Da'on follows after, Ma'tao then says, "We need to go and see if Mapupun is keeping our people as prisoners." Da'on says, "Yes, and we better hurry! Because we need to get back to the group and report our findings!" Sanglo then turns to Ma'tao, points to the path, and says, "Lead the way, Maga'lahi!"

The three now make their way covertly along the mountain trail until they are directly along the backside of Mapupun Village. They stay well within the tree line and proceed discreetly.

Ma'tao notices a group of men standing in a circle under a nunu tree next to a fire that is burning bright and points them out. What all three see next immediately outrageous them from deep within the pit of their stomachs! All six men searching for, both from Ati and Fu'a, are hung upside down from their feet and all beaten to a bloody pulp!

Ma'tao, at that moment, does not even think; he just acts! And with so much ferocity runs towards the group! He zeros in on the leader, the man responsible for beating his people! It is Taiyigi! Ma'tao, now a few feet from him and running with lightning-quick speed, shouts from the top of his lungs,

"Hoi! Lachi na taotao un trabubuka!" Which translates to "Hey you! You messed with the wrong people!"

Taiyigi, at that second, is entirely caught by surprise that Ma'tao could see the whites of his eyes! Ma'tao travels so fast and combined with his strength, and he grabs Taiyigi by his neck with one hand! He lifts him off the ground as if he is a child and slams him so hard up against the nunu tree and knocks him out cold!

Three of Taiyigi's warriors, shortly after try their best to overpower Ma'tao by jumping on his back, but they too were just like children! Ma'tao breaks their hold while propelling himself upward and back with both arms outstretched, grabbing two of them by their hair. He bashes both their heads together that the force it generates is so intense! They are now both wholly incapacitated from the trauma!

Ma'tao now reaches with his right hand behind him for the third man still clinging onto his back! He grabs his neck so tight, brings him up over, and throws him with so much grit towards the trunk of the nunu tree and practically breaks every bone in his body! He then turns and sees a vast amount of warriors from both Mapupun and Sumai surrounding him! He then yells, "You think you're men for what you did to them?! Now try that with me!"

Meanwhile, Sanglo, who is stunned from what he is witnessing, turns to Da'on and says, "My nephew! He is not what I remember him to be.

He was strong, but this display of strength is otherworldly!"

Da'on just looks at Sanglo, agrees, then rushes to assist Ma'tao! Sanglo, who is still in disbelief, runs in right behind him! Ma'tao takes notice and shouts to them, "Free our men! I've got this!"

He then looks upon the warriors who now have him surrounded! He drops to one knee, grabs his Ka'lang then closes his eyes. He focuses and takes three deeps breaths and thinks to himself, *Who are these animals to do something like this? Who are we as people when all respect is lost?* He now only hears the beating of his own heart!

Meanwhile, Taiyigi, who is now slowly getting to his knees, yells, "Get him, you fools! What are you waiting for?!" They all start running in towards Ma'tao, who is as still as can be with no movement whatsoever! They now have him where they want him! Or so they think!

Ma'tao, who is now so focused on that still small voice deep within himself, connects to all he knows is true! He then feels that almighty power from deep within linking to his Ka'lang! The Ka'lang I Man Metgot! Just as the first warrior is within arm's length and about to place his hands on him, Ma'tao opens his eyes! His eyes are now blazing with a brilliance of yellowish gold! He stares deep into that first warrior's eyes while saying with so much bravado, "Let's do this!" Fear instantly wraps that warrior who has nowhere to go with all the others behind him!

Ma'tao, now in a fighting stance, cocks his right arm back, and with so much barbarity, clocks that warrior hard that he flies so far back! Back to where he takes out six of his men that were following him! Ma'tao now raises both hands towards the charging warriors and yells, "Come! Come because now it's my turn to bring the pain!" And bring it he does! He channels the energy again from deep within. And combined with his Ka'lang, directs that energy through both his arms and out of his palms!

As it exits his body, it creates a powerful blast! A wave of dynamic kinetic energy immediately stops the advancement of all the warriors rushing towards him while instantaneously taking them out!

Sanglo and Da'on have just about freed the last man hanging from the nunu tree as they all turn to notice that there are more warriors with torches in hand heading towards their direction! Ma'tao focuses on the warriors attacking from the main path that he does not see the warriors outflanking them!

Sanglo looks to the six that they just freed and then to Da'on while shouting, "There ain't no way that I'm going to spend my last days here! You with me?!"

They all yell back, "We're with you!" They all face their backs towards each other and are prepared to do whatever it takes! They are not going down without a fight!

They are now staring at the torches as they get closer and closer! The closer they get, the more warriors they see! It is now or never! Da'on, with a crazed look in his eyes, shouts, "Chule' magi!

Hamyu manganiti!" Which translates to "Bring it! You evil ones!" Sanglo and Da'on step up to meet the attacking warriors!

Suddenly, Impact! The first wave of attacking warriors greets them! They quickly take them out! With such great skill as fighters and the tenacity in their hearts! The warriors they had just freed join in the fight and are not that bad themselves. But how long can they keep this going?!

Ma'tao, too, has his hands full, keeping the enemy at bay from his position! Their numbers are so staggering and overwhelming!

As soon as they take one down, another takes his place! Ma'tao quickly looks back and realizes he needs to get to them fast! He then clears the way by unleashing a powerful energy blast towards the enemies in front as he moves backward in quick paces towards his men!

He then hears it! Da'on and Sanglo also pick up on it! That all too familiar voice yelling, "So you want to take us on, do you? You mess with one of us! You mess with all of us!"

That all too familiar voice, that could not have come at a better time! It is Aligao! He runs in to join the fight while shaking his coconut rattle with so much intensity that the Sumai and Ma-

pupun warriors closest to him are instantly confused! The power of the rattle then causes them
to start fighting amongst themselves! Directly
behind Aligao rushing in is Atani, Atdao, and
Ina!

Atdao, while shouting, "Let's even up these
odds!" Cocks both arms back, and with extreme
accuracy, throws both Pagasi paddles in a cross
pattern away from his body, which right away
takes out twelve warriors and boomerangs back
to land in his hands!

Da'on shouts, "It's about time!" Ina, with her
spear in hand and such graceful yet powerful
technique, rapidly takes out six warriors herself!

Meanwhile, Ma'tao, now noticing his warriors have joined the fight, yells out to Atani, "Let's put an end to all of this now!" Atani immediately understands what he means, and she, without any hesitation, closes her eyes and raises both hands in the air. She is now centered within herself and focuses her breathing!

She then opens her eyes and channels the power of her Gapot Ulu I Saina! It creates a powerful orange forcefield around Sanglo, Da'on, and the freed warriors!

Ma'tao, now knowing that they are protected, focuses while centering himself once again. While channeling the energy from his Ka'lang, he ramps up his speed! He is now moving so freakishly fast with such grace and fighting technique that none of his adversaries can stop him, let alone see him! These enemies are left beaten, but not before witnessing only streaks of yellowish gold! After seeing that they are no match for Ma'tao and his warriors, all Sumai and Mapupun warriors who remained decide to cut their losses!

They abandon the fight and flee into the jungle! Aligao is about to follow in pursuit as Ma'tao shouts, "Aligao! Let them go! I'm sure we'll meet up with them again soon. We need to tend to our wounded!" Aligao, at that second, turns around and heads to offer his assistance. But not before shouting, "Let this be a lesson! You mess with Ati, you will kumati (cry)! You babies!" Atani looks at Aligao while laughing and jokes, "Babies? Who's the one with the rattle?!" Aligao just looks at her and laughs while saying, "I'll give you that, Atani! That was a good one! And after that adrenaline rush! I'm feeling good to-day!"

Ma'tao looks around at the now-abandoned village as he thinks to himself, *Why would Sumai and Mapupun do something like that? How they tortured and beat those men shows that the darkness is spreading much quicker than I expected among the villages! There is*

only one person who I know of that's capable of that!

He then makes a fist and, with so much anger, punches the nearest coconut tree and instantly breaks into thousands of pieces! He stops! Thinks! Then he gathers himself. This encounter was not by chance, and he is going to get to the bottom of it! One way or another!

Chapter 3

"New Face, New Lead!"

Aligao seeing Ma'tao needs that brief moment to himself, looks around, and notices a very familiar face, and yells, "Sanglo! How have you been Saina' hu?!" He runs up to him so quickly, but Sanglo stops him dead in his tracks! Aligao smirks and says softly, "Yes. I still remember you don't like hugs!" "He does like hugs! Just not from you.", Ma'tao says while chuckling. Aligao jumps onto the back of Ma'tao and straddles him, saying, "But I know you love hugs from me! I know you do!" Ma'tao laughing hysterically, shouts, "Get off from me, you kaduku (crazy)!" They both stop as they notice the rest of their group tending to the six who were beaten. Among them were the two from Fu'a that Mafac spoke about! Amta and Ogogta! Ma'tao then turns to his warriors and asks," Where are Mafac and Gofchegi?" Atdao responds, saying,"I sent them to head back to Fu'a! I had a feeling things were going to get crazy, and I didn't want them to get mixed up in all of it." Amta, with a concerned look on his face, asks, "So Mafac and

Gofchegi are alright?" Atdao responds with a confident, "Yes! And they'll be glad to know that you both are okay as well." Ogogta, so overcome with joy, looks at Da'on and says, "Thanks, Da'on! I knew once I saw you that we'd be alright!"

At that exact moment, Aligao heads over towards Sanglo, who is attending to the other four freed warriors from Ati. Aligao, now with a shocked look on his face, asks,

"Taiasi?! Is that you?" Taiasi, in a soft-spoken yet appreciative voice, says, "Yes, it is Aligao. I want to thank you for assisting in freeing us from those animals! I'm greatly indebted to you." Aligao slowly replies, "Don't sweat it!" He turns, walks towards Ma'tao, and quietly whispers, "Dude! That's Taiasi! What the heck is he doing here?!" Ma'tao replies, "Maga-'lahi Sinahi appointed him to lead the group in bartering with Agofan Village." Aligao now does not hold back. He responds, saying, "Now I know for sure! That the balance in our world or the whole universe, for that matter, is absolutely out of whack! Because who in their right mind would ever place that guy in charge?!"

Ma'tao smiles while saying, "Well, you already know that nothing will move forward in Ati without my grandfather's approval. Don't you at least think he deserves a chance? Look how many I gave you!" Aligao answers sarcastically, "Well, he better stay out of my way because we ain't kids anymore! If he doesn't, I'll definitely rattle the crap out of him! Seriously!" Ma'tao laughs even louder saying," That rattle has definitely gotten to your head! You need to relax!" Da'on then signals Ma'tao. As Ma'tao approaches, he says, "You're going to want to hear what this guy has to say!" Ma'tao looks very curiously at this ulitao, who is beaten black and blue, then says, "You're with Taiasi and the others, yet you're not from Ati! Who are you? Where you from?"

The teenage warrior who is thirteen years of age looks Ma'tao directly in the eyes and answers, "My name is Magogui. I'm from the village of Hanum! I have been looking for you, Ma'tao. That's how I ended up in Ati." Ma'tao. now more confused asks," Why is it that you're looking for me?" Magogui's eyes, now more prominent and staring intensely into the eyes of Ma'tao, he says," It's because I've seen her! I'm not talking about just my dreams! I've seen her in this physical world too! I could be an asset to you in helping to find her! Plus, I know the way to Chochogo' as well!" Ma'tao asks, "Who is she that you say, you know? Who is it that you've seen?" Magogui answers without any hesitation, "Itak! These dreams of her have haunted me these dreams of her for quite some time. That's why I decided to seek you out finally!"

Ma'tao, upon hearing that, suddenly thinks to himself, *How did this kid gain any details about my calling?* Magogui then adds, "As I said, I could help you find her!" Ma'tao quickly responds with a resounding, "No! I can't be responsible if any-thing were to happen to you!"

Though he disagreed with him following, Ma'-tao was intrigued about what he said and asked, "You've seen it? How come you keep mentioning her? How do you even know it's a female?" Magogui answers excitedly, "You may think I'm weird, but hear me out! She speaks to me!" After hearing that, Ma'tao smirks and replies, "Believe it or not! I don't think you're weird. I've had my fair share of conversations with what this physical world can't explain!"

By this point, Atani, who has finished helping to attend to the other injured warriors, joins Ma'-tao. He then introduces Atani to Magogui. And with a very bewildered look on her face, she looks at Magogui then to Ma'tao and says, "Man! That blood in Ati must be powerful among your people! Because you both have the same distinguishing features! It's uncanny!" Ma'tao laughs and replies," That's impossible! He's from Hanum, not Ati!" Atani shrugs her shoulders and replies, "I'm just saying!" She then looks back at Magogui and says, "It's nice to meet you! Are you feeling better?" Magogui, in return, says, "Yes, I am. It's an honor to meet you, and thanks for coming to our aide. I'm not sure how much we all would've been able to take if not for you all!" Atani stops him saying, "Anyone with a heart would've done the same thing! Every single one of them got what they deserved!" Ma'tao fakes a cough while looking at Atani and saying, "Excuse Me?!" Atani looks back at him and immediately knows what he is implying and responds with, "I get you, Ma'tao, but they did!"

Atdao and the rest approach as he says to Ma'tao, "I honestly feel we should leave this godforsaken place!" Ma'tao responds, saying, "I agree! Let's do one last sweep and get out of here!"

They all gather around as he introduces Magogui to the rest of his warriors. While looking at Magogui, he says to the group,

"He will be joining us as we head to Chochogo'. I feel that he could be an asset!" Magogui, with surprise, nods his head agreeing.

Taiasi, who looks exhausted after that ordeal, speaks up, saying, "Is it possible if I say a few words to you all?" Ma'tao looks around at everyone, then back to Taiasi and replies, "Sure. Be my guest."

Taiasi, with so much humility within his presence, begins to address the group, "I want to thank you all personally for being there in our time of need. Because honestly, I didn't think that we were going to make it out of here alive. I'm taking sole responsibility for why we ended up here. It was poor judgment on my behalf in wanting to increase our trade presence and putting the lives of my men in jeopardy when they counted on me. For that, I am truly sorry." He then continues, but not before making eye contact with Aligao and says, "I also want to apologize for the way I may have mistreated fellow villagers growing up. Believe me when I say that I literally saw my life flash right before my eyes! And I now see and have seen for quite some time, the fault in my ways. I hope you could find it in your hearts to one day forgive me. And to you, Ma'tao. You have grown into a great and mighty leader! You have my support one hundred percent! Our world's future doesn't seem so bleak, now that it has you and your warriors as our protectors! Believe me, when I say. Your grandfather and all whom I come across will hear of your marvelous and wondrous deeds!" And at that, he embraces Ma'tao while placing his forehead up against his. Aligao, now changed by that heartfelt speech, walks up to Ta-iasi. And as he turns around, embraces him and places his forehead on his. He then says, "The past is the past! We could forge a better future together!" Taiasi, so grateful, replies," Yes, my friend. I'm also going to be the first to brag about you to Maga'haga Unai!" Aligao laughs and replies, "Please do! Anything to change her perspective about me."

Ma'tao then approaches Sanglo asking, "Saina hu, could we speak for a moment?" Sanglo right away says, "Of course, my nephew! My Maga'lahi!" They separate themselves from the group as Sanglo says, "You Ma'tao have grown into a fine young man! You are doing us proud! Even though Maga'lahi Sinahi may not see it that way right now, You already have those from our village that do! And it's growing by the moment! You have displayed such great skill and speed that I still can't comprehend or explain. All I can say is that I'm glad you're on our side! You stay on your path in life and continue on your quests! Don't worry about Ati and anything that will distract you from it. We'll always be here for you! You hear?" Ma'tao, wholly taken with everything he just said, remains quiet for a second then says, "Saina' hu, with everything you just expressed, you instantly silenced those negative voices within me and have gifted me with so much more peace! Thank you for that!" Sanglo chuckles and replies, "No, need to thank me. Always remember who you are and where you come from! And also, more importantly, and never forget, I helped raise you!" They both laugh while Ma'tao places his arms around his uncle and says, "That I will never do! You have been a significant influence in molding me into the man I am today!"

Sanglo then continues saying, "I would love to join you on your quest, but that is for you to fulfill. I need to make sure that our boys get home safely. Though we will part ways, and until we meet up again, know that you are always in my thoughts and prayers." At that point, Sanglo, Taiasi, and the other two ulitao pay respects to Ma'-

tao and his warriors and head back in Ati's direction. Da'on then turns to Ma'tao while saying, "I need to make sure that Ogogta and Amta get back to their families safely in Fu'a. Also, to see if Mafac and Gofchegi made it back as well. Once I've taken care of that, I'll catch back up with you all."

Ma'tao, in knowing the heart of Da'on, replies, "I understand my brother! Yes, you get them home safely." Aligao overhears their conversation and interrupts, saying, "Da'on! I'm going with you." He suddenly turns to Ma'tao, asking, "Well, only if that's cool with you, my Maga'lahi?

I can't have Da'on go all alone. What if he comes across any Manganiti Man Nanu?" He then laughs as he slaps Da'on on his shoulder. Da'on, who does not even smile or cringe, says, "That's not even funny." Ma'tao snickers in agreement, saying, "Yes, you both go and make sure that all they all are home safely!"

Aligao smiles while saying, "Now, you all be safe! And we'll catch up to you all shortly!" He then turns to Da'on and asks, "You do know the way to Chochogo'? Right?" Da'on smacks Aligao upside his head and signals him to follow while saying, "Yes, I do, Aligao!" At that, Aligao follows while shouting, "And, We're Out!" As they walk off, you could hear him mumbling, "You wait and see! When it comes time to face them. You'll be glad I'm by your side!" Ma'tao, Atani, Atdao, Ina, and their newly joined member Magogui head off on the path towards Chochogo'.

Chapter 4

"Onward To Chochogo'!"

The sun starts to peek over the hills and mountains deep within central Guahan. They follow Ma'tao, who is walking aside Magogui on what they can barely even consider a path. The early morning comes with sounds of fanihi (fruitbat) flying back towards their home in the trees within the deep dark jungle foliage to roost for the day. Combined with the sweet songs of native island birds ushering in the morning.

The caretakers of the night now give way to the caretakers of the day. To be part of and witness that changeover in itself is a wonder to behold. So they savor that moment. Admire and take it all in! It is the first time this far deep within the island for Atani, Atdao, and Ina. All who have spent their lives to this point only along the beautiful beaches of their mystical island home. They are now just witnessing that their splendid island paradise with all its wondrous sights and sounds has so much more to offer! They are not the only ones intrigued, for Ma'tao himself has not walked along this landscape for quite some time that everything seems all so new and foreign to him. To all of them. They also take notice that getting to Chochogo' was going to be no easy task. Because deep within central Guahan are miles of treacherous mountains, with ridges that one could slip and drop off at any given moment! If that were to happen, they would free fall into deep, dark, never-ending caverns. If they are not prepared or guarded, one could easily be deceived by the beauty that this area possesses and play right into her darker side! A darker side that Ma'tao and his warriors are about to acquaint themselves with face to face.

Magogui turns to Ma'tao with extreme caution in his voice says, "We need to stop! For this was not here the last passed this way!" What Ma'tao and his warriors see next could be just as deadly and hurtful as much as it is beautiful. They now stand in awe at this part of the island's number one defenses! This unforgiving area, known as "I Sesonyan Pribidu" (The Forbidden Swamp)! With a constant yearly downpour of torrential rains. The ravines and valleys, combined with the muddy clay soil, are perfect conditions for these mysterious bodies of water. Ever-changing, they could easily take life as well as produce life! The murkiness of her waters a far cry from what an ocean dweller is used to seeing. Yet, it in her ambiguity is where many of her mysteries reside.

This swampland is so vast that it does not seem ever to end!

Atdao, while looking out at the swamp, says, "There have been stories of the Ito'. They are giant catfish like creatures that legend says swallow people whole who are disrespectful in this area! After everything we encountered so far, those stories got me thinking. Has anyone seen any of these creatures?" Ma'tao, who is taking a good look at his surroundings, replies, "Stories. That's all I heard as well, but I suggest we keep our guard up! In that muddy, murky water, you won't be able to see three feet in front of you." Magogui speaks quietly, saying, "I do know of one guy. But I won't mention any names, not to anger any spirits. Along with two others, he and I left Hanum with me to seek you out, Ma'tao. They wanted to join the cause. When we passed an area that is not far from here, we accidentally split up. He was with the youngest in our group, and we didn't see them for almost three days. We stayed in the area, trying to find them, but no such luck. We decided that they probably left and headed back to Hanum, so we proceeded to-wards Chochogo'. It wasn't even an hour later that we found him hiding in a patch of bamboo! He was shaking of fright, completely naked, and shivering like he had been cold for days. He said he saw us calling out to him, and we passed him many times. But I swear! We didn't even see him once, and we passed that same area about more times than I could remember. Upon questioning him on the whereabouts of the young boy. The only thing he kept saying was that they took him and were planning to feast on him! So I asked him who are these people and how do they look? Al he kept mumbling from there on in was Ito'! Ito'. We took him with us as we tried to locate Chochogo', but we kept coming back around and ending up in the same spot for some reason. It wasn't until I decided to pray and asks for protection from my ancestral spirits that we had a breakthrough. Not too long after, our paths crossed with one of the kakhana's of Chochogo'! He performed a ceremony to bring my friend back to life. When he came to, he told us he was heading back to Hanum and never to return. We never did find the young one! The kakhana told us just to let it be. Because to keep searching for him would only draw more attention to us! So we stopped and left this area. I haven't been back here since that fateful day."

After sharing that, Atani and Ina immediately get beside Magogui and hug him while Atani says, "We're here with you now! And whatever or whoever is out there, they now have us to deal with!" Atdao then turns to Ma'tao and says, "I heard that the freshwater eels here were good eating and to die for. But thinking that we might probably die to feed the catfish! Now that's a little too much!" Ma'tao looks at Atdao and laughs hysterically while saying, "Dang Atdao! I didn't know that you had jokes! Look at you." Both men laugh as Atani says, "We should get going. It'll be getting dark soon, and I could use the rest. Besides, I'm famished."

Ma'tao agrees, saying, "Sounds good to me!" They head the mountain away from the swamp and find a nice place to call home for the night. They also prepare a fire that Magogui curls up next to and lays down to rest. Ma'tao then asks Atdao, "What do you say we head back down to that swamp and try to catch some of those freshwater eels you're constantly talking about?" Atdao, without hesitation, says, "Let's do this! I'm down if you are!"

They both get down to the river and prepare coconut fiber fishing line with some shell hooks baited with coconut meat. They toss three lines into the swamp, not far from a fallen tree that they sit upon to wait for a bite. Not even a whole minute goes by when all three lines suddenly come alive! Each of the lines has an eel on it. Atdao jumps in excitement, saying, "Check it out! We're eating good tonight!"

They pull in all three lines to find three very good-sized, healthy-looking, and meaty eels! Ma'tao then says, "I could clean these up if you gather the coconuts and mangu' (turmeric) for their preparation? I also spotted a couple of lemmai (breadfruit) trees up nearby. Should go great with this." Atdao willingly replies, "Your on! Consider it done." Ma'tao then says, "Meet me back here when you find what we need." Atdao heads off to gather the necessary ingredients for their feast.

Ma'tao is knee-deep in swamp water, getting the eels all cleaned, cut up, and prepared for cooking. When suddenly, he senses someone is standing right behind him! He turns instantly to see a very well built man, roughly his height, with long braided white hair. He is adorning an intricately carved hairpiece. Simultaneously, sporting a finely made garment of native bird feathers of the most beautiful colors. The staff he is holding, just like everything else, clearly depicts that he is a person of great importance.

This man standing before him is a kakhana! He then, in a curious voice, asks, "That eel meat looks like it's going to make a mighty fine dinner.

Would you happen to have enough for a guest?"

Ma'tao, without any apprehension, replies, "Only if that guest is a friend and not a foe!"

The man chuckles while saying, "No enemies here. Now that you're here, Ma'tao!" Ma'tao curiously asks, "You from around here? Are you a kakhana from Chochogo'? Are we in Chochogo'?"

The kakhana smiles and says, "What Chochogo' means to one, Chochogo' may mean something to another! Not only is it a place, Chochogo' is a state of mind!"

Just then, Atdao returns with all the ingredients needed to prepare the feast. He looks at the kakhana then to Ma'tao and says, "I see you made a friend!" He then turns to the kakhana and introduces himself by saying, "Saina' hu, I'm Atdao, son of Asiga and Ana'i. Grandson of Maga'lahi Ahgao of Humatak!"

The kakhana then introduces himself by saying, "I'm Tugut. A kakhana of Chochogo'." He then turns to Ma'tao and asks, "And you, Ma'tao! What is your lineage?" Ma'tao, with a confused look, is quiet at first, then speaks aloud, saying, "I'm Ma'tao offspring of Kiighi who I barely even know, son to a mother that I barely even remember and owner to a belly that's very hungry! We best go now and get up to the camp! We have hungry people waiting."

As they all walk up the mountain to the camp, Atdao laughs while saying to Ma'tao, "And you said I have jokes. You get witty when you're hangry." They both laugh as they proceed to meet the women.

As soon as they get to the campsite, Magogui immediately recognizes Kakhana Tugut and rushes up to greet him. Ma'tao then says, "I take it that he's the kakhana you spoke about." Magogui replies, "Yes! It was a blessing he came when he did. Because honestly, I don't know what I would've done if he didn't!"

Kakhana Tugut replies, "This area of swampland could be very deceiving. It has taken many lives by ancient spirits that reside within these waters! Waters that protect the village of Chochogo' and it's people!"

Ma'tao then curiously asks, "Are the Ito' those so-called spirits? Are they manganiti?" Tugut replies," Yes, they are those spirits! But to say they're manganiti would only be a half-truth. In regards to the Ito', there is so much more to these spiritual beings than you think!"

Ma'tao then asks, "As for Chochogo', Is it close? Could you help me to understand more about this village that I'm to lead and become its Maga'lahi?"

At that point, the eel meat, turmeric, and coconut milk, which are cooking on the fire, that Ma'tao and Atdao are preparing is releasing beautiful aromas. The wonderful aroma blankets their camp. The smells alone are enough to have them put that discussion aside, even just for that moment. The moment that they all could enjoy the food and company.

Chapter 5

"Insights Of Truths!"

They are all now filled with that ever so needed, delicious, and satisfying meal. Atdao, so stuffed, says, "From what I heard, eel meat from this part of the island was good. I didn't expect it to be great! It was the best I ever had."

They all agree as Kakhana Tugut smiles while saying, "There are so many things about Chochogo' that make it great. And to you, Ma'tao, many truths that have to be revealed! And so many of these truths are misunderstood." After making that statement, Ma'tao gets up in front of the group and asks, "So can you give us a brief history on Chochogo'? Please enlighten us as to what type of wondrous mystery this village possesses. And what will be in store for me in full filling my duties and responsibilities as your Maga'lahi? Because honestly, I barely even remember living there. So how am I to lead a people? A people that I hardly even know and who barely know me?" Tugut with a very interested yet relaxed look to his demeanor. Primarily upon being posed with a question of this caliber, answers very calmly, "First of all, the items that you bring to the forefront no doubt are essential and in due time need to be addressed. But I think what you should be asking is how do you inspire people? A very primal instinct moves people! A first instinct to survive! Whether it'll be as an individual or the group as a whole. Now how you tap into that will be entirely up to you! But inspiration Ma'tao. Inspiration, I feel, could be a great asset in bringing each individual and helping them bring out the best in their ability to function as a whole. That is one of the central core principles that stand out among our people in Chochogo'! It is also one that has permitted us to stay and flourish so far inland with all its beauty, wonder, and mystery. Side by side with her treacherous, ever-winding, and deadly defenses for so many generations!"

Upon hearing all their talk along with their type of tone, Atani finds herself in a situation. A situation that, regardless of her choosing. She only wants the best for her love, Ma'tao. So she, without any hesitation, asks, "I mean no disrespect Kakhana Tugut or to you Ma'tao, but could you tell us more of Chochogo', where is your main village, along with your people, and why do these swamp creatures work so hard to protect it?" Ma'tao immediately turns to Atani, and with a look that shows his disapproval bites his tongue to avoid any unwanted confrontation.

Kakhana Tugut then turns to Atani, and so taken with her tenacity, replies, "Yes. Atani of Humatak. You who have the heart of a warrior princess and wielder of the Gapot Ulu I Saina. Why wouldn't you want to know those questions? Because if Ma'tao were to assume his birthright as Maga'lahi of Chochogo'. Are you wondering where would all of you fit into this?"

Atani, now wondering if this guy is a friend or foe, asks, "So are you going to answer the question or not?"

Tugut first looks around, then grabs a stick and draws on the ground. He outlines three mountain peaks and, on top of each of them, three circles. He points to the first of the rings and, in an ominous voice, begins saying, "Every three hundred years, a Maga'lahi will be called upon! He will be called upon as the Maga'lahi I Mantatkilu to bring balance ultimately. Balance back to all the islands. Chochogo' is the village that has been around since time eternal! A very ancient village. You all need to know that number three is a very significant number in who we are as a people! A specific Maga'lahi will be selected every three hundred years and tested. If successful, he will be that final factor to bring it all together! Two of this very special Maga'lahi have already existed, but they were not successful in completing their tasks. Specific tasks that only the Maga'lahi I Mantatkilu can achieve! Even with the most skillful warriors at the time by their side! You all here today know of the second one by name, the name of Gadao. Gadao of Inalahan. His feats of strengths are a testament to his prowess, but that alone wasn't enough to correct the misfortune that has befallen the human race. The first warrior to rise from the ranks was never known until just very recently! All information regarding this certain Maga-

'lahi remained a mystery, except that he was from northern Guahan! He was also the closest to date in achieving that prophecy. Even closer than Gadao! Until the all-encompassing dark forces of the manganiti took his soul! He took his soul to use it to accomplish their evil plans by placing it in a just as wicked host! That same dark force unleashed that evil Maga'lahi unto this world! You also know of him. You all already have faced him. He calls himself "Asuli!"

You could instantly see that once Tugut made mention of that name, all are now in disbelief!

Ma'tao then asks, "How can that be? Asuli is Irao's great-great-grandson! He claims that my family is responsible for cheating him from his birthright!"

Tugut responds, saying, "That's the name he goes by today. The dark force of the manganiti is a very ancient spirit. From the time of Puntan. Some even say he's Chaifi himself!" We now know him as Asuli and his fierce band of warriors who would do anything to please their leader. Their Maga'lahi, who led them astray! But a third Maga'lahi has been prophesied to arise. The third was born on this very sacred ground! Nine hundred years exactly to the day that Asuli was. The prophecy speaks of how he is to have all the attributes needed to accomplish what the others haven't, and finally set things right! There are three very distinct mountain ridges in this area, and Chochogo' could reside within any one of them at any given time. The vast swampland connects each of these mountains and their valleys; I Sesonyan Pribidu! Each ridge signifies the rise of one of those Maga'lahi. Since the third Maga'lahi was born into this world, Chochogo indicates its importance on the third ridge. There was another question that you brought to my attention. You Atani asked about the Ito'! The Ito' as they are known, are zombie-like creatures. They are the restless souls of the warriors of the two failed Maga'lahi! Their loyal followers who fought by their sides! They all vowed with a blood oath to stand by the side of each of their Maga'lahi. Through thick and thin. Unfortunately, when the first two Maga'lahi I Mantatkilu failed to accomplish what they were brought into this world to do, not only did the people or their islands suffer. Their warriors sustained the most significant fate of all. The separation of their souls from their bodies! But their souls aren't able to return to the place of their creation. Until the balance shift in this world is made right, they are cursed to live in a dimension between the spiritual realm and the physical realm. Since they could weave themselves between both dimensions and make themselves invisible, they go around lying and deceiving the living!To this day, their zombie-like bodies inhabit and are tormented in and around the murky waters of I Sesonyan I Pribidu! They are said to consume human flesh to absorb their life force! The life force they obtain will allow them to walk in the physical realm among the living! So you see, they all suffer not only from their own doing. They are also paying for the sins of who was responsible for their well being! Their Maga'lahi! But they shouldn't be looked upon as if they are manganiti because by protecting Chochogo', they are protecting the interests of the people of Guahan along with all the other islands!"

Ma'tao, along with his warriors, look on as he asks, "Magogui mentioned that these so-called zombies took his friend. So am I supposed just to let that go and forget it?!" Tugut replies, "I was there to bring his other friend back from shock. And all, including Magogui, claimed that he was taken and repeated what they heard. But non of them claimed to see them eat him! Then again, that swamp is their domain, and we re-spect it wholeheartedly!"

Ma'tao being inquisitive, asks, "Where does Chochogo' stand in this impending war between

Ati and Humatak?" Tugut, as if not showing any interest, replies, "I, for one, know that confrontations are inevitable in society. Chochogo' with the guidance of Maga'lahi Kiighi, has always sought the peaceful path first, which is why peace negotiations have been held here for many generations. But with all recent tensions and the imbalance of energies, I see very new problems that we as a people all have to deal with! As for Maga'lahi Kiighi's stance, he should be the one to let you in on his insights."

Ma'tao then asks, "How much do you know of Itak or the Diyuk Paton Chaifi (Chaifi's Sling Stone), and how is it tied to Chochogo!?"

Tugut, with a big grin, responds, "There is so much more to Chochogo'. So much more, I would like to tell you. But you should hear it from Maga'lahi Kiighi himself!"

Matao, without hesitation, says, "Take us to see my father!"

Just then, they hear rustling coming from down below. Atani whispers, saying, "Please tell me that you all caught that as well. Ma'tao cautiously asks, "Tugut, are you traveling with or

expecting anyone?" Tugut calmly answers, "No!"
Ma'tao then signals them to put out the fire immediately! Atdao does just that without even
question. Ma'tao quietly says, "Atdao, just stay
here, and I'll check out who or what is making all
that noise!"

Atdao adamantly replies, "No, not again! I'm
going this time. Ina, along with Atani, are more
than capable of holding it down here!"
Ma'tao, with a slight chuckle, says, "Ok. Let's go!
If that's alright with the ladies!" They both nod
in agreement. He then pulls Atani closer to him,
saying, "You alright with that, my love?" She

promptly responds, "Yes! Just be careful. Ina and I got this."

As Ma'tao kisses her cheek, he jokingly says,

"If anything, only hurt them! Don't kill them!" He then followed by Atdao heads back down the mountain through a back trail.

With the moon lighting the path and chirps from crickets filling the night, they covertly position themselves up in front of the area where they heard the noises!

After hearing the stories of these zombie-like creatures, Atdao cannot get that off his mind and whispers, "Ma'tao, what are your thoughts on all this? Do you think the Ito' are real? Considering the blood oath we took, we better succeed! I ain't suited to becoming one of them!"

Ma'tao whispers back quietly, saying, "Honestly, whether they're real or not, I have a definite feeling that we'll be finding out soon enough!" Atdao, now with a disgusted look, says," And to think we feasted on the eels!" He then pauses for a moment, smiles, then says, "Nah, I would eat that again in a heartbeat! That was one excellent meal!" Ma'tao chuckles while nodding in agreement, saying, "No Doubt! That was excellent!"

Then they hear it! The rustling of leaves and branches as they make out footsteps heading towards their direction. Then they see it!

A large shadowy figure is getting closer by the moment. Ma'tao notices that it is directly on the same path that they on! So he gets closer to Atdao and whispers, "Stay on this side of the trail while I cover the other. We'll wait for whoever or whatever that large specimen is to cross our path, and when it gets close enough, we'll make our move!" Atdao acknowledges, So Ma'tao quickly yet quietly scurries and conceals himself across from Atdao. Both men, now perfectly camouflaged in the brush, don't even make the slightest sound. Because of how quiet it is, Ma'-tao could now hear his heartbeat. He could also make out the footsteps getting closer and closer!

The shadowy figure starts getting closer until it is just inches away from both of them! Ma'tao takes deep breaths and thinks to himself, *Now! Now is the...*, but before he could even finish that thought, Atdao directly swings the Pagasi with so much force while yelling, "So you think you could sneak up on us you scum-sucking Ito'!" He instantly takes down not one, but two figures! Ma'tao rushes out to assist in finishing them off when at that moment, they hear, "Basta fan! Hafa kao kaduduku hamyu? Hita ha'!"

Which translates to "Hold on, you two! Are you both crazy? It's just us!" They both instantly stop attacking as soon as they realize that their so-called zombie creature is Da'on walking directly behind Aligao! With the moon shining from above and behind them, it seemed as if they were one! Aligao, being upfront, is also the one who yelled after feeling the Pagasi up against his face!

Atdao at once recalls the Pagasi! As it lands back in his hands, he regains his composure. But the thoughts of the Ito' are still running through his mind. Da'on, while assisting Aligao to his feet, chuckles, saying, "You alright? If you asked me, you could pass for an Ito'." Aligao, still shaking it off and regaining his bearings, fires back, "Keep it up Da'on! Keep it up! Because we're now deeper inland. And it's my understanding that the further in we get, the more likely the Manganiti Man Nanu will show themselves!" Ma'tao, while also helping Aligao regain his balance, jokingly adds, "Between getting choked out by Pulonon and smacked by the Pagasi, dang Aligao! You never catch a break! But with all this talk about the Ito' and Manganiti Man Nanu, I'm just glad it's you both!"

Aligao, now more composed, chuckles, saying, "I'm glad to see you too! I was beginning to think Da'on was lying about ever visiting Cho-chogo'!"

Da'on, not moved by that remark, scoffs and ignores Aligao. He does so while greeting Ma'tao and Atdao, asking, "Where's the rest of the group?" Aligao then adds, "Yeah. Where are they? And what is an Ito'?!" Ma'tao replies, "Let's head up to the camp. Are you sure you're alright?" Aligao shakes his head, then responds, "Yeah, I'm fine. You just both better get us up to speed!" Ma'tao assists Aligao as they all make their way up the mountain trail.

They get closer to the campsite as Ma'tao whistles to signal their approach. They then wait for a response. Not too long after, they get it! So they head on in, making their way towards the group. Ina, who whistled, greets them along with Atani, Magogui, and Tugut.

It is still dark out without fire as Ma'tao introduces Tugut to Da'on and Aligao.

Aligao, without any reluctance, asks, "Are you an Ito'?!" Tugut stares intently at Aligao while smiling and replies, "If I were, you'd be my first victim!" At that remark, they all bust out laughing, but non louder than Da'on. Which immediately shocks everyone!

Aligao, while looking at Tugut, smiles and mumbles, "You're lucky you seem essential. Otherwise, I'll rattle you to death."

Ma'tao, now composed, places his hand on Aligao shoulder and firmly says, "Now that we're all altogether again. Tugut now, it's time for us to see Chochogo' finally'! Take me to my father!"

Tugut, without any qualms, agrees and leads the way. Aligao turns and whispers to Ma'tao,

"So this guy is going to lead us to Chochogo'?
You sure?"

Ma'tao then says, "It's an option I have to consider. We need to get to the so-called third ridge.
And unless you know the way, he's our best bet."
Aligao shrugs his shoulders and says, "Shoot.
You know best, but I wasn't joking about rattling
him to death!" Ma'tao, along with his warriors,
follows Tugut as he leads them out the first valley and up the mountain.

Chapter 6

"The Homecoming!"

Some time has passed as they trail behind Kakhana Tugut. They are a little more anxious as they leave the confines of the second valley. So they keep their guard up.

As they head up another mountain, Ma'tao, now looking around at his surroundings, gets up closer and asks, "We're you the kakhana when I was born?"

Tugut looks him in the eyes and replies," At the time of your birth, I wasn't; It was my predecessor Sungot. But I remember that day like it was yesterday. Maga'lahi Kiighi was on edge the whole time your mother was in labor with you. The entire twelve hours! Since the moment you were born, Maga'lahi Kiighi was so proud! That moment I could honestly say was the first time I ever saw him smile. Being Maga'lahi in and of itself is no easy task. But in being Maga'lahi of Chochogo' and so far inland has its challenges like no other! But your father always stepped up to the task. He would go above and beyond to do anything for his people or his village. But I never saw him happier than when he was with your mother. She always seemed to bring absolute peace to him. Your father is a battle-hardened Maga'lahi. One of the fiercest I've come to know or the islands have ever seen! There's so much of him that I see in you. But your mother had a way of cutting through that hardened exterior of his. I recall her being loved throughout the whole village, come now. I've said enough; we need to head in this direction." Kakhana Tugut takes them along the mountain pass down towards the third valley.

It is still early morning with the sun slowly peeking over the horizon. They can barely even see since they are deep within the valley surrounded by the magnificent mountains. It is also still dark enough that they need to be extremely cautious.

Da'on walks up close to Ma'tao and, with a concerned voice, says, "This place looks a little different from what I remember last. We should think about getting to higher ground soon. Because this is a perfect place for an ambush!"

Ma'tao, while turning to respond to Da'on, notices that Atdao moved up to join in the conversation, saying, "We're too exposed out here!" Ma'tao then says, "I feel you both! Tell the rest to be on guard."

At that exact moment, they all hear it! A Scream! A loud, gut-wrenching, blood-curdling scream!

Atani excitedly yells, "What is that?! Where's it coming from?!" Ma'tao yells, "Run! Get undercover! I've heard that before!" Without hesitating. They all run to get under the protection and exterior of the jungle canopy!

As Da'on turns back and looks around to check on everyone, he shouts, "He's gone! Ma'-tao! Magogui's gone!" As they all turn to look for him. Atani yells, "Ma'tao! Tugut! He's gone as well!"

As they gather themselves as to what had just happened, Ma'tao wastes no time and shouts, "Get ready for battle with backs up to one another! Is everyone else here?!" Immediately, they all shout out their names to signify that they're all present and ready for anything,

"Ma'tao!", "Atani!", "Atdao!", "Da'on", "Aligao!"

Aligao then screams, "What in the hell was that?! Was that the Itak?!" They are quiet just for a moment before Atdao yells, "Ina! Where's Ina?!"

They all cannot believe what has just happened! First of all, what created that scream?!

And within just a matter of seconds, Ina, Magogui, and Tugut are now all missing! Aligao yells, "They just vanished! Did that beast take them?!" Atdao, now freaked out, runs off and starts calling out to Ina! They all chase after him with Ma'tao shouting, "Stay together! We'll be stronger as one!"

They catch up to Atdao, who is now stopped and screaming from the top of his lungs! He shouts out into the jungle, "Bring her back here! Bring her back! Ina, if you can hear me, I'll find you and make whoever or whatever did this pay!" Atani grabs her brother and holds him saying, "Yes! We will get them back; we'll get her back!"

Da'on then sees something! He leaves the group and takes off while excitedly yelling, "Someone was watching us! I'm going after him!" He darts off so fast that the others barely made out what he said. They all chase after him frantically!

They find him under a canopy of bamboo trees, standing on top of a boy, no older than fifteen years of age. Da'on has his right foot placed on his neck, which restrains him! Ma'tao, Atani, and Aligao gather around. Ma'tao shouts, asking, "Who are you, and what did you do with our friends?!" The boy grunting in pain, does not answer. Atdao, who now joins the group, quickly walks up to the boy and kicks him hard on the thigh while yelling, "Where's Ina?! Where is she?! If you or anyone hurts her! I'll——" Just then, a voice shouts out from within the surrounding bamboo trees, "You'll what?"

Ma'tao now realizes that the boy was baiting them. Then movements! Ma'tao and his warriors witness actions from all around them! Who are these people?

They have Ma'tao and his warriors surrounded! The voice continues, "What will you do? More importantly, what are you willing to do to free your friends?" Then as to appear out of thin air, Ma'tao and his warriors find themselves completely encircled! These warriors were perfectly camouflaged and blended in perfectly with their environment! They seemed to appear magically! These were no ordinary warriors that they have become accustomed to seeing. One could easily make out that they were so wholly immersed and one with their surroundings and moved entirely as one! It is something so unique!

Ma'tao then takes notice of the voice who called out to them. He seemed to be their leader! He separates himself from his warriors while making his way towards Ma'tao, very proud and ever so boldly! This distinct man draped with ferns, bits of brush, and leaves as part of his elaborate design in military tactical gear. They finally come face to face! To the point that they are now staring deep into each other's eyes. Everyone could quickly feel the tension between both men!. All firmly gripping their weapons in hand in preparation for battle at even the slightest move!

The intensity is at its peak because they are now so close. So close that both men even see beads of sweat running down the side of each of their faces. Silence! Complete silence! Not even a single sound. Then he hears it, "Ma'tao is that you?" Ma'tao, now with his adrenaline hurriedly pumping through his body, takes a deep exhale. Looking deeper into this man's eyes, who is standing directly in front of him. He now takes a deep breath and slowly asks, "Father? Is it you?" They are now both speechless. Ma'tao cannot explain what he feels at this precise moment, but he hears that voice. That still small voice confirms that what he already knows to be true! So he takes a step forward and places his forehead against this man he knows to be his father! Maga'lahi Kiighi!

Without any apprehension, Kiighi embraces his son and pulls him closer. He holds him tighter, saying, "For some odd reason, when my scout mentioned to me last night that there are people camped on the mountain near the mouth of I Sesonyan Pribidu, I had a vision that it was you! So I, along with my warriors, had to come out here and see it for myself. You're home now, my son!"

Just hearing those very words. Ma'tao is now beyond himself! This moment he knew that would one day come, but now that it is here, it is just all too surreal. But even though this is going much more different than he expected, Ma'tao then thinks to himself, *I have so many questions, yet where do I start?*

Ma'tao knows that he needs to keep his composure because his warriors depend on him and follow his lead! Aligao noticing that the tension is still lingering between warriors on both sides, blurts out while looking at Maga'lahi Kiighi, "So now that both of you know each other, could we get your warriors to stand down?" Ma'tao just stares at Aligao as if telling him to shut his mouth, but does not say a word! Aligao then changes his tone and says, "Could you please?"

Kiighi instantly looks at his warriors while signaling and telling them to do so. The tensions die down as Ma'tao now calmly says, "Honesty, I don't even know where to begin. With all that has transpired here today, we just want to get our friends back!"

Kiighi then asks, "Who are these friends that you speak of?" Atdao, still angered, shouts, "Ina! Where is she? Do you know of that beast, or who could've taken her?!" Atani and Da'on right away turn to Atdao to calm him down! Even though he is hurting and angry, he tries his best to control himself. Ma'tao also turns to him and says with as much calm as he could muster, "We will get her back! Right now, you need just to keep it together." Aligao blurts out yet again,

"Also, where's Magogui? What did you have Tugut do with them?!" Ma'tao then grabs the back of Aligao's neck and, giving him a slight squeeze, utters, "Dude, c'mon! I got this!"

Maga'lahi Kiighi, now with a confused look on his face, says, "If you're implying that we had something to do with your friends disappearing, then you got it all wrong! I also heard you mention Itak along with the name Tugut am I correct?" Ma'tao replies, "Yes! Itak! Your Kakhana Tugut! Where is he? and if you had nothing to do with it, why would you have him lead us to you all?" Maga'lahi Kiighi then says, "First of, all let's head to the village. If you want to know where to start, we could start there!" Maga'lahi Kiighi chuckles while saying, "Follow my lead. It's not much further!" They have already walked through two other valleys. So going to Cho-chogo' to rest themselves for a while will be graciously welcomed.

Maga'lahi Kiighi calls to his side one particular warrior who signals the rest. In unison, they all light their torches and form two lines. Aligao starts giggling as he leans into Ma'tao and asks quietly, "Are they losing it? Don't they realize that the sun is now out?" Ma'tao just looks at

Aligao, smiles sarcastically, and replies, "You don't just know when to quit, do you?" Aligao just shakes his head while saying, "Just pointing it out to you! After hearing that crazy scream, who knows what other types of crazies are out here!"

Maga'lahi Kiighi walks in between the two-row of warriors and gestures Ma'tao along with his to follow. The lead warrior heads to the front and signals his Chochogo' warriors to move out! They then start walking even deeper into the canopy of bamboo trees. They walk the entire length of the third valley within the bamboo grove while avoiding getting close to the swamp.

Atani moves up closer to Ma'tao with much curiosity and says, "This place is so interesting! Check out how dark it's becoming under this bamboo canopy. At least if there's a giant bird beast, we'll be safe in here. Now I also see why they need the torches!" Aligao follows up with, "Oh, now I see too!" Atani just smacks him upside the head as Da'on whispers to Ma'tao, "They must've moved their village. This area doesn't look familiar to me. Also, you see their lead warrior?"

Ma'tao then replies, "What about him? Is he someone of concern?" Da'on replies, "His name is Machatlu. I do know he is very loyal to Kiighi. But he is known to have vain pretensions. I would just keep an eye on him." Ma'tao responds, saying, "It sounds like you had a run-in or two with him. Am I right?"

Da'on, now chuckling, says, "Your observation is correct. The last time I was here, he and I went up against each other! We competed against one another to make our Maga'lahi proud and display our village's strength. He is a formidable opponent!

Ma'tao chuckles again while asking, "Did you win?" Da'on smirks while saying, "I bested him when we threw fudfudganom at each other! I caught all his spears while two of mine got him and broke skin! In our second contest, he could more accurately use the atupat and diyuk patu much more skillfully than I and gave me a bruised arm! We were both pretty evenly matched when it came time to display our wrestling skills. It was also one of the most grueling matches that I have ever been in! We both wouldn't stop until both Maga'lahi Kiighi and Maga'lahi Dadau declared a stalemate!

Ma'tao, now showing more interest, says, "Stay sharp and rested! We just might revisit that later on!"

Da'on, just as excited, replies, "Honestly, I have been waiting anxiously for a rematch against that guy!"

They are now heading deeper into the bamboo canopy, and if not for the torchlight, they all will be in complete darkness. Machatlu now leads them all into a cave! This cave connecting to the bamboo canopy heads deep into the heart of the third mountain that they now have come across. The dark, damp underground cavern path that they are on starts to narrow.

As it narrows and now hugs only the side of the cave walls. This very narrow path causes them to form a single file line for them to pass.

Ma'tao thinks to himself, *If this is the entrance to Chochogo', then this cave combined with the swamp will surely make it hard for an enemy to overcome these defenses that I've seen so far!*

As they all steadily walk down the narrow and winding cave passage, they come to a row of six torches. On each side and standing next to each torch is a Chochogo' warrior. Each one of them dawning the elaborate tactical gear that is reminiscent of that of Maga'lahi Kiighi!

As they come to the last pair of warriors, Ma'-tao notices a light off to the left of him. The light barely enters the cave due to the enormous trees and lush vegetation surrounding the outer cave walls! Machatlu, Kiighi, and all their warriors head in that direction. Aligao, looking around in awe, asks Ma'tao, "Are we there yet?!" Ma'tao, admiring their surroundings, replies, "As if I know. I haven't been around these parts in years."

Maga'lahi Kiighi turns towards Ma'tao, and as they exit the cave, he says in a very majestic voice, "Welcome to Chochogo'! Welcome home, my son!"

The sun greets them again as they exit the cave. The thick vines and the lush vegetation drape over their bodies and face to expose a whole other world within the island! Ma'tao is now walking side by side with Atani; both are in awe!

For Chochogo', just like the other places they both have been since their adventures began, stands out as a place so unique that one probably would not imagine ever-existing! Especially after leaving behind the hot, humid swampland! And not to mention the bamboo canopy's black enclosure into the deep, dark, damp, and dreary mountainous cave. Chochogo' in itself is a sight to behold!

Ma'tao instantly takes notice that the village is strategically situated. From where he is standing, they have to walk uphill on the path they are on. For Chochogo' rests just below the mountain crest. The same mountain that they walked through. One could easily see that this is a village well designed to defend itself against enemy attacks. One could easily forget about all of that once you lay your eyes on her surrounding beauty! Rolling hills and giant native trees encircle the village and add to her protection. But within the jungle canopy, a wide array of flora and fauna only enhances while accentuating her beauty!

As they take in all her wonder, it is short-lived. Atdao, who is now more agitated about Ina's whereabouts, very impatiently says to

Ma'tao, "I know this is a place you longed to be back to for so many years! But we need to find and locate Ina! If I have to leave and do it alone, I'll do just that!"

Atani tries to console her brother while Ma'-tao, who could feel the worry in Atdao's spirit, empathetically replies, "I understand." Then without putting it off any longer and from right where they stand, Ma'tao calls out to Maga'lahi Kiighi, saying, "Maga'lahi! My warriors and I mean no disrespect, but we must find our friends! We need to make sure that they are safe and that no harm befalls them!"

Maga'lahi Kiighi calls to his warriors, "Saga! Saga guennao ni tumutogi hao!" Which translates to "Stop! Stop right where you stand!" He then walks up to Ma'tao and his warriors with a concerned look and says, "I understand you want to get them back! But you must hear what I have to say in regards to where they' might be. If you're to stand a chance, then follow me up to my village and you'll get the answers you'll need on who took and how to recover your friends! To ignore this advice will be futile to all of you and your efforts!"

Ma'tao looks into his father's eyes, and that instant connection reassures him that they need to heed his advice. He then turns to Atdao, who still is so distraught, and says, "My brother, let's just head into the village to gain more insight on what we'll be facing! You also know for a fact that we shouldn't run out there blindly. We need to find out who or what took Ina and Magogui!" Atani, who also understands what her brother is feeling, adds, "You out of anyone know how close Ina and I are with one another. I also know she could protect herself! That's not to say we're not going to do anything about it. With everything we've been up against so far, we can't risk losing anyone else!"

Atdao looks into his sister's eye and, while still feeling reluctant, replies, "And you know that I'm not one just to sit around and wait for things to happen if I could do something about it!" Atani agrees and says, "Yes, I do! And we respect you for that, but let's be smart about this!" Atdao, now at least listening to reason, looks at Ma'tao and his companions while gesturing that he understands and falls in behind them.

They now all make their way up towards the village. Ma'tao then turns to Atani, saying, "My heart goes out to your brother. If it were you who went missing, I would react the same way, if not worse!" Atani agrees and says, "I feel the same way you do! We do need to know more about who or what we are facing. And once we do, we need to get back out there and find both her and Magogui!"

As they all approach the crest of the mountain, they enter another canopy of bamboo trees. Aligao looks to Ma'tao and jokingly says, "Not this again!" Ma'tao just looks ahead as Da'on responds, saying, "It's not. I could see some warriors standing at the village entrance!"

As they proceed, they all could now see those warriors. But more importantly, Chochogo'! Ma'tao, now filled with so many mixed emotions, finally gets to lay his eyes for the very first time in the village of his people! The moment he has longed for, for so many years.

As he starts to let it all soak in, Machatlu yells out, "Hoi! Warriors of Chochogo! It's I Machatlu! Along with our brave and humble leader, Maga'lahi Kiighi! Prepare the way for our Maga'lahi and honored guests!"

The sun starts beaming down on this now beautiful clear day as they enter the renowned village of his father's clan. Once they pass from under the bamboo canopy, they see it! Cho-chogo'! The village itself is clean and pristine. The entrance is between two strategically placed lat'di huts. Guarding those huts are six well statured and equipped warriors ready to attack at any given notice! The dwellings are different as opposed to the houses on the coastlines and are perfect for the region. Beautifully crafted, their lat'di are made from much different rocks, yet seem to be just as durable. The posts carved out of ancient native trees are what they construct their huts with, and one can easily see that it gives off the strength that this village possesses!

The villagers and warriors of Chochogo' look on with such curiosity as Ma'tao and his warriors parade down the village paths.

The layout of the village is so elaborate. Any attacking force will be hard-pressed to have to come face to face with the defenses and the warriors of the area.! The huts are strewn all along the mountainside of this ridge. That they have a perfect view of the valley below! Thus giving their warriors and villagers the advantage of higher ground when attacking. As for their weapons. Within the short time that they entered the village. Ma'tao could immediately see that each hut is so fortified with all types of weapon-ry.

All sorts of training implements and weapons never before seen are used by these warriors. Young men are training throughout as the elderly gathered to discuss daily or future ongoings. Indeed, this is a village of warriors!

Ma'tao, at that moment, feels a sudden jolt of energy coursing throughout his entire being. Something deep within himself reassures him that the spirits of his ancestors are surrounding him with their blessings. It is as if they are announcing the Maga'lahi of the future has arrived! Ma'tao can not even explain into words what this day means to him. So he just lets it all set in naturally, for deep within his heart, he knows he is home!

Maga'lahi Kiighi calls to Machatlu, saying, "Take care of our guests! Whatever they want and need, be sure to provide!" He then calls over a bunch of women from the village while he walks over to Atani, saying ever so politely, "If it'll be alright with you? I would like to catch up with my son. He and I have a lot to talk about. These women will take care of you; just let them know if you need anything, and they will get it for you."

Atani looks at Ma'tao then to Maga'lahi Kiighi and replies, saying, "I appreciate it, but I'm fine." She then looks back to Ma'tao and says, "I'm here if you need me!" Ma'tao responds, saying, "I'll be alright, just make sure and tend to Atdao. I won't be far. Be sure to get me if anything!"

He then turns to Maga'lahi Kiighi, heading towards his hut, situated in its very own impressive ridge. This ridge allows Maga'lahi Kiighi to have a bird's eye view of his village and people, overlooking the whole valley down below. Ma'tao, now doing something that he has only dreamed of for many years, follows his father's lead!

Chapter 7

"A Long-Awaited Reunion!"

As they get to the top of the ridge and closer to the hut, Ma'tao notices that it does not rest on any lat'di whatsoever. There are no lat'di stones upon this entire ridge! Maga'lahi Kiighi then calmly says, "We're here." Ma'tao nods and looks around. He also has to focus his eyes to see the hut because it blends so naturally and perfectly with its surroundings. The house is fairly decent sized, and at first glance, one could quickly think that it was pretty bare. They might probably even mistake it for any regular villagers hut and not the dwelling of a Maga'lahi.

Yet for one to think that would be very misleading, because what it may not possess visually, it certainly makes up for in functionality! So to even consider it simple could result in dire consequences!

Maga'lahi Kiighi enters into his hut while Ma'tao enters right behind him and instantly notices all types of weapons and trophies Kiighi has collected from previous battles. With everything that Ma'tao has witnessed so far, he at once senses that whatever it is that Maga'lahi Kiighi finds true to himself or what he stands for, that the same passion burns deep down inside of himself! A little something that gives him that extra ounce of reassurance that this is where he needs to be at this moment in his life.

Ma'tao looks at his father while saying, "This moment is so surreal! I've looked forward to stepping into Chochogo' for so many years. If it wasn't for us needing to go and find our friends, something I feel so deep down inside doesn't want me to leave!" Maga'lahi Kiighi smiles and replies, saying, "That's because of you! My son, you are so deeply tied to this land. From the day

I first held you in my arms, I felt that greatness within you! You Ma'tao, are destined to do great things!"

Ma'tao, though happy to hear those words from his father. He is suddenly saddened while replying, "And what of my mother? Who is she? I don't even know her name? What happened to her?!"

After asking those heart-wrenching questions, Ma'tao could easily see it on Kiighi's face, that look of hesitation. Hesitation in that he was not even sure if he should answer those questions.

There was an awkward pause before Maga'lahi Kiighi opens his mouth to say, "Your mother!

My wife! Meant more to me than anyone will ever know, nor will anyone ever mean as much to me again!" Ma'tao could see that his father was not comfortable talking about this matter, but regardless he presses forward and asks him ever so strongly, "Tell me about her! What was her name?! No one in Ati ever speaks of her. Not even her own family! They don't even mention her name. It's like she never even existed. She's a ghost to me!"

Kiighi could now see that his son needed to know the truth. He could feel his pain burning from deep down within to get some answers finally. And no one else other than himself is capable of giving it to him!"

He then looks deep into his son's eyes as he gestures to him to sit on the guafak mat in front of them. Kiighi then takes a deep breath and, while still profoundly gazing firmly, says, "That's all because they still hold me responsible for what happened to her! Your grandfather never spoke to me after her leaving!" Ma'tao, with a dumbfounded look on his face, replies, "Leaving? What do you mean by her leaving?"

Kiighi, while still with that profound eye connection, says, "Her name, my son was Lumu'ina! She was a very free-spirited woman and always has been since the very day she was born. She had a very different way of looking at our purpose as a people in this world! And with that point of view, not everyone took to her way of thinking. I'll say that she had a unique way of shaking things up! She always knew how to get the best out of me, and she was very instrumental in making me the leader I am today. Your mother, Ma'tao, was a fierce leader, and boy did she love you so much!"

Ma'tao, upon hearing that blurts out, saying, "Well, if she loved me so much, why did she leave?! Where did she go?!" Maga'lahi Kiighi holds his son's hands to calm him down while saying, "That's where things get very confusing! It's not like she decided to one day get up and say, I'm leaving, or I'm out of here! It's more like she disappeared" Ma'tao getting even more upset, yells out, "Disappeared?! Are you telling me that my mother disappeared while she was still with you? Did you not go and look for her?"

Kiighi looks down, pauses again, then looks back to his son, saying, "That's all I did, but to no avail! I ended up so consumed with it that I neglected my duties as Maga'lahi while sacrificing my relationship with you in the process! I know she didn't just decide to up and run away!

I've always believed that so firmly in my heart! Recently, I started to recall these tales of Asuli. These thoughts flooded my mind and fought for my attention! When I was growing up, Asuli was a name only reserved for legends and folklore. I had no idea how so much more real these actual stories or myths are. While pregnant with you, she'd mentioned how she has seen a great force of evil looming and lurking over Chochogo' trying to prevent her from giving birth to you. Because she'd also say that if you are to come into this world, any chance they have of taking control of it will be mightily opposed! She never spoke of how or why; she'd say that it just was!

It was the way things needed to fall! Your mother, Ma'tao, was the most selfless person I've ever met, even to this very day, and I will give up my duty as Maga'lahi to even spend a moment with her once again! She would disagree, but I miss her so deeply!"

Ma'tao, hearing the sadness in his father's voice, brings his tone down while asking, "Do you think the disappearances of Mother, Ina, and Magogui are connected?"

Kiighi then nods his head, saying, "I do not doubt that they are connected! The people of Chochogo', my ancestors, are the ones who have given that creature his name! Itak, as they called it, is a massive black beast of a bird! It has a horrendous scream! When I was growing up, the Itak would show up only on certain hours if a female in the village was pregnant and didn't inform her family. Long gone are the Itak of those days! Villagers have claimed to have spotted Itak much more frequently! And according to them, it is getting much bolder! Back in the day, it would only appear during midnight hours. But more recently, sightings have confirmed that it has been seen more frequently during dusk as the sun is rising, as you all attested too! This beast is known to cause fear, strife, and resentment among people and villages! It could even drum up more tensions to war!"   Ma'tao then says, "Sounds like she's getting braver and more powerful while spreading more fear!"

Kiighi looks at his son curiously and asks, "I'm not sure if I heard you correctly? Did you say, She?"

Ma'tao, with a little smirk, says, "Yes, I did. Itak might be a female!" Kiighi, now more curious, asks, "How's it that you know that?" Ma'tao replies, "Magogui! He mentioned that Itak appears in his dreams and is the reason why he sought me out. He also led us most of the way here. We need to find them soon! There's even more that I need to tell you!" Kiighi scratches his head as he wonders what else does his son have to say.

Ma'tao holds his father's shoulders while saying, "You might want to brace yourself for what I'm about to tell you."

Kiighi acknowledges that he understands as Ma'tao continues saying, "It's Mother. I think she's still alive!" Maga'lahi Kiighi, hearing those words, is now beyond himself! Notably, hearing that from his son, whom he had just reunited with very recently. His whole world, which was once instantly shattered, may now have a chance of being whole again!

He then gets much more deliberate as he asks, "Are you positive? If so, how could this be?!" Ma'tao, with a bit of a smile, shakes his head, saying, "In all honesty, I'm not sure, but this is a powerful feeling within me! I also know that we needed to be here. And with everything we've been through so far, I know the answers rest here within Chochogo'!" Kiighi glances into his eyes and snickers, saying, "In all honesty, that's one trait of a great leader and being able to admit that you don't know or understand it all. But having enough sense to follow what you know to be true while considering the people's thoughts and feelings! That my son, you came to terms with much earlier than I."

In hearing those words from his father, Ma'tao instantly feels grateful yet humbled at the same time. Kiighi then continues saying, "If your mother is still alive, we will find her! We need to speak with my lead warrior Machatlu. He is the eldest son of my closest and now deceased friend Sungot. If anyone knows about Itak and where to locate it or her, it'll be him!"

Ma'tao, with interest, asks, "Wasn't Sungot your kakhana?" Kiighi, now with sadness in his eyes, replies, "Tugut murdered him! Tugut was an apprentice under him for many years. He also was an abandoned child found by Sungot near the swampland. He and Machatlu are about the same age and grew up together and were like brothers. Some say the reason he killed Sungot was because of jealousy! Machatlu, just like his father, received the gifts of a seer. And he was destined to become the Kakhana of Chochogo', someone that Tugut was also aspiring to become. One day Sungot and Tugut got into a heated argument regarding the matter. And in a fit of rage, Tugut took his hima adze to Sungot's head and split it open! He was instantly killed, right on the spot! Villagers witnessed it. They also mentioned that Tugut fled back towards the swampland, where he was first found, after committing that heinous act! He ran back into I Sesonyan Pribidu!"

Ma'tao, now baffled, replies, "Tugut?! Is this the same Tugut we're speaking of?" Kiighi, a bit confused with his son's reaction, responds, saying, "I only know of one Tugut, and if you meet him by the swamplands, I'm pretty sure that was him!" Ma'tao shakes his head in confusion, saying," The Tugut we saw was an old man! Not the same age as Machatlu!" Kiighi smirks and says, "All the more reason to believe he finally got what he probably was searching for all along. Some mystical power! Even if it is evil. You see, son; this proves that Asuli is starting to get a stronger foothold into this world and is now going to more extraordinary lengths to achieve it! It also doesn't matter who he uses. Tugut is just a pawn to do his bidding!" Ma'tao then asks, "Do you know of the Diyuk Paton Chaifi? Because it was part of my calling that also led me here!"

Kiighi, perking up with interest, exclaims, "It does exist! I have seen it once as an ulitao! But I, too recently, have been visited by dreams the past few days. Visions of that exact sling stone! Chaifi created it to search out and kill the soul that stole fire from him! But Fu'una protected that soul for many generations. Also, in my dreams, Itak was present flying over villages that were burning after many battles! These dreams would shake me to the core and awaken me to cold sweats in the middle of the night! If any weapon were to defeat Itak, it would be the Diyuk Paton Chaifi! One more thing. I know where it was last known to reside. But to retrieve it will be no easy task or for the faint of heart! For the one who is to recover, it must be of royal blood! And here you are, standing before me today, and I do not doubt that the prophecy is speaking of you!"

Ma'tao shakes his head in disbelief, but he agrees, saying, "Father, this is pretty uncanny!

But all this talk about prophecy, you have to admit, it's a lot of responsibility!" Kiighi smiles at his son, saying, "Even before you were born, your mother already knew. She knew that the path of our islands and people uniting runs through Chochogo' by way of Ati! It was a dream she received from Fu'una herself. I didn't have any clue of what she was speaking of until that day you were born. Sungot prayed a blessing upon you, and at that exact moment, I finally felt and understood what she envisioned! The strength and energy that you emitted, even as a baby. I have never felt anything like that ever again until I laid my eyes on you today! I now know in my heart that you are the true destined Maga'lahi I Mantatkilu! But that still has no precedence until you accept or believe that yourself!"

Ma'tao is still in awe after finally reuniting with his father and says, "I know there is so much to learn, but I know that I'm up to the task. I still also have to one day face my grandparents in Ati!" Kiighi chuckles, saying, "Believe me when I say, I feel you, son! Your grandparents are a pretty hard sell! And Maga'lahi Sinahi's sister Unai! Dang, that lady! Let me tell you! She needs a man!" They both burst out laughing!

As the laughter quiets down and gets more serious, Ma'tao looks back to his father and says, "But first things first. I want that meeting with Machatlu along with my warriors to formulate our next plan of attack!" Maga'lahi Kiighi agrees and heads out of his hut. He signals an ulitao who is nearby. He then informs the ulitao to summon Machatlu and the other warriors to his place for an important meeting! The young warrior heads off to do just that.

Chapter 8

"Man And Beast!"

Ma'tao greets his warriors and Machatlu as they enter Maga'lahi Kiighi's hut. Kiighi then gestures them to sit on the bamboo flooring. He then has one of the villagers serving them breadfruit in coconut milk and fresh eel meat in mangu' (turmeric) and cooked with coconut milk. They all take to the meal and replenish their energy after their long journey.

Maga'lahi Kiighi, now satiated, says, "I hope you all had your fill, so now we could get down to business. We also won't be making any rash decisions due to hunger!" He laughs as he continues saying, "Machatlu! You are my second in command, and I have a job that is suited for you. It's something only you are capable of fulfilling! You are to escort Ma'tao and his warriors while assisting them in locating and retrieving the Diyuk Paton Chaifi!"

Machatlu looks at Ma'tao then says, "So you must be going after Itak?! Because the Diyuk Paton Chaifi is the only thing that could take it down!" Ma'tao replies, "Yes, we need to get to

Itak as soon as possible! Because the lives of our friends are at stake!"

Machatlu immediately responds, "If Itak has them, it won't be an easy task to try and rescue them! Because Itak preys on strife, fear, and resentment! It craves it! Yet to even have a chance against Itak, you'll need to retrieve the Diyuk Paton Chaifi. And that in itself will be no easy task! You first need to head deep into the heart of I Sesonyan Pribidu! A place that I have not yet even ventured. And I grew up around here. My father Sungot, even though he didn't enter the heart of the swamp, he is the only man that I know of ever to get that close and return home to talk about it! The Ito' is said to reside deep in the area. They will gladly rip out your heart and feast on it to satisfy their insatiable need for human flesh! My father mentioned that when he was thirteen years of age. He was out one-day gathering kangkung (swamp cabbage) in the swampland and lost his way. It was getting dark, and he knew that it would be hard for him to see his way back to the village with the new moon. He didn't want to light a torch because he didn't want to draw attention to himself. So he camped where he stood and decided to make his way out in the morning to avoid getting more lost. In the middle of the night, strange growling noises had wakened him abruptly! He opened his eyes right away, and luckily he did. Because within that split second, he noticed a large group of zombie-like creatures, which we now call Ito' from a distance! His curiosity got the best of him, and he followed them. From a safe space, he climbed a nunu tree and watched them from above. He found them gathering around a massive lat'di stone that was still erect, with other stones that have fallen around and beneath it! And resting atop of that last standing lat'di was the most beautiful shimmering black with gold-flecked sling stone he had ever seen! It was also just shining ever so bright! So bright that it lit up the whole lat'di stone and the Ito' around it! He told himself he had to have it and that there was no way he was leaving without it! As he started thinking of ways to possess it. He heard a horrific scream! He said the scream was so terrifying that it instantly made his skin crawl and stomach turn. That's when he looked and saw a vast dark shadowy mist! As it hovered over the lat'di, he noticed that this dark hazy mist was deeply frightening! So frightening that he could feel his heart beating out of his chest! This evil abomination instilled so much fear into him that he just froze where he stood from sheer shock! He then said this dark shadow took the form of an enormous beastly blackbird! It had deep ebony pitch-black eyes and thick leathery type of feathers! He mentioned that the claws and talons were so large that it could easily rip a full-grown man into shreds! The wingspan of this creature could easily blanket three Maga'lahi huts with space to spare! But then, as he was telling me all this. That is when I could honestly say that this was the very first time that I ever saw fear in my father's eyes! He said that dark shadowy form of evil which transformed into that beast of a blackbird transferred yet again into a very beautiful young woman!"

Aligao, who was so attentive and intrigued up to this point, couldn't help himself. He cuts off Machatlu and blurts out, "Why? Why was he afraid?! Does he like guys?!" Atani, with her quick reflexes, slaps him upside the head!

Machatlu ignores him and continues saying," My father also said if this form of pure evil could transform so quickly, who's to say that it isn't already in our midst?! And that's what frightened him! He was afraid for the safety of his village and his family!" Ma'tao interrupts him there and curiously asks, "So this evil shadowy force can shapeshift? And if so, could Itak be Tugut as well?"

As soon as Ma'tao mentions Tugut's name, all present quickly notice how Machatlu's body language changes. One could easily see that the name Tugut struck a nerve in him. But he keeps his composure and responds, saying, "From all the knowledge I gathered from our elders and witnesses throughout the years. Yes! Itak is a shapeshifter! My father and others whom I trust witnessed it. One thing very fascinating yet disturbing at the same time is that Itak could only shapeshift into human forms of people that it has taken prisoner! With that sort of power, it can infiltrate and influence with dire consequences! And with the more fear and hatred it instills, the stronger Itak becomes! It thrives on negative energy!"

Ma'tao, now even more curious, then asks, "So it could take the form of a man or woman?" Machatlu quickly replies, "Yes! As long as that person is a prisoner!" Ma'tao then asks," Does Itak live in the swampland? Also, what else did your father say that might be of any help to us?"

Machatlu, now with a conflicted look, replies, "Now that I can't answer. I do know that most of the sightings have been in and around Sesonyan Pribidu. But after one grueling battle with Tomhom village six months ago. My warriors and I took a different route back to Chochogo'. The area we found ourselves in was not familiar to us. We kept walking until we found ourselves on a clifftop. On top of that cliff, we found one of the most massive caverns ever seen! As if Chaifi himself carved it out. It was very dark out, and with the thick foliage covering the entrance, it was tough to see. I was wounded pretty badly, so three of my men went ahead to scout out the area while I and the others attended to our wounds. When they came back, they repotting that one of the warriors would have fallen to his death if not for that horrendous scream he heard at the last minute! As the three of them looked up, they saw Itak! It emerged out from deep within the island! When they returned home, they told me about it. I wanted to investigate it for myself, but tensions are still high between Chochogo' and Tomhom. But now might be a good a time as ever to head there!"

Atdao then yells out, "Here, there or whatever! Can it be killed?! Tell us! How do we kill this Itak!" Atani looks at her brother and not only see's his pain but feels it as well and adds, "If there is a way, you must tell us! Whoever or whatever it is has our friends!" Kiighi then steps in, saying, "From what I know, Itak is a monstrosity of pure evil! And the Diyuk Paton Chaifi is capable of killing it!'

Machatlu nods, then he continues saying, "Yes! My father mentioned as he saw Itak transform into that beautiful young woman. She could not even get close to that lat'di stone! Powerful bolts of lightning emitted from the sling stone struck her as soon as she stepped next to it! She then belted another horrible scream and yelled to the Ito' to get it out of her sight! She also told them to secure it where no human being will ever find or get their hands on it! If there's any chance of recovering your friends, we must locate and retrieve the Diyuk Paton Chaifi!"

Ma'tao then asks, "We will! How did your father survive the ordeal and get back home?" Machatlu then, with a smile, says, "He honestly didn't even remember. He just said that he heard some voices talking around him! So he decided to climb down the tree to find out who or what it was. When he got to the bottom, he turned, and that's when everything turned black, and he fell asleep! When he awoke, he had a horrible headache and was right outside Chochogo'! It was kind of weird!"

Ma'tao then asks, "Are you willing to assist and follow us? Well, first of all, that's if it's alright with Maga'lahi Kiighi?" Machatlu, who eagerly wants to join them, first looks at his Maga'lahi. Who at that second gives his approval right there on the spot! Aligao asks Maga'lahi Kiighi, "Aren't you going with us?" He then answers, "As much as I would love to, my duties as Maga-'lahi dictate otherwise. With Ma'tao and Machatlu with you all, I'm as good as there."

Atani then speaks out, saying, "So what is the plan? Where are we heading to first?" Atdao adds, "Yes! Whatever it is, we need to get going and soon!" Da'on looking on, agrees by nodding.

Ma'tao then says, "For some reason, I'm feeling something so strong from deep within! It's as if my Ka'lang is telling me that we need to head deep into the heart of I Sesonyan Pribidu! The answers for what we're searching for will reveal itself once we're near the deep center of the swamp!"

Maga'lahi Kiighi says, "I feel that should be the first course of action. Whatever you need, my son Chochogo' will provide!" Ma'tao gestures to his father that he appreciates the support, then turns to rest his warriors saying, "We don't have much time to spare! Ina and Magogui need our help, and we're not going to let them down! We still have a couple of hours of daylight left. We should leave now!"

None of them have any qualms with that decision as they gather up their weapons and belongings. They also make one last check. Kiighi, who is now watching as they prepare to embark on their journey, turns to Ma'tao and Machatlu, saying, "You both are sons of Chochogo' be safe and watch each other's backs! And that also goes for the rest of you. Blessings from our ancestors and return safely!"

Ma'tao, followed by Machatlu and his warriors, each place their foreheads on Kiighi's as they prepare to leave. He then signals them to follow as they all head on out to I Sesonyan I Pribidu!

Chapter 9

"Onward to the Swamp!"

They move as one more swiftly and stealthily now they have been together for quite some time. All while keeping a steady pace. The warriors follow Ma'tao while walking parallel with Machatlu back down the mountain of Chochogo' towards the cave on which they entered.

As they start back up, the cavern walls towards the overshadowing bamboo canopy Ma'tao with a bit of curiosity, asks Machatlu, "I now know it's going to be just a matter of time that we'll come across these Ito'. If they're zombie-like beings, could they be killed, and what type of damage are they able to inflict upon us?"

Machatlu, while still pushing the pace up towards the canopy, turns to Ma'tao, saying, "Even though they're all known as Ito', there are different castes, along with various types of them. The Pa'chang, as they are known, are the lowest ranking and slowest among them." Machatlu pulls out a small woven pandanus packet from his satchel and tosses it to Ma'tao, saying, "The Pa'chang are not much of a problem if you hit them with this! They instantly are immobilized and will no longer be a threat."

Ma'tao then replies, "What is in it?" Machatlu smiles and says, "Good old fashion salt! The salt in each of those packets will instantly burn them once it touches their skin!" Ma'tao shakes his head, saying, "That's pretty cool! I was wondering what was in all those extra satchels that Da'on and Aligao are carrying."

Machatlu responds with, "Yes! You could launch it from your atupat or have it make contact on their skin! After that, they shouldn't be much of a problem. Next are the Entalo'! These Ito' are the mid-ranking and will be a little more of a challenge. These walkers are pretty fast and could quickly put up a fight! The salt will stun them, but it won't stop them! For them, you'll need to be a bit more creative because you'll need to snap their necks to stop their attack!"

Ma'tao listens intently to every detail of Machatlu's instructions while signaling to Aligao, who is goofing around, to do the same. Machatlu then continues saying, "As for the highest-ranking among them, you will surely know who they are once you see them!"

Ma'tao, now more intrigued as he is curious, asks while chuckling, "Why? Are they skilled fighters? Can they talk?" Immediately Machatlu responds adamantly,"Yes! And so much more! They could also disappear and reappear at will! This class of Ito' are known as the Figo'! The salt will only irritate them. If you break their necks, they could still come back! There is only one sure way to kill them. And I've only seen it once. It was when my father and Maga'lahi Ki-ighi stopped one from entering Chochogo'! They hit that creature with so much salt! Yet it still attacked! They also both beat that evil thing into a bloody mess, but it still wouldn't die! It wasn't until my father took his fisga (spear) and speared it directly into its heart! At that exact moment, that evil creature burnt up within itself! It was like it burst into flames! The flames burned bright purple! And completely incinerated that creature! It then turned into ashes, then it completely disappeared! I freaked out! But from that night on, we knew! We knew that we could now take out all forms of the Ito!"

Ma'tao asks Machatlu, "That Figo', did you notice if it was wearing a necklace with a black stone pendant around its neck?" Machatlu thinks for a moment then says, "Yes, it did! That was where the fire started after my father stabbed its heart!"

Ma'tao then looks back at his warriors, asking, "Does hearing of those purple flames remind you of something? Or who we're up against?!" Without hesitation, they all reply,"Asuli!" Atdao then says, "If we took him out when we had the chance, Ina would still be with us right now!" Atani responds, saying,"We don't exactly know that for sure, but I do know Ina is a survivor, and we'll get her back!"

Machatlu, now with a surprising look, turns to Ma'tao and asks, "So you know of him as well?!" Ma'tao, with a severe tone, replies,"Know of him?! Let's say we have history! And after what you told us, he must be behind this! They must have a leader that's calling all the shots. And from the sounds of things, he's involved some- how!"

Machatlu continues saying, "They're also more active at night. I suggest that we camp for the night at the area we first met and head into the swampland first thing in the morning!" Ma'tao looks to his warriors, who nod that they agree with his decision except for Atdao, who angrily replies, "Why wait?! Don't you think it'll be bet- ter to proceed once we get there? There's just too much waiting and stalling!"

Ma'tao heads over to Atdao, who now looks thoroughly irritated and says, "C'mon Atdao! We all need to be together with this! I understand you're worried, but we will get them both back!" Atdao looks at Ma'tao and replies, "You do what you have to do, and I'll do what I have to!"

Ma'tao looks at Atani, who shrugs her shoulders as if to say she tried her best in reasoning with him to no avail. He then looks back to Machatlu, who signals that they just reached the bamboo canopy. They all stop for a quick breather and to refuel their torches before proceeding,

Aligao then says to Da'on, "I can't wait to run into those Ito'! Because once I do, I'm going to rattle the hell out of them!" Da'on smirks, replying, "You need to start listening and stop messing around! Didn't you hear what Machatlu said? I think it might work with some of them, but I don't know about those Figo'. They sound like they'll be a real challenge!" Aligao laughs while saying, "When they meet me, they'll be saying that!" Da'on scoffs and continues working on his torch.

At that moment, Atani brushes up against Ma'tao and says, "This keeps getting more interesting! These Ito' especially those Figo' he mentioned seem like they might be a problem. Did you ever hear anything about them before? Or their connection to the Itak?" Ma'tao looks back into his love's eyes and replies, "I've heard stories growing up regarding zombie creatures, but nothing quite like this! Whoever or whatever force we'll be facing, be that Asuli or someone else. I feel that the Ito' may be being controlled by him, but with Itak, I'm still not quite sure. From what I've gathered so far, we need to find a way to bring more peace between our island villages! Because of all the negative energies that ensue from the chaos it produces. Itak will not only get more robust; it will not stop until it rips our island and our people apart!

Atani grabs her loves hand, saying, "We won't let that happen! We can't let that happen!" Ma'tao pulls her close, saying, "I feel what you're saying and wholeheartedly agree. Will you be alright going through with this?" Atani whispers, saying, "I'll be fine. It's Atdao. He has me worried!" Ma'tao holds her hand and responds, saying, "I understand. But you know as well as I do that he won't rest until we find her!"

Machatlu then calls out, saying, "We should get moving. Is everyone ready?" Ma'tao kisses Atani's forehead to reassure her and says, "You just let me know if anything! I got you! We need to get going." Atani acknowledges as the head towards the swamp.

Ma'tao heads back to the front next to Machatlu as he asks him, "After finally meeting my father and hearing about yours, it seems they were close." Machatlu nods, saying, "Yes. Just like many of us, they both grew up together as ulitao. My father could commune with our ancestors and knew that Kiighi would be an important factor in the survival of our people, village, and island. So he vowed to be by his side and made sure he became Maga'lahi. And during that time, he also became his kakhana!" Ma'tao then adds, "My father also really thinks highly of you! I could see that you are a great asset to Cho-chogo'." Machatlu shows a slight grin upon hearing that and replies, "I appreciate the observation. But everything I do is for my Maga'lahi, my village, and my people! Your father took me under his wing during those dark times in my life and helped to point out my purpose in this life! He is one of the most esteemed and well respected Maga'lahi that Chochogo' has produced!"

Machatlu turns to Ma'tao, looks him in the eyes, and adamantly says, "What I admire most about Maga'lahi Kiighi is that war with him is always the last resort! He would always seek out a peaceful way to de-escalate problems. Fighting to him is always the last resort! But don't be mistaken. Because in battle, he is one of the fiercest and most tactical fighters that I've ever had the privilege of fighting beside! I know he would love to be here fighting alongside us. But the constant threat of war lately with all the other villages, he knows that he needs to be present within Chochogo'!"

Saddened for a brief second, Ma'tao shakes his head. Because he understands that same feeling and Machatlu picks up on it and reassures him, saying, "I could see you've faced that same dilemma before. I also see that within the short time we met, that you have that same sense of duty between you and your warriors! They highly respect you for that!" Ma'tao then says, "It's not easy in trying to do what you know in your heart feels right. There always seems to be someone or something standing in the way!"

Atani overhears them speak, interjects, and adds, "Standing in the way. Like that swamp?!" Ma'tao looks over to Atani, who is pointing at I Sesonyan Pribidu! Machatlu then says, "Yes! We're here! We should camp up ahead for the night." Aligao utters in excitement, "About freakin time! Now I could finally get to catch and try those eels that Atdao was telling us about!" Atani laughs, saying, "Only you Aligao could think of eating at a time like this!" Aligao smirks while replying, "Itak! Ito'! I will say! Fill my belly first; then, we'll play!"

They all laugh as Aligao, Da'on, and Atdao head to the swamp shore to catch eels. Ma'tao, still laughing, looks at Atani and says, "Well, we do need to eat, and it might as well be now." Machatlu then adds, "We could just set up camp here for the night."

They all agree as Ma'tao and Atani start a fire and gather up some food.

Chapter 10

"An Informed Visitation!"

As the beautiful orange, yellow sun scatters its rays throughout and sets within the valley. The smell of charred wood fills the air with the crackling sounds of the fire burning right in front of them.

Ma'tao, his warriors, and Machatlu have now eaten their fill and start settling in for the night in preparation for what is ahead. Da'on grabs a clay cup, fills it with laulau (porridge), and offers it to Machatlu as he sits crossed legs next to him.

Machatlu smiles while he takes the cup from Da'on and says,"How are things in Fu'a these days?" Da'on smirks while saying, "Just as with Chochogo', we too are feeling the threats of war constantly on our borders. I got to say, though; you also seem to be coming into your own from the last time we met!"

Machatlu laughs, saying, "I knew when I saw you that you'll probably still be harboring feelings from our last meeting! Da'on, the great warrior from Fu'a in a draw with Machatlu! We're still on the same side, you know. You need to learn to let that go!" Da'on scoffs with a bit of a smile, saying, "You're right, but we could still spar for old times sake!" Machatlu laughs even louder saying, "Of course! I could never turn down a good butt whooping! Just for old times sake. I always love some friendly competition! But we first need to save our energy for I Sesonyan Pribidu."

Da'on agrees as they place their foreheads together. Aligao laughing in the background, asks, "So it's on?" They both turn to look at Aligao as he continues saying, "This should be some good stuff! Even though I've never seen Machatlu scrap. But from what I heard in Chochogo', I think Da'on will have his work cut out for him! I'm going to take some bets! Atdao, would you like to wager?" Atdao ignores Aligao and lays down while closing his eyes to get some rest.

Ma'tao then interjects, saying, "There won't be any sparring or betting! The only thing that we'll all be doing is getting some well-needed rest! Aligao, you take first watch since you're always looking for some action!" Aligao rolls his eyes, heads to a small patch of bamboo trees in the center of the camp to post up for the night. Ma'tao lays down on his guafak mat beside Atani as they start to doze off.

The cold chill of the night air as it rolls off the waters of the swamp chills him to the bone. He starts tossing and turning while thunder and lightning bolts fill the night sky. It will be so blindingly dark out if not for the intervals of lightning flashes ever so often! He tosses and turns! He gets more restless by the moment! Beads of sweat start running down the sides of his face! Flashes of lightning followed by those thunderous claps! A woman is screaming! Shadowy figures are crossing in and around the jungle around him! He starts spinning faster and gains more momentum after every turn!

He thinks to himself, *What's going on? What's happening?* A bright brilliance of white light! Followed up by a deafening thunder crash, and suddenly he stops!

He is now standing, facing I Sesonyan Pribidu with no one else around! And in a very calm setting. But off to the left, out of the corner of his eye, he spots a bluish flame burning in the distance, and he takes off to follow it! As he observes, walking at a quickening pace, whoever is holding the torch is trying to elude him. So he picks up the pace even faster, to the point where he catches himself in a full-on sprint!

Ma'tao now thinks to himself, *Who is this person? Where is this person going? Should I be in pursuit?*

As he contemplates those thoughts, he starts to pull back on his speed. But not before noticing that the person veered off down into a lower valley, then takes a hard right turn and completely disappears!

That instant, Ma'tao comes to a complete stop and decides to walk down the hill and be extremely cautious. He approaches the hill's bottom, and notices dug deep between a patch of bamboo trees is a cave!

Luckily that fleeing mystery person causes him to look in that direction. Because he easily could have missed it! The cave is dark, yet there is something to this area that makes it feel so inviting. Ma'tao gets drawn to it and enters ever so curiously but cautiously. He could no longer see the blue burning torch! He then starts to hear water trickling and could barely make out that it is coming off the side of the cave walls.

The water gathers together into a small stream, which draws his attention even deeper. His eyes follow the flow towards the cave floor as it becomes more prominent as it flows into a cavernous pool. Ma'tao then thinks to himself, *This is odd, considering this is a type of cave found only along the coastline!*

Not even a split second that he thinks that thought while staring deep into the fresh underground pool. A loud thunderous clap fills the cave! Simultaneously the blue torch lights back up and brightens the once empty cave! So bright that it blinds Ma'tao for a brief second! As he starts to refocus, a voice calls out from across the pool, shouting, "Put fin matto hao magi. Maolek i karera-mu?" Which translates to "So you finally made it here! How was the journey?" Ma'tao, startled, immediately thinks to himself,

Could it be?

For the voice sounds so familiar, but he had to be sure! The figure slowly draws the torch closer to his face to expose his appearance. Ma'tao now sees his face! It is who he thought it would be!

He then shouts from the top of his lungs across the pool, saying, "I knew it was only a matter of time that you would show up!" The man shouts back, saying, "So now you had a taste of power! Has it gone to your head?" Ma'tao yells back, "Why don't you come over here and find out!" No sooner has he said that Ma'tao was now standing face to face with that him as he shouts, "Saina hu! You know how to make an entrance!" Ma'tao grabs him as they embrace and place their foreheads onto one another.

It is Maga'lahi Hineti! Ma'tao is overcome with joy and says, "Since you're here, I can only assume that I'm in between worlds. With my physical body probably still asleep?" Hineti responds, saying, "You guess correctly!" Ma'tao, with a slight chuckle, says, "It always amazes me and goes to show that there's still so much to learn on how to be more attuned." Hineti laughs in reply, saying, "Yes, my son! There is still so much to learn, but where you stand today, it's so much further than you were yesterday!" Ma'tao looks down, shakes his head, and says, "You don't know how much I needed to hear that. It feels like more weight of the world is placed upon my shoulders!" Hineti, now much more serious, says, "It's through all those trials of adversity that we discover who we truly are! Those trials also create visions that produce choices. Those choices that define us!"

Ma'tao, who is usually very calm and composed now speaking with weariness in his voice, says, "It's just that I have so many questions! First and foremost, my friends. We need to find them! And this Diyuk Paton Chaifi, is this sling stone as powerful as they say it is? What can you tell me about it? Also, with the Itak and those Ito' we have to face. I have yet to see any of them! Yet they sound like they'll be a big problem? Will they be a hindrance? And with these visions of my mother, what am I to make of that? And to top that off, with not being able to visit Ati without backlash! It's like so many things hitting me at once!"

Ma'tao looking now more confused than ever, looks down. Maga'lahi Hineti places his hand on his great-great-grandson, saying, "Breathe Ma'-tao! Just breathe, my son. I know how all that responsibility can become so overwhelming for just one person, but remember what I said!" Ma'tao looks up and makes eye contact with Hineti. Hineti continues saying, "It's all a choice!

Now just like the choices you made in the past! Are you going to claim what's rightfully yours and stand up for those who can't stand up for themselves? Or are you going to cower at first sight of adversity?"

Ma'tao takes that deep breath and looks at Hineti dead center in his eyes and asks sarcastically, "Really?! You're asking me that?!" Hineti now laughs while saying, "I honestly didn't think so! It would be best if you pace yourself. Take each one of these obstacles and deal with them as they come! Don't worry about the past because it could drum up the pain. Don't focus too much on the future, for it could lead to fear and uncertainty! This moment! This moment is what's important and where it all happens! Live it, Ma'tao! Live in it!"

Now feeling those positive vibes that his great-great-grandfather is emitting. Ma'tao regains his composure while saying, "Tomorrow first thing in the morning, we head into I Sesonyan Pribidu!" Hineti then strongly pronounces, "Hence why I'm here. You need to be extremely cautious once you enter deep into that realm! Things within that area are not always as they appear to be! They could dull your perception of what you know to be true! Listen to who you are. I will not be able to assist you within its boundaries.

Your Ka'lang I Man Metgot will help you discern elements that you'll encounter once you set foot into that swamp. It will also help you in attaining the Diyuk Paton Chaifi! They are opposing forces, and each creates a perfect balance with the other! Take this!"

Upon saying those words, Hineti opens his hands. And within them are two weapons! One is a beautifully woven atupat(sling). The most beautiful and intricately woven sling with designs that Ma'tao has never before seen! Hineti places it in his hands while proclaiming, "Here I present to you the Atupat Aniti (Spiritual Sling)! This sling will make it possible to use the Diyuk Paton Chaifi once acquired! Any attempt to try and launch the stone otherwise will be futile. That stone is capable of so much destruction! When Chaifi created it, he did so with so much hatred and malice towards the human race! Not only was it meant to destroy the soul that stole fire from him. But also to kill all people who advanced their knowledge because of it. And since fire helped propel the livelihood of people so far forward. Chaifi vowed to destroy every single person walking the face of this earth! And his Diyuk Patu was created to do just that! Now how to acquire it, that in itself will be a real test!"

He then presents Ma'tao with another very unique weapon. It is a very crude-looking adze with two deadly slashing points! Hineti then says, "This here is the Higam I Saina (Ancestors Adze)! This weapon is a special type of adze! It will serve you when needed. Fashioned from the bones of the very first warriors, whom Puntan had selected in advancing the human race!"

Ma'tao looks on in awe as Hineti presents him with these exceptional gifts!

Hineti then continues saying, "Some of these Ito' as you know by now, are former warriors of past Maga'lahi I Mantatkilu. They who, in their whole beings at the time, swore a blood oath to their Maga'lahi. One could say they stood by him to the point they had no choice! Their undying loyalty and obligation made them a viable force when they were human! It was their strong will and belief to protect! They still carry that within themselves! They won't go down without a fight! Especially the Figo'!"

Ma'tao, taking everything he heard into account, replies, "If they were once loyal warriors to their Maga'lahi, is killing and stabbing them through their hearts the only way to eliminate them?" Hineti responds, saying, "As we speak, right now, their loyalty lies in protecting and securing that stone! I'm also going to have to say when you're in that moment, the moment when you're most unsure, confused, or even hesitant! That's when the answers you seek will start unfolding itself unto you!"

Ma'tao looks Hineti dead in the eye and, with a chuckling smirk, says, "There ain't no straight answer with you, is there?"

Hineti laughs aloud after hearing that and says, "Now Ma'tao, what kind of a great-great-grandfather will I be if I just gave you all the answers?

If I did that, you wouldn't know what it feels like to step into your destiny! But heed my words! Once within I Sesonyan Pribidu, all your perceptions of what you know to be real in this physical realm will surely test you and your warriors at every corner!"

Hineti then takes the Atupat Aniti along with the Higam I Saina and says, "This sling and adze are just like your Ka'lang! They were birthed by thought, by Puntan himself! Strengthen and interwoven with hair from Fu'una, which will allow you to harness the power from the Diyuk Paton Chaifii! Chaifi created this weapon to harm our people and our islands. But this unique, powerful stone in the right hands. Could be used for the greater good!"

As he places the Atupat Aniti and Higam I Saina back into the hands of Ma'tao, he says, "Take these, my son. You now possess the power of our creators backed by our long line of ancestors! Once you obtain the Diyuk Paton Chaifi, you'll have all the elements you need to help bring back balance and the truth to have it ascend!"

Hineti grabs the hands of Ma'tao and, while squeezing them, says, "I also want to leave you with something always to remember!"

He then stares more profound into the eyes of his great-great-grandson, and with such sincerity, continues saying, "Annai kinenni hao nu'i hinemhom, eyugui na gotpe matto i manana!" Which translates to "When the darkness seems to have overtaken you, that's when the light comes bursting in! Always remember that! And with that, I must now leave you. For now, it's time, and I must go. Everyone around you will be up soon!"

Ma'tao, though left with still so many questions, laughs as he says, "I understand! But right when it starts to become a little clearer, you need to leave." Hineti then replies, "We'll see each other again real soon, my son! Remember, everything you need is already within you!"

As he says those very words, Hineti starts to dissipate into hundreds and thousands of little white orbs of light. And as quickly as he came, he disappears!

Ma'tao feels sad to see him go, but knows in his heart that they will meet again. While clasping the Higam I Saina, he could automatically feel the incredible power and strength that this special adze possesses! He then looks at the Atupat Aniti and is still so amazed by all its beauty. While analyzing all its intricate details along with its woven patterns, he finds himself getting very sleepy. So sleepy that he decides to lie down to just rest for a brief moment. He finds a comfortable corner along the side of the cave. It is so comfortable and inviting that he closes his eyes to soak in everything he discussed with Maga'lahi Hineti. He then drifts off into sleep.

It could not have been but a few minutes until he hears, "Get Up! Ma'tao! Get up now!" As Ma'tao opens his eyes to see what all the commotion is about! He awakes to a panicked stricken, Atani! While trying to gain his bearings as to his whereabouts. He immediately just zeros into her expressive eyes, and excitedly asks, "What's the matter?! Is everything alright?! Are you okay?!" Atani, with grief and fear in her voice, responds worriedly, saying, "It's not me! It's At-dao! He's not here! I fear that he might have entered the swampland all by himself to try and locate Ina! We need to go, and we need to go now! We need to hurry and find him!"

At that exact moment, Aligao also catches wind of what is going on and says, "He must've slipped out after he finished his watch!" Da'on, now joining in, adds, "After we switched shifts, he mentioned he was going to sleep over there because of Aligao's snoring!" As he says that, he points over to a guafak mat. It is located in an area alongside a mound of rocks with a makeshift bamboo stick frame. Atani heads over to that direction, pulls up the guafak mat only to expose more rocks while exclaiming, "This! Is this the Atdao you were watching over!" Da'on scratches his head while saying, "I mean no disrespect, Atani! But Atdao is now a man! And I ain't no babysitter!" Ma'tao, in seeing tensions start to rise, steps in and says, "All of you relax! We need to get a grip on our emotions! It's not going to be beneficial to anyone if we let it take over!" He then looks at Machatlu and says, "I feel it's time to head in without a moment to waste! We can't afford to lose anyone else!"

Machatlu agrees and responds, saying, "Alright! Let's head on in, but make sure to grab all satchels and supplies! Also, make sure to remember what was said before we head on in! More importantly, remember to stick together! We'll be stronger in numbers!"

They all acknowledge what Machatlu just explained. They all then look to Ma'tao, who signals for them to move as they make their way ever so cautiously into I Sesonyan Pribidu!

Chapter 11

"The Forbidden Swamp!"

That smell! A very distinct smell! One could only liken it to the smell of fear! Better yet, the stench of death! So distinctive is it that Ma'tao thinks to himself, *If anyone of us were to have any apprehensions at all of entering the forbidden swamp, then this would be the moment that those thoughts would arise! I must not entertain or pay any attention to that myself!*

The sun is starting to rise as they head into and come across the muddied grasslands of the swamp. It is now barely able to peek through the thick, dense fog hovering over the water's surface within the swamp!Machatlu then says, "Even though it's daylight, Certain areas within the fog and jungle foliage will get dark! Remember to always be on full alert!"

By just being there, they all understand what he means. At brief moments, one cannot see a mere three feet in front of them.

The ice-cold wind blowing through the swamp disperses bone-chilling temperatures effortlessly that they instantly feel! But still, they all press on, for what they all know is at stake!

Aligao then says aloud, "This place is a whole other world!" Ma'tao again, then thinks to himself, *A situation like this could prove very deadly for all of us if we encounter any Ito'! We might be able to fight, let alone see them because of this dense fog!* Ma'tao then says, "We need to burn our torches brighter! We need the heat to help dissipate this fog!" They all pause for a moment to refill and ignite more bamboo torches. The torches' flames instantly dissipate the thick, dense fog around them while the heat they produced provides some welcomed warmth.

But not even thirty feet from where they lit the torches, Aligao says, "Check it out! This fog is getting so much thicker and rolling in faster! Is this normal?" Machatlu replying with, caution says, "No, not really! It's not something I usually see!" Ma'tao, without hesitation, shouts, "Get in close! And stay together!"

As they create a circle with their backs to one another, they not only feel the fog creeping in, there is something else! Da'on then says, "Guys, there's something out there!" Aligao adds, "These torches are useless!" As he throws the torch, he was holding into the thick, dense blanket of fog! He then, with surprise, asks, "Did you guys hear that?!" Da'on says quietly, "Hear what?" Aligao then just as quietly replies, "There! Listen." At that precise moment, they all start to hear it! The pitter-patter of feet! Little feet! The chatter of little voices all around them, talking, laughing, and getting closer by the second!

Atani, who is now next to Ma'tao, grabs his hand asking, "You hear that, right?" Ma'tao softly replies, "Yes." Atani responds with, "Are you thinking what I'm thinking?" Ma'tao quietly asks,

"You or me?" Atani then says, "You take it this time." Ma'tao picks up his voice says, "Everyone! Close your eyes!"

He then takes three deep breaths and focuses on them. Around them, all could hear the chatter of those little voices getting louder in a gibberish language that none of them could make out! But none of that phases Ma'tao as he draws that inner strength from deep within! He opens his eyes and, while shouting from the top of his lungs, proclaims, "Ginen I Minetgot Puntan Yan I Na'liheng Fu'una!" Which translates to

"By The Power Of Puntan And Protection Of Fu'una!"

As soon as he proclaims those words, he opens his eyes, which are now blazing yellowish gold; the power from within flows through his Ka'lang I Man Metgot! The all-powerful energy creates a blinding yellowish gold force field that instantly surrounds Ma'tao and all with him! Simultaneously he creates a great energy blast emitted from the force field so powerful that whatever was surrounding them is suddenly all thrown back! The explosion is so intense that it cleared a sixty-foot radius all around them! From where they are standing, they could now only make out banyan and bamboo trees! Whatever it was making their way towards them had completely disappeared!

Aligao, while snickering, yells, "That was awesome! What were those things? They completely had us surrounded! They also sounded weird, and they didn't even seem human?" Machatlu, while still standing in a defensive position, says, "Hold on! Did you all hear that?" Da'on nervously replies, "Hear what?" He then turns to Aligao, asking, "What do you mean, not human?" Aligao looking all around, then says, "I just have a very good feeling, my friend, that today you are going to come face to face with all your fears!"

Da'on, now even more nervous, utters, "Wh..wh..what do you mean all my fears!"

Ma'tao then anxiously says, "Get in position! Be on full alert!" No sooner than he said that, something dropped from an overhanging bamboo branch above and landed perfectly on Da'ons shoulders! Da'on screams in such a high pitched squeal, and that catches everyone by surprise! Because it was Da'on! Aligao laughs so hard that he falls to the ground!

Aligao's reaction is short-lived. Because out from within the bamboo trees, an army of evil, hideous, and vile little creatures with stick and stone weapons rush charging towards them!

Machatlu yells, "It's the Manganiti Man Nanu! Use the packets of salt! It will take care of these creatures, as well! And don't get bit by them! Their bite is very toxic and could even be deadly!"

He then takes his spear and easily takes out six of them with such accuracy and refocuses on others taking their place! Aligao runs towards Da'on, who is still so freaked out and flailing around! He yells, "Keep still and stop screaming like a little girl!" Atani hears him and yells, "I resent that, Aligao! Hurry and take these things out!" Aligao then moves with so much quickness, he grabs the Manganiti Man Nanu by its neck off of Da'on and looks it in the eyes! And with a disgusted look on his face, he yells to the creature's face, "Damn! Pili was right! You creatures, are so freakin UGLY!" He then takes a salt packet and shoves it down that little beast's gullet! Not even a second later, the creature explodes violently, scattering bluish-purple blood, guts, and brains all over the place onto every one of them as well!

Da'on, after witnessing what Aligao just did for him. Regains his composure! He now looked like the Da'on they all know! He is so inspired and grateful after what Aligao had done and says, "Thank you! I now know what to do!" Aligao, though appreciative, turns back to him and shouts, "Thank me later! Let's eradicate these damn ugly things now!"

Da'on does not give it a second thought and takes immediate action! It was as if his girlish scream never even happened! He then hurriedly takes out six of those ugly, disgusting, vile creatures so rapidly as he swings his nasa with so much technique and elegance!

Ma'tao, while taking out thirteen of these creatures on his own, turns to Atani and shouts, "No joke! These are some ugly crazed looking things! I think we might be wearing them down!" Atani yells back, "You just jinxed it and spoke too soon! Look!" Right as those very words leave her mouth. The second wave of these purple-haired, grayish skinned, and purple-eyed creatures with these grotesque crazy looking sharp fangs for teeth, emerge from the bamboo trees and rush towards Ma'tao and his warriors! They are now so overwhelmed with these Manganiti Man Nanu, and the situation is starting to get out of control! Also, the risk of them getting bitten and infected is getting more serious by the second!

As all this craziness is going on, something completely unexpected happens with another problem added to the mix! Something stuns Ma'-tao, as he thinks to himself, *Why can't I move?!*

What's going on?! I can see what's going on around me, *but my arms, my feet! What did they do to us?!* Ma'tao is now completely paralyzed!

Ma'tao then sees a bunch of these little monsters swarming at his feet! Each one of them using the other as a step to scale up onto him! He also notices that his warriors are in the same predicament! Though these creatures are little, they make up for it in quickness and speed! Ma'tao could hear their chatter as they approach higher up his body while he feels the sharp points of their finger and toenails digging into his skin! And their smell! They have such a strong, pungent smell to them! They reek of death!

He again thinks to himself, *This can't be it! It can't end this way!* He then starts slipping out of consciousness! The Manganiti Man Nanu are so fast and persistent! They also have Ma'tao and all who are with him covered and taken out!

Right then, when all seemed lost. There is a loud and resounding Ku'lo blast! The blast is so loud that it right away catches the attention of Ma'tao, and he quickly resists passing out! Then another blast is heard! This one much louder than the first one and from a type of Ku'lo that was very unfamiliar to them! Suddenly bit by bit. Ma'tao can see again! The ugly vile creatures disappear one by one, making it easier for Ma'tao to both see and breathe again! He thinks to himself, *What's going on? What or who is causing it?*

Though his vision is blurry, he gets a glance at a beautiful little warrior that smiles at him, and in his mind, he hears her say, "Don't you worry, Maga'lahi! We got you!" Ma'tao is now so dazed, drifting in and out of consciousness. But he does manage to say, "Pili! Is that you! I'm so glad you're here!" He then passes out.

But not long after, he is awakened by other little warriors hitting him with white bamboo sticks! He opens his eyes and is about to scream, but before he does, one of these warriors force liquid from a clay cup down his throat! Ma'tao is about to get even angrier until he instantly notices that he could move again! He rapidly jumps up and also realizes that he can see perfectly fine and speak again! He looks around and notices that the little warriors were also tending to his warriors and Machatlu.

They, too, are starting to gain back their mobility and senses. Ma'tao then hears, "Glad to have you back Maga'lahi!" Ma'tao turns to see who is speaking to him and sets his eyes on a group of Taotao Man Nanu! A warrior clan of Taotao I Man Nanu outfitted with awesome gear and weaponry! They have shown up at just the right time and eliminated that group of Manganiti Man Nanu!

Their mighty female leader steps forward to introduce herself. She is so beautiful, with long flowing bluish hair with three braids off to the right side of her face. Her skin, like the rest of them, also has a radiant bluish glow to it. One can readily see that she has the true essence of a warrior, emanating from her entire being! And with the weapons she possesses, along with the gear she is wearing, she is not one to be taken lightly!

But before she could say another word Ma'tao still a bit dizzy, asks, "Pili is that you?" She then replies, saying, "My name is Tiani, Maga'lahi. Pili is my older sister! She and our clan leaders instructed my warriors and me to join up with our allies here on Guahan. And in doing so, assist you in your efforts! Because we received word that Itak has been showing up more frequently in this region. And causing so much more havoc while spreading its reign of terror, negative energies, and influences towards war! With all that fear present, it also means that the Manganiti

Man Nanu are uneasy and being stirred up as well! Where ever Itak flourishes, so do they! Hence why they attacked you all!"

Atani and the others now join Ma'tao. Who are also so grateful for the Taotao Man Nanu arriving on time! Tiani looks at them, then back to Ma'tao, and continues saying,"Ma'ga'lahi, you and your warriors all have the power and ability to unite all beings, villages, and islands finally!"

Just then, another Taotao Man Nanu warrior also steps forward. This battle-hardened warrior outfitted with the most skillfully crafted weapons and tactical gear. His beautiful bluish hair is long and intricately braided. He then says, "I'm Pigan!

I'm the lead warrior of my clan. I've known of you ever since you were born, Ma'tao. My people reside in Chochogo' as well, and we have been watching over you and your people for generations! It's an honor to present ourselves to you, Maga'lahi, finally!"

Ma'tao, now more composed, replies, "The honor is all mine! Thank you all for showing up when you did! They were small, but moved with such ferocity and quickness!" Aligao then adds, "Those things were crazy and ugly as hell! Talk about strength in numbers!" Pigan responds,

"They were once like us. But they were seduced by the darkness!"

Ma'tao curiously asks, "What was it that they did to us? All of a sudden, we became paralyzed, and no matter how hard we tried, we couldn't move!" Atani then adds, "Yes, what was it that they did to us?" Pigan responds, saying, "It's in their blood. If you got it on you or in you, it causes paralysis within seconds. That's why we hit you with these special white bamboo sticks! They have the power to reverse the paralysis because of a particularly special blessing prayed onto them. Like us, the Manganiti Man Nanu still possess the ability to communicate if they wanted to telepathically. Unfortunately, that's what happened to you, and they infected all your minds! The drink that we had to force down your throats is called Lo'degao (Medicinal Tea). It has the special ability to reverse the process if caught in time. Luckily we did, or you would turn out exactly like the Ito'!"

Ma'tao looks him dead in the eyes and excitedly asks, "So you're familiar with them?" Pigan replies, saying, "Yes, Maga'lahi. We have battled them for so many generations. Protecting not only Chochogo' but Guahan as well. We keep them contained within I Sesonyan Pribidu." Pigan pauses for a minute, looks around, then back to Ma'tao and, in a concerned voice, says, "But very recently and with Itak getting so much stronger. For the first time, I could honestly say that I don't know how much longer we'll be able to contain them." Ma'tao then asks, "Is it true that when the last two Maga'lahi I Mantatkilu failed to complete the unification of our islands and people, that their warriors turned into the Ito'?" Pigan responds, saying," There is some truth to that. For as long as I can remember, there have always been poor souls that turned into the Ito'! It was just those extraordinary and specific warriors that turned and became the Figo'. Out of all the Ito', they are the hardest to eliminate. And have been the most challenging to contain within this realm! But with you obtaining the Diyuk Paton Chaifi, you Ma'tao could finally help swing that balance to our favor!"

Ma'tao then asks, "So how did you know that we are searching for it?" Pigan points to what Ma'tao has on his waist, then continues saying, "I noticed that you already had obtained the Atupat Aniti. That's the only way you'll be able to control the trajectory of the Diyuk Paton Chaifi."

Ma'tao then asks, "Do you know happen to know its location?" Pigan replies with a resounding, "Yes! It's located deep within the heart of the swamp and protected by the Figo' themselves!" Da'on, after hearing that smirks and says, "Why am I not surprised!"

Aligao smacks him on the shoulders and says, "Hey! You already conquered your fears with the Manganiti Man Nanu! Now you can do anything!" They all share a laugh while Ma'tao turns back to Pigan and says, "We're also searching for Atani's brother Atdao. He might have passed this way hours before we did." Atani, now more worried, adds, "We need to find him! I fear for his safety with all this craziness around! Will you help us also locate him?" Pigan bows and says, "If Maga'lahi doesn't mind, it'll be our pleasure to escort and assist you all." Ma'tao looks at Pigan," With all your knowledge in dealing with the Manganiti Man Nanu along with the Ito!, that's something we're not passing up! So, where do we go from here?"

Pigan then says, "We need to head deep into the heart of the swamp, but first let me speak to the rest of my clan members and warriors, then we'll head out." Pigan then turns to speak to them. Upon doing that, Ma'tao notices that the majority of them head out. Tiani and her three warriors stay back, as well as Pigan and three of his warriors. Pigan returns to the group as Ma'tao asks, "Is everything alright? Where are they going?" Pigan replies, "They'll be splitting up as well because we need to make sure that all the banyan trees along the border of I Sesonyan Pribidu are thoroughly protected and defended! We can't afford to leave them unmanned because they are entry and exit ports between realms! My warriors will notify us immediately if any dark force tries to exit or enter the area! Come, we must hurry!"

They all proceed! All heading deeper into I

Sesonyan Pribidu!

Chapter 12

"Peace Amidst The Chaos!"

They all come across the waters of the swamp as Pigan gestures for them to stop! He then says, "From here on out, the only way to get to our destination is through these waters!"

Aligao sticks his foot in the water and shouts out, "Are you for reals! This water is freakin cold!" Da'on, laughing, looks at Aligao and says, "Why don't you quit your whining! If I could overcome my fears, so could you!"

Aligao smirks and replies, saying, "And that coming from someone who not too long ago was screaming like a girl! Wouldn't you like to know what I'm afraid of? It sure ain't this dang water!" He then puts on a much more conflicted look as he says quietly, "Let's go." Da'on laughs and shakes his head.

They march on in with Pigan and Tiani riding on Ma'tao shoulders. Along with their warriors atop Aligao, Da'on, and Machatlu's shoulders. Aligao looks to one of them and asks, "How were you all planning on crossing these waters if we weren't here?" The Taotao Man Nanu warriors on his shoulders keep quiet and diligently scan their surroundings. Aligao then remarks, "Oh. The strong silent types! Never mind. I could relate."

Ma'tao, overhearing Aligao's question, turns to Pigan and asks, "I'm just as curious myself. How would you traverse these waters if we weren't here?" Pigan looks at Tiani then back to Ma'tao and chuckles while replying, "I thought you'd never ask, now let us show you! First, set us down on that thick, dense patch of kangkung leaves."

Ma'tao then places both his arms on the kangkung patch of floating leaves. As soon as he does that, Pigan and Tiani run down each arm onto it. They then both shout, "Now stand back a bit!"

The group stands back as Pigan blows his Ku'-lo. It creates that beautiful pitch and frequency that they all heard earlier. It is a very distinct sound that is so much more different from the Ku'lo they use. Within seconds after making that call, the murky swamp waters around them start getting very busy with movement. The cold brackish water starts churning up all around them!

Ma'tao, still staying calm, asks in a very concerned voice, "Tiani? Pigan? What in the world is happening? Is this something we need to worry about?!" Tiani excitedly says, "Just stay where you stand!"

Atani then looks at Ma'tao, and with a puzzled look on her face, whispers, "What's going on?" Ma'tao reassures her by saying, "Don't move. It'll be alright!"

Aligao is now getting more anxious as the water around him starts churning more rapidly. He starts excitedly, calling out, "Ma'tao?! I don't know about this?" Just then, something with scales and sharp nails brushes up against his leg! Then he feels it! A tail! Whatever it is, it just swam right between his legs! Aligao is so flustered and freaks out to the point that he can barely even scream! And without giving it a second thought, he immediately jumps out of the water with lightning-like speed! He bolts with so much quickness! As everyone turns to look for him, he is already out of the water. And into the waiting arms of Da'on!

Da'on laughs as Aligao yells out, "What in the freakin world is down there?! It brushed up against me!" Da'on laughs even louder, and while swinging his arms in a rocking motion, asks, "Aww! Does the little baby want me to put him to sleep?"

Da'on, right at that moment, stops laughing and shockingly says, "Hey! What was that?" Aligao looking all around them, shouts, "Don't you dare put me down!"

As he says those very words, out from the cold, murky, brackish water arise, eight hilitai (monitor lizard)! Once these lizards rose to the surface, they lined up alongside one another. Each one of these fantastic lizards sports a beautiful saddle made from bamboo. And for strength, they are all lashed together with the roots of the banyan tree. These are no ordinary hilitai as well. They obey every gesture and listen to every word that the Taotao Man Nanu relay to them! It is something very unique that Ma'tao and his warriors have never seen with hilitai.

As Pigan, Tiani, and their warriors mount the hilitai, Tiani says, "Now this is the best way to travel in a swamp!" Pigan then looks to Ma'tao and shouts, "Now to heart! Follow us!" Ma'tao and the rest of them follow the lounge of lizards. Immediately Atani takes notice and says, "Tiani's right! Check out how fast and graceful they are in the water. Those hilitai are so stream-lined that they move so quick with such little effort!"

Aligao joking says, "I wish that I had a giant hilitai to ride!" Ma'tao shakes his index finger in the air and replies, "Be careful with what you wish for, Aligao! With everything we've come across so far, I wouldn't want a monster hilitai to be something we come face to face and have to deal with!" Aligao scoffs and shrugs his shoulders.

They walk for a couple of hours when they come across what appears to huge lat'di stones. These lat'di have fallen over time with the haligi (base stone) and the tasa (cap stone) strewn about the area. They sit on a small patch of land that is now barely peeking out of the murky water.

Machatlu takes a hard look in that direction and asks, "Pigan! Those lat'di over there! Do they have any connection with the Diyuk Paton

Chaifi?" Pigan, without any hesitation, says, "Yes! That's exactly where it use to reside." Machatlu then says, "My father, Sungot, told me about this place. He mentioned this is where he saw the stone for the first time. Along with Itak and the Ito'."

Pigan, now side by side with Machatlu, says, "I know of your father! He was right! He did see the Diyuk Paton Chaifi at that location. An alliance of my ancestors, your ancestors, and together with all the animals along with plants of the land. Created and erected those special lat'di! Coming together as one is what the four lat'di represented. That all life forms could live together in peace and harmony! Back then, our islands and way of life had balance." As they continue treading through the brackish waters, Machatlu just received a revelation as he excitedly asks, "Wait a minute! Are you saying you knew my father?! Are you? Did you—?"

Before he could even finish his sentence, Pigan says, "Yes! Yes, it was my brothers and I who found him! We were following Itak from a distance that night when we came across him watching Itak and the Ito' from that banyan tree! We put him to sleep and took him back home to safety. You should be glad we did! Because if we left him there, you probably wouldn't be here!"

Machatlu just shakes his head, saying, "So that's what happened! Thanks, Pigan."

Pigan then says, "I also sense that you inherited his gifts as a seer as well!" Machatlu, with a shocked look, asks, "How could you tell?"
Pigan humbly replies, "I too have been gifted with particular abilities, and one of them is sensing that within you."

Just then, Ma'tao takes notice that the water is getting deeper! It is to the point where it already passes their waist while moving towards their chest in some areas! In contemplating their situation, he calls out to Tiani and Pigan, saying, "Wherever we are heading, I hope we get there soon! We will be left defenseless in this situation! We must get to higher and drier ground now!" Pigan then shouts while pointing, "It's just up ahead!"

Up ahead, in the distance, all they see are flickering lights. And not sure what to make of it, Atani asks, "Those lights?" Ma'tao, who also sees it, asks, "Where are those lights coming from?" Aligao interjects, asking, "What lights? What are you looking at?"Da'on joins in, also asking, "Yes, what lights? I don't see anything other than the lights from our torches!"

Pigan turns to Ma'tao, along with Atani, and with a sense of shock, says, "That's right! You two can see those lights! In acquiring your pen-dants, you both are now able to see realms and dimensions that other humans can't. Interesting!"

Tiani then says, "Those orbs of flickering lights are the life force energies of those individuals who are now the Ito' and the Manganiti Man Nanu! They are trapped here in this world and aren't able to ascend!"

Ma'tao curiously asks, "How long have they been here?" Pigan then continues saying, "Since as long as you humans and us Taotao Man Nanu have walked this earth! Upon making their choice after becoming seduced by the darkness.

Their life force separated from their bodies. Leaving behind a soulless moving corpse!"

Ma'tao then asks, "So we're heading towards the orbs?" Pigan replies, "Yes! Directly under those orbs is an island! Within the island surrounded by bamboo trees is a huge crater. That crater is the heart of the swamp! What's interesting is years ago, that crater was barely big enough to engulf a breadfruit tree, but through the years, it has widened immensely and gotten so much deeper! It also exposed a system of extensive underground caverns that run throughout the island. We have come to know that area as the Liyang Taifinakpo' (Never-Ending Cave)!"

Aligao very inquisitively looks at Pigan then asks, "So we're supposed to go in there? In the dark? Where more of those dang ugly creatures may be hiding to ambush us again?! Don't take that the wrong way, Pigan, but I don't know if I could take that again!" Da'on then adds, "Sounds fun! Don't worry, Aligao. I got you!" Aligao sarcastically replies, "Whatever, Da'on?!"

Even though it has been dark so far, the evening is starting to befall them as Pigan says, "I feel more confident heading in there because we have the power of the Ka'lang I Man Metgot along with the Gapot Ulu I Saina on our side!"

Aligao shakes his head in disagreement, saying, "I don't know about that! They didn't help us too much with our last run-in with them! Those things are nasty!" At that instant, he screams out, "Hey!" As Ma'tao slaps him upside his head. Aligao chuckles while asking, "Why did you do that? You know I'm just joking."

Ma'tao very seriously says, "Keep it up, and I'll tell Maga'haga Unai that you're the one who stole her pugua' (betel nut) stash! And this time, I'm for reals!" Aligao playing up to Ma'tao, says, "C'mon, don't do that! With that lady, I'll never hear the end of it!"

Pigan then continues saying, "We'll be prepared for them this time. Yet they'll be aware of that! So we need to be extremely cautious! I can't emphasize enough how alert we need to be; the Ito' and the Manganiti Man Nanu could be lurking around every corner! We need to gather ourselves for a moment and formulate a plan."

Ma'tao then says, "I agree. Let's head over to the lat'di to come up with that plan. We also need to get out of this water as well!" So they all make their way towards the lat'di. But before they get too close, Tiani stops them saying, "Let me and my warriors head there first to make sure that it's safe. Stay here and don't move until I give you the all-clear!"

Tiani, along with her warriors, then move ever so swiftly through the swamp towards the islet of lat'di. No one makes a sound while they stay put awaiting their signal.

Atani then excitedly says, "There! I see it!" While pointing towards a blue torchlight that one of Tiani's warriors lit up. Without delay, they all decide to join them!

The islet of lat'di may be small, but once they all step onto it, every single them instantly feel a sense of peace and calm surge through their be-ing! It is a very welcoming presence considering they are in a place with so much chaotic energy surrounding them!

Immediately Ma'tao says, "Before we venture any further in this sacred space, we need to ask permission and blessings from our ancestors!"

No one has any qualms with his request as they all join hands in a circle. But before Ma'tao could say anything, Machatlu speaks up, asking, "Ma'tao, if you don't mind, could I be the one to say a few words?" Ma'tao, while gesturing for him to proceed, replies, "Please do the honor. I understand what this place means to you!"

Machatlu then takes his place in the center of the circle and asks,

"Mañaina-hu, pot fabot kao un sedi ham ya bai en liheng guini na lugat? Minaggem korason-mami entre pa'gu na yinaoyao. Pot fabot echa i dinanña'-mami kumu un hinasso! Kosakisiña bai en atbansa kumu un tah'taotao yan animas!" Which translates to "My ancestors, could you please allow us to use this place as refuge? With peace in our hearts amidst the chaos. Please bless us in coming together as one mind! So that we will collectively move together as one body and one spirit!"

The prayer and blessing in which Machatlu spoke upon them is something they needed at that moment and in moving forward!

Ma'tao then asks Pigan, "In all your years in dealing with the Ito' and especially the Manganiti Man Nanu, how would you suggest entering Liyang Taifinakpo'?"

Pigan looks at Ma'tao then signals his warriors. Tiani and her warriors join them. Together they form another circle within that circle. Pigan stands in the center of it and replies, "Why tell you when I could show you!" He then grabs his satchel and pulls out three beautiful shiny stones.

He places them neatly into a triangle around himself and says, "These are Guinifen Acho' (Dream Stones). They were given to me by my father. Not only do some of us have the ability to communicate telepathically, but I could also separate my spirit from my body momentarily and walk within the dream realm. While my spirit is scoping out an area, I can focus my thoughts to enter these stones. And from what I view from within the dream realm will be projected from the stones into this realm! It's what we used to find you!"

After hearing that, they curiously observe as Pigan crosses his legs and sits within the triangle. Two of his warriors position themselves behind him. Pigan then closes his eyes and takes deep breaths while he slips into a deep meditative trancelike state, all while his warriors keep a close watch on him and the surrounding area!

It is not too long before Pigan starts mumbling words in the language of the Taotao Man Nanu. He then shouts, "Show me!" Instantly his body goes limp as his warriors hold and keep him propped up! Simultaneously the dream stones glow bright blue! Tiani then tensely says, "Pigan has now entered the dream realm."

Ma'tao strangely asks, "How's it that you can tell?" Tiani just points towards Pigan's lifeless body. Which now has a vision of moving images that the dream stones have cast up above him! All present are in utter amazement! Pigan's spirit is viewing it, while everyone around the dream stones is witnessing it!

They are all left speechless and unsure of how this is possible. Yet these visions and images are appearing right before their very eyes!

Tiani then yells, "As amazing that this is to witness for the first time, we need to quit the gawking and quickly interpret what he's visioning! Because even though he is invisible in the dream realm, with all the threats looming around and among us, we can't be this vulnerable for far too long! We all need to remember as much of the details that we can gather!"

At that Atani, says, "I see what seems to be an entrance. There! Behind those bamboo trees!" They all gather closer as Ma'tao points, saying, "Yes! I see it too! The entrance to Liyang Taifi-nakpo'! I see some guards out front. About six of them!" Machatlu points and says, "Yes, I counted six as well. And by the looks of them, I'd say they are Pa'chang! We could take them out!"

Ma'tao then says, "Machatlu, Da'on, and Ali-gao! You three are responsible for taking them out!" All three agree. Shortly after, Aligao points saying, "There! After the last guard! I see a pathway leading down into the earth!" Tiani then points out as she says, "There are three caves from that first path! He takes the middle! Now here's where it becomes more interesting!"

Atani replies, "Why? What did you see?" Tiani responds anxiously, "Look alongside the walls of the caves! Do you see it?" They all look harder as Atani replies, "I'm not sure. All I see are glowing purple stones scattered throughout the cave walls."

Tiani replies excitedly, "Those aren't purple stones! Look again!" They all stare harder as Pigan gets closer to what Atani thought were purple stones. Aligao is so focused on a set of them himself that he inches towards the images with every passing second. Concentrating harder on it, but they suddenly disappear.

Pigan is now right about where those purple stones were when right out of nowhere, they rapidly reappear! Aligao, now much more focused, freaks out and screams, "What the?! It's a Manganiti Man Nanu!" He jumps back so fast while yelling, "I now know which cave I'm avoiding!"

Da'on, a bit shocked, adds, "There are hundreds of them in that cave!" Ma'tao curiously asks, "Are you sure they can't see him? He's pretty close to them!"

Tiani responds, saying, "He does get up close and personal!" Aligao very adamantly adds, "Dang! You Taotao Man Nanu really need to understand the word Privacy!" They all laugh aloud. Machatlu hushes them and excitedly asks, "Wait a minute! Did you all see that?"

Not sure about what he saw, Ma'tao asks, "What are we looking at?" Machatlu earnestly says, "More Ito'! Those are the Entalo'! They appear to be guarding another cave." Da'on excitedly adds, "It's more like caves! Check it out!" He points towards a whole series of caves and caverns!

They all continue looking on as Pigan ventures much further. Ma'tao then looks at Tiani, saying, "You're right, this is getting more interesting by the moment!"

Atani then asks, "Everyone! Please keep an eye out for Atdao!" Aligao then says, "This cave system is so vast that I don't see it ever ending!" Ma'tao, while focused and studying the images, says, "There! The third cave on the right after he passes the Entalo'! There seem to be much more Ito' guarding that third cave!"

Machatlu then really zeroes in and exclaims, "The Diyuk Paton Chaifi is in that third cave!" Ma'tao surprisingly asks, "How exactly do you know that?!" Machatlu responds, saying, "Because now we're dealing with the big boys! Those Ito' are the Figo'! And I could guarantee that they are guarding that stone in that room! We need to hurry and get down there!"

Tiani adds, "Machatlu's right! Those Ito' are Figo'! Plus, when you look at that cave, it's the only one that seems so much brighter!"

Ma'tao then says, "Only if Pigan could get by those guards!" No sooner than he said that, Pigan passes the Figo' without them sensing his presence. The tension is practically unbearable as they watch him slip past those adversaries without being seen! Tiani looks at all their faces and snickers, saying, "It's like we're waiting for him to get caught! It's Pigan's spirit; guys, those things have no clue he's there!"

Ma'tao then shakes his head in disagreement, saying, "If, by any chance that Asuli is involved, it wouldn't be very wise to keep your guard down! He seems to do his best work when underestimated!"

Tiani replies, "You're right! I best not get ahead of myself!" Da'on then says, "This cave Pigan is in keeps getting brighter! Also, so far, I've counted twelve Figo'!" Ma'tao then excitedly adds, "Hold up! Make that thirteen!" As he points to the most prominent and scariest looking Figo' of the bunch! Aligao stares deeper into that image of the Figo', and with much intensity, says, "Dang! That is one huge gaga' (animal) of a man or whatever they are! And damn, is he ugly! Ma'tao, that dude's all yours!"

Ma'tao just smirks while he continues saying, "And check it out! Look what he is guarding!"

Immediately they all get to see what was lighting up the cave walls finally! Placed very distinct and secure atop three black stalagmites, it's the all-powerful Diyuk Paton Chaifi! The magnificent stone is shining ever so brightly in all its splendor!

Aligao, in awe, says, "It's so beautiful!" Ma'tao, gripping tighter onto the Atupat Aniti hanging off the side of his waist, seriously says, "Yes, but beauty in that sense comes at a price!"

They all still look on in amazement as Ma'tao continues saying, "Remember that stone has extraordinary and sacred powers! I must be the only one to handle it, lest we be in trouble!"

He then looks towards the images while saying, "We all need to work together in remembering every single layout of Liyang Taifinakpo'. My gut feeling tells me that we seriously need to prepare for what we will come across!"

For right, as those words flow right out of his mouth, the images of Pigan start to flicker. As if something or someone was on to him! Da'on points while exclaiming, "You guys! Am I just imagining things? What's that huge shadowy figure overtaking the light?!"

They all turn to see what Da'on is pointing out! And all take notice as the flickering of images worsen! The huge shadowy figure surrounds Pigan's spirit within the cave! Simultaneously, Pigan's body starts shaking violently within the dream stones! Suddenly the images cease appearing, and his body immediately stops convulsing!

Ma'tao anxiously asks, "Is he dead?!" One of Pigan's warriors, who is still holding his body, instantly says, "He's still alive! But barely!" *What just happened?* They all think to themselves.

As they gaze upon one another with complete and utter silence, something catches them off guard! They instantaneously hear and feel gusts of strong wind from up above that rapidly shatters the silence!

Aligao yells while points in the night sky, "Something's up there, and it's heading our way!" Atani shouts, "I don't have a good feeling about this!"

As they all stare and try focusing on what they are seeing, Machatlu looks up above then cries out, "It's Itak! And it's heading our way!"

Ma'tao then yells, "Everyone! Get behind the lat'di! Because from what I see! It's not alone!"

Darting as fast as they can towards the lat'di, they all see a flash of purple lightning followed by loud thundering clashes! Sparks start flying in the air all around them! As purple lightning bolts and electrical sparks crash down from the heavens above and all around them. A set of bolts separates Ma'tao and his warriors from the Tao-tao Man Nanu and Machatlu! Ma'tao could see them struggling to try and move Pigan's body from harm's way!

Atani, with her quick thinking, takes deep breaths! She quiets her mind and focuses her thoughts! With her eyes now flaming bright orange, she channels her energy from her inner being and Gapot Ulu I Saina! The energy pulsates through her arms and out from her hands! She creates an orange force field, just in time to protect most of the Taotao Man Nanu! But a little too late to cover Pigan along with his two warriors!

Ma'tao shouts, "Take cover!"

The cause of all this chaos has now shown itself! It's Itak! And it's not alone! Someone is riding this monstrosity of a bird!

Ma'tao now gets a clear view of who it is! And he too sees Ma'tao!

Ma'tao screams aloud, "It's Asuli!"

Ma'tao tries to focus and bring his power to the forefront. But he is now caught in a deadlock stare with Asuli atop Itak! He then, within that moment, closes his eyes, focuses his breathing. Then with his inner strength and while shouting from the top of his lungs proclaims, "Ginen I Minetgot Puntan Yan I Na'liheng Fu'una!"

Which translates to "By The Power Of Puntan And Protection Of Fu'una!"

Ma'tao then opens his eyes, which are now blazing yellowish gold! The power he channels from within and his Ka'lang exits his right arm. It leaves through his palm which, is now facing Asuli! The mighty concentration of yellowish gold energy connects with Asuli's purple bolts! The sound they make upon clashing together is deafening all around! While the power that they both generate is so strong that it even causes the ground to shake!

It is just enough time for Machatlu, Tiani, and most of the Taotao Man Nanu to take cover behind the lat'di. But sadly, Pigan and his two war-riors were still in harm's way!

As Ma'tao gathers himself and focuses, he could now see that Asuli controls every move that Itak makes. He directs that giant of a bird towards Pigan! Both warriors never even had a chance to escape! Itak swoops down with light-ning-fast speed and grabs all three of them! Pi-gan's lifeless body just dangles as Itak tightens its grasp!

The warriors wince in pain as the giant bird's nails sink deeper into their bluish-gray skin!

Ma'tao would like to have another chance to knock Asuli off Itak! But does not want to risk hitting Pigan or his warriors. So he holds back with all his might and shouts, "Really, Asuli?! Why don't you come down here and face me!"

Asuli just follows that up with an evil, devilish laugh and shouts back, "In due time, Ma'tao! In due time! I still have a score to settle with you! Trust me! Pigan has been a thorn in my side for quite some time. And will be a perfect pawn in the ranks of the Manganiti Man Nanu! Unless I decide to kill him first! And soon, all the Taotao Man Nanu will be under my control!"

As those words spew out of his mouth, he looks towards Tiani and her warriors while he delivers another mighty blast of purplish lightning! The electrical bolts crackle with so much ferocity! As it tears up the ground in front of Tiani and her warriors! But they are protected behind the strength of the lat'di!

Asuli laughs even louder and says, "Follow me, Ma'tao! Follow me if you dare! Come you all and meet your true fate!"

Itak, with that god awful scream, screeches off as they disappear into the dark black abyss of the night sky! All in shock as to what they just encountered, only lessened by Taiani screaming aloud, "No! Don't do this! Pigan, wake up!" In not wanting everyone around to feel defeated. Ma'tao shouts, "We need to go now! We need to push on! We will get them back!" And with those words now backed by more pain, he leads them all as they push! Push towards the cavernous hell holes of Liyang Taifinakpo'!

Chapter 13

"To The Heart!"

With no time to waste! Ma'tao, his warriors along with Machatlu, Tiani, and the Taotao Man Nanu traverse with much haste through the waters of I Sesonyan Pribidu to the heart of the swamp.

They soon find themselves along the bamboo treeline. Knowing that right behind the grove of dense trees is the entrance of Liyang Taifinakpo'!

Up above and moving in such unison. Are the orbs of life energies longing to reconnect to the now soulless bodies of what beckons below! The Ito' and Manganiti Man Nanu.

They stop for a moment as Atani asks, "Now that we're here, how do you suggest we take down those Pa'chang?" Aligao joins in, saying, "I know Ma'tao, you said for Da'on, Machatlu, and I to take care of those Ito' which is fine by me. Just don't expect me to be the bait again!"

Tiani speaks up, saying, "No need to worry! Leave it to us. We'll draw them out!" Aligao, who is now relieved, says, "Thanks, Tiani! I didn't want to be the one to have to set the pace for this mission!"

Tiani smirks, saying, "Don't thank me yet! The quicker we draw out the Pa'chang, the quicker it'll be for you to face the Manganiti Man Nanu once again!"

Aligao looks down and shrugs his shoulders while responding, "I was afraid you'd say that!" Ma'tao smacks Aligao on his back, saying, "Got to hand it to you. You didn't think that through! But what can I say? No guts! No glory!"

Atani laughs, adding, "Yup! Walked right into that one!" Aligao laughs harder back at Atani, saying, "That's where you're wrong! And I did think this through. When we last met them, they got the drop on us because they were so quick! Considering how fast those damn ugly things are. We need to be faster! Better yet, let their strength become their weakness! My all-powerful rattle will cause them to be confused while having them fight amongst themselves!"

Machatlu asks, "So do you think that'll work?" Da'on vouches for Aligao, saying, "I have faith that it will! I've seen what that rattle did first hand to Sui'hans men. And without much effort from us, they took themselves down! I got you, Aligao. My nasa and I will be right there by your side!"

Machatlu then replies, "Next on the list will be the Entalo' and the Figo'! I will do what I need to, but let's not forget that big bad boy guarding that Diyuk Paton Chaifi!"

Ma'tao, with confidence, adds, "When he shows, I'll be ready! If we're to succeed, we need that sling stone! No two ways about it! We, at the least, have a rough idea of what's standing in our way. What will be the deciding factor is how well we execute it! We all need to support one another once we enter the deep dark underworld! With the power and the blessing on my Ka'lang I Man Metgot, I will lead until it's time for each group to take care of their responsibility. Atani, with

the power of the Gapot Ulu I Saina will be behind us to make sure that nothing catches us by
surprise!"

There is this brief pause just for a second. But
that brief second seemed like an eternity considering the challenges that lie ahead beyond the
dense bamboo grove!

Ma'tao then takes the opportunity within that
moment to look deep into each person's eyes.
Upon making that intimate connection, he says,
"We may be a small force! But a small force that
I'm one hundred percent willing to protect and
lay down my life for! It's these small daily heartfelt actions that will one day be the stuff of leg-

end! All because of a few! A few who risked everything! Everything that they have to get behind a cause. A cause that they believe in and are willing to fight and die for! I don't know for sure what's up ahead, but I can promise every one of you that I'll give it my all!"

With not another word spoken, they enter the bamboo grove. With the eerie, somewhat spooky feeling within the bamboo, it only makes sense to want to do a last-minute check with their gear and themselves.

It is at that moment that Ma'tao feels a gentle tap on his shoulder. He turns to find his love standing there in all her strength and beauty! The moon's reflection enhanced every aspect of why he fell in love with her in the first place.

He whispers, asking, "Are you alright?" Atani replies, "As long as we're together, I'll always be fine." She then looks deeper into his eyes as she grips his hands tight! She continues saying, "Isn't it crazy? Crazy that we're going back into harm's way. But as long as we're in this together, I feel a great sense of calm deep within me. A true reassuring peace!" Ma'tao pulls her closer and holds her tight. He does not say much except for, "You be safe, my love!" Atani knows that it is not those very few words that he spoke that made the difference. It is how he made her feel as he said them! The connection that they share after everything they have already been through is even more substantial. Within that space in time. Their space in time!

They all now find themselves standing along the tree line and staring deep into the Liyang Taifinakpo' entrance.

Ma'tao then says, "Tiani, when you head in there and draw them out. We'll be waiting and ready to take them all out!" Tiani, without saying a word, just nods as the remaining Taotao Man Nanu gather behind her.

Ma'tao, along with the rest of them, keep themselves out of sight behind the bamboo trees and wait. They are so quiet and still while blending in with their surroundings!

Tiani, with so much stealth and speed, moves alongside the cave entrance. While being followed by the other Taotao Man Nanu, they take the first steps to infiltrate the mysterious Liyang Taifinakpo'!

Ma'tao signals all of them to stay still where they stand. He waits for the slightest detail from Tiani to dictate that next move. They wait. Their waiting does not last too long before they start to feel the wind start picking up all around them! The bamboo trees start swaying with much violence back and forth! Dirt and leaves are whipping up all around when Ma'tao notices blue flames accompanied by electrical crackling noises emerging from the cave entrance! Within seconds, the blue flames now trailed with reddish-purple ashes billow across the cave entrance!

Ma'tao, puzzled about what he is seeing, keeps calm while gesturing to the rest of them to stay still and stand firm!

The wind starts dying down as the ashes also begin to clear. One Taotao Man Nanu warrior peers out the cave entrance, simultaneously waving a blue flame torch in the air. Ma'tao then looks at Atani, who signals to everyone else to follow their lead as they approach the cave entrance. When they get there, what they encounter is unique!

At first glance, Ma'tao could already see that this is no ordinary cave! For one, it is right in the middle of I Sesonyan Pribidu, on an islet, surrounded by all this murky water. Despite the gloomy surroundings, the rocks on the entrance are shimmering with beautiful yellowish gold and purplish flecks! Which shines brighter, the closer they get from the reflection of their torchlights.

Ma'tao thinks to himself, *How unusual!*

That thought short-lived as he feels a tug on his hand as Atani says, "We need to move! Tiani is calling us!" Ma'tao quickens the pace as he leads his warriors to shorten the gap between themselves and Tiani. At the same time, Atani follows from behind to ensure that they do not get ambushed.

Da'on then asks, "Did any of you get a chance to see any of those Pa'chang?" Aligao replies, "Not me! Tiani and the Taotao Man Nanu wasted them before I could even blink!" Machatlu then says, "Their weapons must contain salt within them because that stench we are smelling is proof of that!"

While proceeding deeper into Liyang Taifinakpo' Aligao calls out to Ma'tao, saying, "Check this place out! Those images through Pigan didn't do this place justice. Compared to what we are supposed to encounter, this place is mesmerizing!" As he points out and refers to the walls lined with the thickest, greenest, and plushest lumot (moss) that any of them had ever laid their eyes on!

They catch up to Tiani and the rest of the Taotao Man Nanu as they are about to enter the area that contains the series of caves! The series of three caves, in which Ma'tao recollects Pigan entering the middle.

They all gather in front of the entrance of the middle cave. Atani falling in last as Tiani jumps onto the shoulders of Ma'tao, saying, "Are you ready?" Ma'tao, with confidence, responds, "It's now or never!" As he looks at Atani, she signals with a nod that she is ready. Aligao, Da'on, and Machatlu look at each other then towards Ma'-tao, gesturing him to proceed.

The other Taotao Man Nanu also carry out something out of the ordinary! They glow! They glow a beautiful blue that is so hypnotic. It signifies that things are about to go down! While their battle-ready faces and stance only further confirm that!

Ma'tao then steps forward and crosses the threshold of the middle cave. Tiani, still standing on his shoulders, starts glowing brighter as they slowly inch their way forward. She gets ready to leap off at any second while positioning herself. In that instant, as if out of nowhere, a horrific, very childlike battle cry fills the cave! Rushing past them like a bat out of hell, it is Aligao!

He is gripping his rattle, making a mad dash towards the center of that space! Once he gets there, he stands shouting, "Maila' Manganiti! Maila' Manganiti! Guahu si Aligao! Sa' hagu bai hu paniti!" Which translates to "Come you evil ones! Come you evil ones! I am Ailgao! I am going to be the one to hit your face!" After he states that claim, there is complete and utter silence! No sign of any Manganiti Man Nanu!

Aligao, with his arm raised, gripping his rattle, is still super pumped and full of bravado. But cannot help focusing on that awkward silence. He takes a complete three hundred sixty degree revolution in preparation to spot a single soulless life form, but non appear.

He then turns to Ma'tao, chuckling while shrugging his shoulders, saying, "They must've come to their senses and ran off! Once they realized that messing with Aligao was bad for their itty bitty soulless bodies!" Aligao chuckles even louder! That he does not pay any attention to some sort of sticky clear liquid. A moist, smelly, gooey liquid that stretches down from above and drips onto his shoulder. He then feels it.

It is so slimy! And with much curiosity, is now drawn to look up.

He now comes face to face with the source! And the realization that the sticky clear liquid is drool! Drool from a soulless itty bitty life form! But not just one!

Ma'tao yells, "Torches up!" Everyone raises their torches simultaneously towards the top of the cave, exposing hundreds of Manganiti Man Nanu!

They are all clinging to and dangling from the cave ceiling! Their purplish glowing eyes in unison now illuminate the cave! While the smelly stench of their breath flowing past their grimacing evil smiles, and sharp fangs coated with drool fill the air!

Aligao, still standing right under them, is frozen from shock! The growls from the Manganiti Man Nanu echo throughout as Ma'tao whispers, "Don't flinch! Stay completely still!"

Ma'tao then signals Atani, who is already aware of what she needs to do! Ma'tao, Machatlu, and Da'on prepare themselves for what is about to come. The Taotao Man Nanu are now glowing brighter blue as they prepare for the fight!

Just then, a loud squeal of a scream by one of the Manganiti Man Nanu is blood-curling and so ear piercing! It seems to be one of the leaders. It starts making its way towards Aligao at a hurried pace! Aligao could now feel the adrenaline rushing through him at great speed as his heart seems to be pumping right out of his chest!

Ma'tao then yells, "Now!" At his command, Atani already centered, and focus opens her eyes, burning orange while holding out her palms facing Aligao! She channels the power from herself and the Gapot Ulu I Saina in his direction!

The orange force field could not have come at a better time! The rest of the Manganiti Man

Nanu are now following that individual leader! They all start to descend with so much ferocity and speed upon Aligao!

The force field protecting him angers the Manganiti Man Nanu even more! While most of them still look for a way to get to Aligao, the leader and others start to focus their frustration on Atani and rush towards her!

Tiani and the Taotao Man Nanu create a protective circle around her! Then with so much speed and gracefulness, start to eradicate every single Manganiti Man Nanu without prejudice!

Their salt infused magical weapons turned those Manganiti Man Nanu into purplish burning ashes and dust!

Ma'tao then focuses his breathing and centers himself. Then with his inner strength and while shouting from the top of his lungs proclaims, "Ginen I Minetgot Puntan Yan I Na'liheng Fu'una!" Which translates to

"By the power of Puntan and protection of Fu'una!"

Ma'tao then opens his eyes, which are now blazing yellowish gold! He projects a blast of powerful kinetic energy in Aligao's direction. It not only blasts those little demons off the force field but also incinerates them into purplish burning ashes and dust! Which delights him because it was very unexpected!

Ma'tao then yells, "Our turn!" As he follows up with his supernatural speed! So mind-boggling fast that he now is the one who catches these evil little demons by surprise!

Machatlu is so amazed and intrigued with all that he is now witnessing that he cannot contain himself and shouts to Da'on, "Let's get Aligao!"

Both men rush towards the orange force field and assist one another in clearing the path and taking out many evil little monsters in the process!

Da'on now feels the Gapot Ulu I Saina's strength flowing into his specialized weapon, the nasa! So he pulls it off from around his body and whips it with much savagery! It takes out thirteen little demons while knocking out the leader in the process!

Machatlu follows that up with a spear thrusts that completely incinerates them all! Aligao then regains his composure and signals Atani that he is alright! She lets down her orange force field shield from around Aligao!

He, too, notices that his unique coconut rattle has come alive by the Gapot Ulu I Saina! And with no hesitation whatsoever shakes it like there is no tomorrow!

All the Manganiti Man Nanu pick up on the frequency it generates! It cuts straight through their pointy purplish-black ears and causes immediate confusion!

From that moment on, they are so confused! So confused that they all stop dead in their tracks, attacking Ma'tao, Tiani, and all their warriors! They now turn on each other and start fighting amongst themselves! Nothing else matters as they are now so driven to destroy each other! And destroy one another is what they do!

But Ma'tao, Tiani, and the rest of the warriors do not wait around to see it happen! They all follow as Ma'tao rushes leading the way out of that cave, which is now full of plumes of purplish ashes along with black dust! Remnants of disintegrated Manganiti Man Nanu!

They all make their way into a large cavernous space where for a brief moment, they catch their breath to compose themselves!

Within this space, more caves exist. And within one of those caves, the Diyuk Paton Chaifi!

The scent in the air is now starting to reek of blood mixed with moss and dirt! With caution, they enter the cavernous space.

Their rest break is short-lived! They start to get bombarded by large boulders from up above!

Ma'tao yells, "Take cover!" Not knowing who or what is throwing the boulders all back into the cave, and re-evaluate the situation. Ma'tao then asks Tiani and Machatlu, "Could those be the Entalo'?" Machatlu responds, saying, "More than likely! Remember, if it is, they won't be as easy to take out as the Pa'chang!"

Tiani agrees and says, "He's right! Those Ito' are much more skilled and aware! To eliminate them, we need to sever their neck from their bodies!" Atani then says, "I'll lead us in there and use the force field to protect us!" Ma'tao then adds, "Once we're in there, we need to pinpoint exactly where the boulders are coming from, so I could blast them off their ledge! Once they're incapacitated, we need to be quick and take them out where they lay!"

Tiani looks at her warriors, then back to Ma'-tao and with much confidence, says, "That just might work, but we must prepare if things don't go as planned! I've had run-ins with the Entalo'. And though they are no Figo', they put up a damn good fight!"

Ma'tao then asks, "Did anyone at least see how many we are up against?" Da'on replies, "From what I was able to assess, I'd say about six!" Ma'-tao then says, "I have no doubt we could take them out if we work together!"

From where they stand, you could hear the boulders come crashing down and reverberate throughout the cavernous walls! They could also feel it shake the very ground they are standing on!

Atani yells, "We better hurry! The longer we wait, the more time they have to call reinforcements!" She then gets in front of the group and centers herself. She then focuses her breathing, and while channeling her energy with the Gapot Ulu I Saina, she raises her arms in the air and creates another force field. But this time, around the whole group! Atani's eyes are now burning that beautiful orange hue as she leads the group out of the cave.

Ma'tao stands behind, supporting her with every step she takes, and everyone else trailing after.

As they exit the cave, no time is wasted from their assailants as boulder after limestone boulder comes crashing down onto the force field! The noise is so loud and nerve-racking! Also, the pressure that it creates within the force field is bone crushing! Bone crushing to the point that Aligao screams out, "The noise and the pressure!

This pain is excruciating! I don't know how much of this I could take!"

Ma'tao shouts aloud, "How many Entalo' do you see?" Da'on then yells, "Like I said, six! I counted six! They are all situated up along the ledge and all around us! If you decide to blast! Do it now! And do it fast! Because this pressure, combined with all this piercing noise, is becoming too much to bear!"

Ma'tao, who is also starting to feel the pressure building up within the confines of the force field, shouts, "Atani! Are you ready?!"

Although Atani is very focused on keeping the force field around them from collapsing, she too is starting to feel the strain. The strain from the constant bombardment! So she shouts aloud, "Yes! More than ready! On your count!"

The pressure is getting more excruciating by the second as Ma'tao shouts out, "Everyone! On the count of three, get down and be prepared to attack with no remorse!"

Ma'tao holds on to Atani's shoulders! He then continues shouting, "On my count! Get down!" He then closes his eyes and focuses his breathing once again. Even amongst the chaos going on around them, he is in total coherence!

He is now thoroughly centered as he proclaims, "Ginen I Minetgot Puntan Yan I Na'liheng Fu'una!"

He places one hand on Atani to signify that it is time to transition! He opens his eyes now blazing that beautiful yellowish gold and shouts aloud once again, "One! Two! Three! Get down!"

As Atani powers down her force field, Ma'tao simultaneously guides her out of harm's way, between him and his warriors. He then raises and stretches out both his arms! At that exact moment, all torchlights burn out! It is complete utter darkness!

Three bright, brilliant flashes follow it up! A loud roaring boom follows the third flash as he creates one of the most potent energy blasts thus far! The discharge he produces contains so much powerful kinetic energy it picks up and slams all six of the Ito' up against the cave's limestone walls! Powerful luminous yellowish gold lightning bolts also from within exited his arms! It causes the limestone walls to explode upon impact and quickly obliterates it! Large rocks, pebbles, and dust scatter all around and fill the large cavernous space!

Ma'tao, at that moment, thinks to himself, *My powers! They're growing! I'm feeling so much stronger!*

He does not let that thought stop him as he yells, "Stay down!" He sends another blast of lightning bolts from both arms, where he notices movement on the ledge above the cave entrances! All actions seize as he shouts, "Let's do them a favor and send them off properly! Their souls are waiting for them up top!"

Tiani, along with her warriors, does not waste any time and seek out the first Entalo'!

Ma'tao leans over to check on Atani and asks, "Are you alright?" Atani gets up, and while dusting herself off, says, "I'm fine! In considering what just happened! Your powers have increased so much in such a short amount of time! Those flashes? Aren't they the flashes you recalled in your dream?!"

Ma'tao, while helping dust her off, replies, "Yes, now that was uncanny! But are you alright?" Atani grips his hands tight and says, "Yes! Now let's deal with these Entalo'! I have a strong feeling Atdao, Ina, and Magogui are somewhere nearby."

Machatlu starts shouting, "Let's not get ahead of ourselves! We still have these guys to deal with!" He then runs full force towards a figure in the distance! Da'on and Aligao follow in pursuit. Ma'tao, anxious to join in the fight, is about to take off after them when he hears Atani scream!

He turns to see her being picked up by a gray-ish-white zombie with glowing red eyes. They have now come face to face with the Ito' for the very first time. And an Entalo' for that matter! This Entalo' is big and foul looking! He also reeks with the stench of sulfur and death! He lifts Atani, who now has both arms pinned against her side!

She screams, "Ma'tao! Get him off of me!" Ma'tao takes hold of both this creature's arms and overpowers him while breaking the grip he has on her! Atani can slip out and whips around the Entalo' so fast while whipping out her two bamboo blades, slices both his joints from behind his knees!

The injury causes this foul sulfur smelling being to fall back onto himself! Ma'tao does not waste any time. Within a nanosecond, he positions behind the Ito', and while having him in a headlock, snaps his neck! As he lays the Entalo' down, he and Atani witness first hand the rest of his life force exit out his body! It is in the form of tiny orbs of pure white light. They both get a small glimpse of how this person once looked before his grotesque transformation. Then that form breaks back into tiny orbs of light as they all float up in unison while exiting Liyang Taifinakpo'! Finally, to unite with his soul floating above the swampland! That Entalo' is now finally able to leave this realm and find eternal peace!

Within that moment, the remaining husk bursts into flames of purplish-red ashes and disintegrates before Ma'tao and Atani's very eyes.

Tiani and the other Taotao Man Nanu take out two more Entalo' who are utterly knocked out by that all-powerful energy blast created by Ma'tao. They just complete the process and send them off to a much more peaceful existence!

Machatlu, Daon, and Aligao, on the other hand, now have their hands full. Because of the other three Entalo' that are now confronting them! They only had the wind knocked out of them, and all three are now fully recovered! And by how they are positioning themselves, they are not about to go out as easy as the others!

Ma'tao, seeing that, lines the zombie confronting Aligao up in his sights. He again takes deep breaths and focuses. He is so centered and focused as he launches the True Spear towards that Entalo'!

He launches the spear with so much fortitude! That whatever it comes in contact with, the True Spear is sure to inflict some serious damage!

It slices through the air towards its target. It is traveling so fast that when the Entalo' notices it, it is already too late!

The True Spear, with much precision, slices through the right arm of that Entalo' and completely dismembers it from his body! The True Spear then boomerangs back around into the hand of Ma'tao.

He and Atani notice that despite not having his arm, the Entalo' does not show any signs of feeling any pain! So they are not about to wait for him to attack and press the situation!

Ma'tao runs straight at him at full velocity. He gauges his distance and speed. He is about three feet away as he takes a deep breath, focuses, and cocks his right arm back. The Entalo' tries to move again to avoid the onslaught, but Ma'tao is just too quick! He releases his arm and follows through with his whole body! Ma'tao, with such accurate precision, places that punch that he shatters the creature's jaw! It also launches him high up in the air.

Atani takes advantage of the situation, and with much speed herself, she maneuvers her way to where she is right behind that Entalo'. He has not even hit the ground as she again uses the two bamboo blades. And in a cross fashion, she slices his neck off! It is such a clean and masterfully executed technique that his head rolls towards the feet of Ma'tao while the body lands with a massive thud to the ground! And just like the other Entalo' before, his body burns up and disintegrates! While his remaining life force joins his soul above.

Aligao then shouts, "Thanks for the assistance! But honestly, I had that covered!"

There is no time to rest as they both proceed to assist the others! The two Entalo' left seem to be giving Machatlu and Da'on a pretty good fight!

Ma'tao yells, "It looks like you both need help! Are they both that troublesome?!"

Machatlu smirks as he somersaults into a back-flip and lands strategically behind the Entalo'! He then takes his spear and jams it hard into the backside of the creature's neck, hitting his jugular vein! Blood starts splattering all over the place!

Da'on after witnessing that, yet still engaged in a fight and not to be outdone! He leaps with such agility onto a boulder off to his side. And launches himself into a backflip over the Entalo' he is facing! As he is above him in mid-air, he uses the cordage from his nasa as a noose! Then with such fluid-like movements, wraps it around the neck of that Entalo'! As he lands back on his feet, the loud crackling snap of the creature's neck-breaking fills the cave! Then with so much vigor throws his adversary from up over himself, hard up against the cave wall, causing his head to separate while coming clean off!

He then turns to Machatlu and asks, "How'd you like that?!" Machatlu just scoffs and says, "It was alright."

Both of the zombie bodies then burn up! Their ashes are now the only remnants as both their life force energies float away.

Aligao, flabbergasted, looks at both of them and says, "Damn! That was a bit excessive. But it was awesome!"

He then tries to downplay it, saying, "I was about to take care of my opponent that way, but lucky for him Ma'tao and Atani got in the way!"

Atani just laughs it off as Ma'tao replies, "Everyone alright? We better get going!"

Chapter 14

"Through The Heart!"

As they all head deeper into Liyang Taifinakpo', Ma'tao looks around the area. He then recognizes the cave where Pigan entered. He points, and with much excitement, says, "There! That's where we need to go! That's where we saw the Diyuk Paton Chaifi!"

He leads the ways as the others follow. Atani, who is right behind, but a couple of feet away, hurries to catch up to him. Ma'tao enters first!

As soon as he crosses the entrance, there is a loud thundering crash, and the ground starts to shake! The earth beneath their feet is throwing them left to right! The rock wall behind him comes crashing down and separates him from everyone else!

Ma'tao turns and starts shouting, "Atani! Ali-gao! Can you hear me?!" Dead silence! He hears no response! Due to this massive rock pile now separating them!

It is now very dark, pitch black! He starts to feel a very uneasy feeling rise from the pit of his stomach. He begins to worry, more so about everyone else on the other side of the cave! Ma'-

tao thinks to himself; *I hope they're alright! I need to get out of here and back to them!*

He attempts to relight his torch when he starts to hear a cracking hissing sound and movements within the darkness of this space!

That dead silence breaks as he hears a wicked sinister voice call out to him, saying, "Now Ma'-tao! Now I have you exactly where I want you!"

Ma'tao could now hear his heart pounding as he stays very still. He also does not make any abrupt movements to give away his location.

Meanwhile, on the other side of the fallen rocks, Atani, Tiani, and the rest of the warriors try to move the boulders. And clear a way to get to Ma'tao!

Atani, getting more worried by the moment about being separated from her love, yells, "Ma'-tao! Ma'tao! Are you alright? Can you hear me?" No answer.

Then from behind them, they start to hear rocks moving, and static crackling hissing sounds coming out from the caves all around them!

Aligao then whispers, saying, "Something is coming our way! And by the sound of it, I don't think they're friendly!"

Da'on then says, "Get closer and stick together!" Tiani and her warriors position themselves in a circle around Atani and the rest of them. They also start glowing brighter blue and signal that they are ready to take on whatever is coming!

Machatlu, who is also ready to scrap, says, "Just by the sheer smell of rotting flesh in the air, I have a compelling feeling we are about to meet the Figo'!"

No sooner than he said those very words! Appearing out from behind the boulders, they become surrounded! By giant muscled pale-skinned creatures with long flowing black hair and flaming red eyes!

Though they are Ito', they do not carry themselves like the Pa'chang or Entalo'. They seem to have a sense of more awareness and a much scarier sinister look to them!

The negative energy within the area is now getting so intense and very uncomfortable at the same time.

They all could feel it trying to overcome their energies as the Figo' start drawing closer towards their circle! Tiani yells, "Don't look into their eyes! Don't look into their red eyes! These creatures have the power to put you in a trance and possibly take over your body!"

Aligao, now more anxious, shouts, "Not that again!" Atani then notices that all six Figo' have on something very familiar. She then, with excitement, yells, "Look! On their necks! They're all wearing the same dark stone pendant! It looks just like the pendants controlled by the Ka'lang I Manganiti! Asuli's Ka'lang I Manganiti! We need to deal with these guys and get to Ma'tao!"

Da'on then adds, "That's how they're able to control or possess others. It's through Asuli!" Aligao shouts, "We need to destroy those pendants. There ain't no way I am going to go through any of that again!" Machatlu then says, "Then we need to take them out like the others completely. Remember to use the salt! Complete-ly sever their necks and impale their black hearts!" Da'on then cries out, "What are we all waiting for?! Attack!"

At the same time, on the other side of the cave. Ma'tao stays very still while listening to every single movement that this Ito' is making. The static crackling hissing gets louder as the creature approaches closer!

Ma'tao works his hand into his pouch to grab ahold of Dark Sight. Sensing that whatever spoke is very close, he places the turtle shell goggles over his eyes. He can see! But his joy is halted as his assumptions are correct. The Figo', this vile and sinister-looking creature, is now right in front of him! And breathing on Ma'tao with his cold rotting flesh breath that it expels. Grotesque saliva is dripping down from his fangs, which falls onto the chest of Ma'tao.

Ma'tao is freaked for a second as he and this abomination stare deep into each other's eyes. He is the Figo' of all Figo'! The Ito' of all Ito'! And the master of the other six in the other cave!

He grabs Ma'tao! He picks him up with such ease and throws him up against the limestone wall! Ma'tao, now with the wind knocked out of him, is dazed as to what just happened. Though he is stunned, he hurries to compose himself! He gets his footing back under him and gains his bearings. But this Figo' is so quick that Ma'tao cannot pinpoint his exact position!

Then with a loud crack, Ma'tao absorbs a stiff, big knee to his face delivered with such precision by this monster! His Dark Sight goggles then go flying through the air as blood spews all over the cave walls! He hits the ground so fiercely, and this time struggles to get back up!

Ongoing at the same time on the other side, Atani advances on towards the ugliest female she has ever laid her eyes on! She is the Figo' close to her. Before she gets too close, that creature in a devilish voice screams and speaks in some chaotic language they do not understand. Her cry is.so loud that Atani is stunned for a second!

However, a second is all that female Figo' needed! From her red eyes, she emits red energy beams that create a force field around and paralyzes Atani when it touches her!

Tiani, along with her warriors, try to assist Atani but are thwarted by two of these monsters who cast a magical net over them that contain them and their powers! Da'on, Machatlu, and Aligao are each confronted by other Figo' as well.

As their battle ensues, Da'on immediately finds out that Machatlu was right. As the Figo' he is facing blocks his first punch with not much effort! He then gets picked up, flipped like a child, and slammed to the muddied ground! That Ito' just looks at him, then laughs while forcefully stepping on his neck!

Machatlu, on the other hand, connects with a couple of kicks to his opponent's body! But they are not enough to do any damage as that Figo' unleashes a couple of kicks of his own! And those blows make a considerable difference! Machatlu drops to his knees to catch his breath while that Ito' gets behind him and places him in a viselike headlock!

In seeing this, Aligao raises his coconut rattle in hopes of confusing their adversaries! But before he could even give it a slight shake, the Figo' he is facing leaps on all fours into the air! He grabs the rattle out of Aligao's hand in mid-air by his mouth and sharp teeth! Then in a spiderlike fashion clings to the cave wall upside down! Before Aligao could make out where he is at, that Figo' leaps back over Aligao and uses the rattle to hook Aligao's neck within its hoop! It instantly chokes out Aligao, who almost passes out from the lack of oxygen!

The Figo' then backflips on all fours onto Aligao's back! Aligao is now completely pinned down on his belly with the very agile Ito' positioned on his back! They are all now incapacitated!

Meanwhile, back on the other side, and with a wicked sinister laugh, the head Figo' says to Ma'tao, "I applaud you for making it this far! But I must say, I thought you would put up more of a fight! You're pretty disappointing!"

Then with one hand, he picks Ma'tao up by his hair, and with the other, punches him so hard in his torso! A loud gut-wrenching thud echoes throughout as Ma'tao is now on his knees and starts coughing up more blood!

The Figo' now feeling victorious, pushes his long stringy black hair from his face while walking towards Ma'tao, bragging, "By now, your friends should be begging for their lives! After I rip your heart out you, my fellow Figo' and I will feast on all your flesh and bones!"

Ma'tao now recalls that this monstrosity of a being was that sizable shadowy figure in Pigan's images. He could now feel the skin on the back of his neck crawl while his heart thumps like crazy within his chest!

But despite all that is going on, he knows the truth! The truth of what is now staring at him dead in the face! So he takes his deep breath and focuses! And even though the pain is unbearable, he focuses on the thought of Atani and his destiny! And the truth in knowing that the greater the fear, the more he must make a stand against it!

He then gets up to his feet while clinching both fists tightly. He opens his eyes and could now see this freak of nature all so clear!

Ma'tao then very confidently says, "Are you going to talk forever? Or are we gonna dance?!" He then shouts, "Ginen I Minetgot Puntan Yan

I Na'liheng Fu'una!" Then with an all-powerful earth-shattering yell in that standing position, he cocks his arm back! He then, with all his might, throws a powerful punch that cracks the monster square across his jaw!

The colossal creature gets knocked back a couple of feet as his head flings back, and purple blood flies through the air! He then readjusts himself while sarcastically saying, "Now we got ourselves a fight!" Ma'tao then runs full force towards the Figo'! He then leaps off the lime-stone wall and onto the monster's shoulders!

Ma'tao then straddles his neck between his thighs! The momentum that Ma'tao generates forces the Figo' down! They hit the ground so hard that it dislocates the monster's shoulder on impact!

As painful as it looks, it does not hinder the giant Ito' one bit! He stands up and with his working arm. Swiftly grabs Ma'tao, who is still on his shoulders by his hair! And with such great strength flings Ma'tao with such ferocity onto the ground!

Ma'tao is shocked! In shock that he was not affected one bit by that hard throw! He just shakes it off and gets back on his feet. He is now moving so fast! The monster loses track of him just for a split second. But within that second, Ma'tao positions himself and lands one of his most brutalizing kicks to the side of the creature's face! And with a thundering blow backed with a powerful lightning kick, the head Figo' is propelled clear across the cave! He smashes into the fallen limestone rocks with such great force that it clears an opening between both caves! It is a big enough opening that Ma'tao can see Atani and the rest of his warriors, who are now in trouble!

In witnessing that, he does not stop. He darts straight to the Figo' who is now dazed

Ma'tao, now angered by seeing his love in that position, shouts, "No more playing around! This message is for Asuli!"

He gets behind that giant of a beast and straddles him with his powerful legs! While holding the giant monster's face tight to one side, he firmly grasps the Higam I Saina! Then along with an almighty shout, he slashes the neck of the lead Figo' with the all-powerful adze! It cuts through the creature's neck like butter!

He then follows through by snapping the monster's neck! Not stopping there, he jumps on his chest, and with another loud shout, slashes a hole into the monster's chest! Ma'tao then reaches into the Figo' and rips out his heart!

Ma'tao witnesses the creature's life force leaving its body, but he does not see it as ascend! He does not overthink it as he rushes to assist his warriors!

Upon witnessing what just happened, the other Figo' are stunned for a moment! The female Ito' flinches as her powers weaken for a second. That second is all Atani needed to refocus and find that strength within herself! And with confirmation that Ma'tao is alright, she realigns with her pendant!

She raises her right palm and screams, "Now feel this!" She unleashes her energy blast! It overpowers the creature's controlling beams and blasts her in the face as she falls to her back against the cave wall!

Ma'tao then grabs the magical net off Tiani and her warriors while shredding it in half! The Taotao Man Nanu turn up their speed and attack the two Figo' who are now both confused by how fast they are moving!

Ma'tao takes salt packets from his pouch and slams it hard onto the back of the Figo' on top of Aligao. The salt burns through the creature, who screams in severe agony while it lets go of the rattle and releases the hold on Aligao's neck!

In response, Aligao does not waste any time! He retrieves his rattle while shaking and focusing all his thoughts on the remaining Figo'! They all scream as if they are confused and in pain! The Figo' stepping on the neck of Da'on laughs aloud then shouts, "That won't work with us! Our minds are stronger than you think!" He then continues taunting Ma'tao and says, "Now that I'm in this body! Let's go another round!"

Ma'tao, curious as to what just happened, pauses as Tiani yells, "The life force from that giant Figo' you defeated! It entered the body and joined with the life force of that Figo' on Da'on! We need to act quickly and kill the rest of them to prevent them all from combining and getting stronger!"

Da'on starts gasping for air while wincing in pain! The Ito' has gotten more robust, and he is not holding back!

Atani summons her strength from within and focuses all her power onto the coconut rattle! Immediately Aligao feels the increase in its capacity and shakes it like never before!

All Figo' except for the one on Da'on are affected! They fall to the ground, confused, and start screaming in pain! While they all convulse vigorously, trying to block their ears!

Machatlu yells, "It's working, Aligao! Keep it going!" He does not waste any time as he jams his spear through the throat of the Ito' he is facing! He then, with such quickness, spins around while thrusting the bone spear hard and straight through his heart! He then turns, and with such celerity, he takes out the Figo' that had Aligao pinned down!

Tiani herself acts while she slashes the throats of the two Figo' closest to her! Her warriors then rip out and stab their hearts! Now there are only two of these deadly creatures remaining!

The Figo' on Da'on is now more irritated than ever. He steps off Da'on and runs straight towards Atani! Ma'tao shouts, "Protect Atani! Don't let him get to her!"

Da'on gets up coughing as he rushes to assist in protecting her! Ma'tao dives for the monster's legs to trip him up! It is like tackling a large limestone boulder because this creature is like solid rock!

Ma'tao slows him down but does not stop him! He tightens his hold onto one leg as that powered-up Figo' drags him across the cave!

Da'on quickly makes a lasso with the rope from his nasa and throws the noose around the hefty beast! He then pulls with all his might to try and help restrain him!

Machatlu, from where he is standing, slings three packets of salt with such accuracy that it hits the monster dead center on his chest! Though he is showing signs of pain, he still moves forward!

Tiani and her warriors also rush towards them and assist! They slash at the monster's joints with their weapons but barely make a scratch! Because of his formidable scale-like skin!

The creature, now more determined, persists and keeps moving forward! It is all happening so

quickly that when Atani finally realizes the Figo'
is near her, it is too late!

The monster picks her up with one hand and
chokes her tight! He immediately cuts off her
circulation, and she cannot breathe. She struggles while fighting for her life!

Ma'tao, seeing Atani is in grave danger, is now
so worried and more enraged than ever! He lets
go of the monster's leg and repositions himself.
He once again summons his power from within,
and that combined with his pendant, he then
feels that electricity surge! That all-powerful energy! It transmutes and flows from his body
through the Higam I Saina. But is he too late?

Atani stops kicking, and her body now looks lifeless! Ma'tao moves even faster as he reaches around the neck of the Figo' and secures him tight onto himself! Then with such precision and brute force, Ma'tao thrusts the Higam I Saina deep into the chest of this powerful Figo'!

The monster screams and lets go of Atani! Ma'tao rips the adze out and thrusts it again, but this time into his throat! As he pulls it out as Da'on simultaneously pulls harder on the rope of the nasa! Their combined movements bring down the creature! It also causes a large gash to open up while causing blood to spew everywhere!

Machatlu, Tiani, and her warriors scramble to protect Ma'tao, Atani, and Da'on from the female Figo' who looks to be getting up after that blast Atani gave her earlier. Atani herself is still not moving as all the worse thoughts Ma'tao could think of are now unfolding right before his very eyes! He thinks to himself, *How could I let this happen?!*

The Figo' though bloodied and injured, gets back up to his feet. He rips the rope of the nasa off his neck! He releases a loud, blood-curdling scream while saying in a devilish voice, "You Ma'tao will join her!"

Those words do not even phase Ma'tao as he focuses on Atani! She is all that matters now! He takes a deep breath as he channels all that rage and uses it as fuel!

Ma'tao then yells to his warriors, "Stay back and attend to Atani! This fool of a Figo' is mine!" They all do just that.

Ma'tao zeroes in on this monster! This monster who may have just taken the life of his love! And now he sees nothing but red and screams, "Ginen I Minetgot Puntan Yan I Na'liheng Fu'una!" He then rushes towards the Figo' as he lowers his shoulder towards the creature! He drives his shoulders into this hideous creature's torso, and while grabbing the back of his legs, picks him up! Ma'tao then carries the gigantic beast with so much momentum and plows him hard into the jagged rocks within the cave wall!

The creature slumps down with the wind knocked out of him! Ma'tao picks him up with one hand by his long straggly hair. And while standing in front of him, looks him directly in the eyes! Ma'tao is so full of rage that he does not say a single word! He tilts the monster's head to the side as he thrusts the Higam I Saina into the gash within the creature's neck! He feels the jugular, and with such great force, rips it out! He rips it out so hard and fast, causing the Figo' to collapse and fall to his knees!

Ma'tao, now thinking the worse of what might have happened to Atani, yells, "You crossed a line, and now you're going to pay!"

With so much rage while in so much pain, he thrusts the Higam I Saina deep into the monster's chest! All hear the sounds of bones crushing and flesh ripping apart! Then with such brutal force and quickness, he pulls the Higam I Saina out from the creature's chest, which still has his bloodied heart stuck within the weapon!

The lifeless body of this once mighty Figo' now lays dead. Dead and strewn across the feet of Ma'tao.

He then rushes to Atani's side. Ma'tao worriedly thinks to himself, *Has she met the same fate? No, this can't be?*

The other warriors are still ready to fight because they are not out of harm's way yet! The other Ito', the female, is still left. So they all band together! They are not going to let her get anywhere near Atani or Ma'tao!

Ma'tao calms his breathing as his adrenaline starts to settle. The realization of everything that just happened comes to the forefront of his mind!

He starts breaking down! It is all too much to bear as his tears start rolling down his cheeks and onto Atani's body. He whispers in pain, calling out to her, "Get up, my love! Get up! We still have things to do. We're not finished yet."

Aligao places his hands on Ma'tao to try and comfort him. All could feel and sense the grief that he is feeling at that exact moment. They are also starting to feel the pain with just the thought of losing Atani.

Tiani, still glowing bright blue, says to her warriors, "Stay alert! Nothing gets close to Atani or

Ma'tao!" after she mentions that one of her female warriors calls out, "She's moving!"

Machatlu then turns to them, saying, "Guys, the Figo'! She's approaching!"

Ma'tao yells, "Take care of her! Or I'll kill her myself!"

Da'on, unsure of what to make of it, says, "She's gesturing something. I don't think she wants to fight!" Aligao asks, "Do you think we should put our weapons down?"

Ma'tao then shouts, "Don't you dare put down your weapons! Take her out! Or I'll kill her myself!"

Machatlu intervenes, saying, "Please, Maga'lahi hold on a moment. She's trying to say something."

Tiani then says, "Be careful! We still need to take precautions!"

They all back down a bit and are also not as tense, as they notice that the female Figo' is not showing any signs of aggression anymore. As she moves closer, she bows her head down lower. She finally comes to the point where she is down on her knees. She is also speaking in a language that Ma'tao and his warriors cannot understand.

Tiani then asks, "Are you all able to make out what she is saying?" They all gesture and reply, "No."

Tiani then translates, saying, "She is saying that her journey has finally come to an end. The prophesied Maga'lahi I Mantatkilu has now come to relieve her of her burden. A burden that she has carried for so many years!"

Tiani then looks to Ma'tao and asks, "Could you please trust me and rescind your decision to kill her? We should give her a chance to explain her part in all of this. It could be beneficial to our cause!"

Ma'tao, still wrought with pain, looks to Tiani and nods as he agrees while saying, "You all be on guard! I'll let her speak, but make no mistake! If she does anything to rub me the wrong way or any wrong move. I'll end her myself!"

With everyone in agreement, Tiani signals her to come forward. The female Figo' carefully gets closer as Tiani then tells her to step within their circle slowly. She gets closer to the ground until she is on her knees in the center of their ring.

She then speaks as Tiani translates, saying, "Please forgive us, Ma'tao. When I took my oath to serve my Maga'lahi I Mantatkilu, this is not where we intended to all end up! I, too know, of such a love. Have faith! For you shall see her again! It's time for me to depart this world and to do my part in helping you to bring back that balance."

In not knowing what she meant by that, Ma'-tao looks in her direction with his face covered in tears and says, "What do you mean?" She does not respond. Ma'tao then shouts to Tiani, "Ask her what does she mean by that?! When will I see her again?!"

As Tiani is about to translate the question, the female Figo' stands straight up! She stretches out her arms while closing her eyes. A blinding bright white light shoots out from within and all around her, filling the once dark space!

She floats up as the light gets bright. So bright that everyone has to shield their eyes to keep from going blind. The wind within the cave also starts to pick up! Aligao starts yelling, "What's going on?!"

Ma'tao, now shielding himself along with Atani, shouts, "Does anyone see her?" Da'on calls out, saying, "Everyone! Gather around and protect Ma'tao!"

The whole cave is now beaming bright white that they are not able to see each other! The earth also starts to shake again with so much violence under their feet! They reach out to grab ahold of one another! Then just as quick as it started, it all of a sudden stops as the bright white light from the female Figo' also begins to dissipate.

They are all now able to see her silhouette as she starts to reappear. As the bright white light surrounding her disappears, they all take notice that she is not the same hideous-looking monster she once was! Standing right before them now is a beautiful Chamoru woman, adorned in the finest warrior attire that they all have ever seen.

This Chamoru woman warrior is also holding in her hand something exceptional and of great importance! It is one of the most fascinating yet deadliest weapons known to man! The Diyuk Paton Chaifi!

They all stare in astonishment as she starts walking towards Ma'tao. She kneels in front of him, bows, and presents herself by saying, "My name is Hanumta! Thank you so very much for freeing us all from our prison! Our living hell!"

Ma'tao looks at her with tears still in his eyes and a blank stare. As Tiani and their warriors still surround him looking on. Hanumta then says, "May I?"

She then stretches out her arms, reaching for Atani. Ma'tao, still in a state of grief, just looks back towards Atani as Hanumta kneels beside him.

She places her arms around Atani and looks to Ma'tao while saying, "You Ma'tao! You might be able to bring her back!" Ma'tao, bewildered, looks at Hunumta and asks, "How? Please tell me, how could I bring her back?" Aligao then says, "Yes! Tell us! Tell us what we need to do!"

Hanumta looks at Ma'tao then says, "It has to be you! The Diyuk Paton Chaifi could only be surrendered to the prophesied Maga'lahi I Man-tatkilu. Also, only you and Machatlu being sons of Chochogo' and having blood ties with the ancestors of that specific village, are the only ones who could proceed with this mission. Everyone else here is a prisoner to this cave! So from here on out, if Atani is to have the slightest chance of coming back. You, Maga'lahi Ma'tao, who is the destined Maga'lahi I Mantatkilu. Assisted by Machatlu, who is destined to be Kakhana Machatlu, have to be the ones to face this daunting task!"

Ma'tao then looks at Atani then back to Hanumta, and with much concern, softly asks, "Is she dead?"

Hanumta looks back into the eyes of Ma'tao and replies, "A powerful Figo' separated her life essence in this realm! Just like I am in this moment, her life essence has yet to ascend. And because of that, her physical body is in suspended animation."

She then looks at the Diyuk Paton Chaifi and says, "This sling stone, since its creation, has always had the power to take and claim lives. With all the centuries that have come and gone, I have seen it cause so much death and destruction before my very own eyes! But you Ma'tao could use it to help save lives! I have only come to witness one other time within only one other person, the same strength and power that lies within you!"

Ma'tao, without hesitation, asks, "So what do I need to do?!"

Hanumta then says, "You need to face Itak! And you need to kill that monstrosity of pure evil! Not only can Itak bring about death and destruction to our world, as it disguises itself in different forms. Itak also has the innate ability to persuade the thoughts of all men! Persuade them in a way that will make them lust for power and control to the point it will drive them crazy until they attain it by any means necessary! That is what happened to my Maga'lahi! The very first

Maga'lahi I Mantatkilu! You all have come to know him as Asuli! He made his choice, and by that choice, is how I, along with the rest of his warriors, ended up here. Because of the blood oath, we all swore!"

They all are now in utter shock as to what she just said!

Aligao, with much concern for his childhood best friend, asks, "If that is so, and it's up to Ma'tao. What will make him able to resist what Asuli could not?" Da'on then adds, "Yes! That is why we need to follow and protect him!"

Hanumta then says, "I understand your concern! But this is not just a physical battle! It is also a battle of the mind! Ma'tao, you are going to see things. Things that you probably won't be able to explain! You might even think they are there but are just created within your mind, your imagination! Like I mentioned. You possess that same strength and power within you! But unlike him, you will need to resist whatever Itak does to tempt you! You have already proven you have a heart for your island and its people by acquiring your Ka'lang I Man Metgot. But you also need to have the power and control over your thoughts! Because your thoughts are what will become a reality for you, for our people, and our islands! Itak is standing in the way of all of it. Destroy

Itak Ma'tao! And you will release its hold over humankind and save Atani and countless others!"

She then says, "I see that you have the Atupat Aniti! You are going to need it. Because once I relinquish the stone over to you, the Atupat Aniti will be the only sling that will be able to control the trajectory of the Diyuk Paton Chaifi!"

Ma'tao then asks, "Itak! How do I kill it? And where does it rest?"

Hanumta then says, "First of all, you need to face Itak with a clear conscience and a balanced state of mind. You will not be able to defeat it otherwise! Itak can easily sense fear, pain, and hatred! If you're there strictly bent on wanting to take revenge, not only will it give you away, it might be the end of you or whoever it has taken prisoner! There is someone more significant than ourselves out there. Someone or something that we all need to focus on that will help us all accomplish that goal! Remember, Itak feeds on it all! The Diyuk Paton Chaifi is the only thing that is cable to penetrate its thick leathery feathers! I also know that it also possesses other special abilities that you soon find out! You will need to use it in conjunction with the Atupat Aniti to take down that monster of a bird! As for Itak's great nest, all these caves connect with chambers. It's as if they are never-ending deep within the earth! Yet Liyang Taifinakpo' has an exceptional series of caverns located within the cliffs of Tomhom village! Within those caverns, you will find Itak!"

Ma'tao then says, "That may take hours to travel there!" He then turns to Tiani and asks, "Is there any way you could transport Machatlu and me to Tomhom village? We need to locate the entrance to the caverns right away!"

Tiani looks at both her and Pigan's warriors. And with uncertainty replies, "Though I haven't reached Pigan's level of creating portals. I will need all of my fellow Taotao Man Nanu's help in creating a portal large enough to transport you both through Liyang Taifinakpo' to a banyan tree closest to the entrance to the cavern."

Machatlu exclaims, "Just get us to Tomhom. And I'll get us to its exact location!"

Hanumta then continues saying, "The rest of us will stay right here and look after Atani! It's important, Ma'tao! Important that you trust us and don't worry about her! I can't stress that enough!"

Ma'tao looks at Atani with tears still in his eyes, then back to Hanumta, giving her a nod that he understands. Hanumta then says, "All that's left now is to relinquish the Diyuk Paton Chaifi over to you!"

She then helps Ma'tao place Atani down onto a bed of soft green moss as the others assist. She then bows and postures herself with one knee down while putting her hands together over her head, presenting Ma'tao with the impressive stone!

Ma'tao, now standing, takes the Atupat Aniti and centers the sling over the stone. As soon as he makes that connection, a bright flash of white light appears around Hanumta! The bright white light of pure energy makes its way from within Hanumta. The light travels up through her arms and over to the powerful weapon.

As soon as the light reaches the Diyuk Paton Chaifi and the Atupat Aniti, it shines brighter than ever that all have to shield their eyes!

The transference of power back into the sling stone is now complete, and Hanumta is now free from that burden!

Ma'tao wraps the Diyuk Paton Chaifi within the Atupat Aniti and places it inside his pouch.

Hanumta regaining her composure and energy, says, "All that power Ma'tao is now with you! It must not get into the wrong hands! You need to hurry and deal with Itak before Asuli figures out you have the stone!"

He walks over and kneels by Atani. He then bends down and kisses her forehead, whispering, "You hold strong, my love! You know we already went through something like this before. Nothing could ever take me or ever separate my love for you! I'll be back shortly, so you better be waiting for me! I love you!"

Even though she does not move or make a sound, he knows that she heard him in his heart. Ma'tao then gets up with much more zeal in his spirit! He looks to Hanumta, Aligao, and Da'on and says, "Take care of her, be safe, and be strong! We'll be back!"

Aligao runs up to Ma'tao and hugs him tight while saying, "She's in good hands! You just get back here as soon as you show that overgrown Aga (Marianas Crow) who is the true Maga'lahi of these islands!"

Da'on embraces them both and adds, "Yes. You do just that, and hurry! You won't want to keep Atani waiting. And I'm not sure how long I'll be able to put up with Aligao and his whining!" Aligao smacks Da'on, then smiles as the three share a brief chuckle, and Ma'tao nods, agreeing.

He then looks to Machatlu and Tiani, takes a deep breath, and with his significant commanding presence says, "Let's do this! Take me to Itak!"

Hanumta looks to Tiani as she points to a path saying, "At the end of that path, there is another series of three caves. Enter the cave in the middle! That cave is directly under a grove of banyan trees where you'll be able to harness their energies!"

Tiani and the Taotao Man Nanu warriors lead the way towards the caves as Machatlu follows. Ma'tao kisses Atani on her forehead once more while saying, "Hang in there, my love! I'll only be gone for a moment."

He then proceeds to catchup to Machatlu and Tiani, only looking back to take a quick glimpse of his love.

As Ma'tao catches up to Machatlu, he says, "We need to locate that entrance as soon as we get to Tomhom!" Machatlu replies, "Don't worry. I'll get us there. Keep your thoughts on taking out Itak!"

They both quickened their pace while Tiani and the Taotao Man Nanu get to the end of the path. They now make their way into the middle cave that Hanumta mentioned.

As Ma'tao and Machatlu enter the dark cave, an earthly smell of wood bark and moss fills the air. They walk into a circle that Tiani and the Taotao Man Nanu immediately created and closed off once they are in the center of it.

Tiani then has her and Pigan's warriors all join hands, close their eyes, and lift their arms. They start chanting in their language while placing themselves in a deep trancelike state.

Ma'tao notices that they all start glowing bright blue once again, which illuminates the once dark cave.

Machatlu, who is now in awe, utters, "Amazing! Check out these cave walls." He refers to the tremendous thick roots of the banyan trees, which are upon the surface! Their thick massive roots, indicative of centuries of growth. They also have created a unique network within the Liyang Taifinakpo'! These ancient roots completely cover the cave roof and the cave walls, while others are resting, and others penetrate through the rugged cave floor.

As the Tiani and Taotao Man Nanu harness the banyan trees' energy, they glow brighter and brighter! Their chanting also gets louder and louder! Then out of nowhere, a portal between Ma'tao and Machatlu appears!

Ma'tao pushes Machatlu back a bit as the portal grows larger. They both stare deep within it, but everything is hazy and are not easily identifiable!

Tiani shouts to her warriors, "Louder! Chant louder!"

The wind starts picking up within the cave as they all increase the volume! The portal is also growing in size! It is now so noisy as the wind blows hard in the cave. They all have to secure their footing while holding on to each other tight!

Ma'tao then excitedly points into the portal while shouting, "Machatlu! Could you make out that place? Is it Tomhom?"

Machatlu focuses on the portal where they both notice trees, a cliff line, and a beach! He then spots something familiar, and with much excitement, shouts back, "Yes! Yes, it's Tomhom!"

Ma'tao then looks in Tiani's direction! She and the other Taotao Man Nanu are holding firm to one another to keep the portal open!

He then shouts, "Tiani! We're here! It's Tomhom!" She opens her eyes, and while yelling back, says, "Be strong Ma'tao! It's your destiny!

Save them all! Quick you must hurry! We can't hold it open much longer!"

Ma'tao looks at Machatlu, and with all his might leaps into the portal! Machatlu follows right behind him! Within that instant, all goes dark! Then, dead silence!

Chapter 15

"Tomhom!"

Dead silence! As the typhoon winds dissipate, that is all he hears. Nothing! He opens his eyes to find himself within the hollow of a banyan tree.

Ma'tao now finds himself peering out into a majestic scenery of jungle foliage backed by a serene cliff line overlooking the beautiful Pacific Ocean.

He then turns around to find Machatlu still passed out yet breathing. Ma'tao walks up to him a gives him a slight tap to his face saying, "Hey, get up! We are here, and we need to hurry!"

Machatlu opens his eyes then hastens up to his feet while peering out of the banyan tree, saying, "It appears that we are! But we still need to be cautious! If anyone finds out we are from Cho-chogo' their Maga'lahi might have us hunted down!"

Ma'tao ignoring what Machatlu said, exits the banyan tree and starts climbing to the top on its huge branches to get a better lay of the land!

Machatlu, not far behind him and trying to hold back from yelling, calls to Ma'tao, saying, "Did you not hear me?! We need to be careful!"

Ma'tao looks back down at him, saying, "Quit your whining! The sun is about to set, and it's getting dark out. Plus, we need to know precisely where we are! Does this area look familiar? Is the entrance to Itak's lair far from here?"

Machatlu climbs with much speed as he pulls himself up to the same branch where Ma'tao is intensely scouting out their position. He looks out to gain his perspective while saying, "We're close by!" He then points up towards a steep path along the side of the face of the limestone cliff wall while saying, "There! That path along the cliff line. Do you see it?"

Ma'tao nods, then, while pointing further up, says, "Check it out! Up along the cliff line!"

Machatlu looks to where he points and locates what Ma'tao spotted. Smoke! He then says, "That area where the smoke is coming from, that is a place we need to avoid once we get to the top of that cliff! That is one of the Tomhom warriors men's houses! The cave entrance is three miles west from there!"

Ma'tao then says, "We'll make our way along-side that path staying within the jungle. By the time we get to the top, we'll have the cover of night on our side."

Machatlu replies, "Yes, I agree! We should start making our way. It's going to be pretty dark soon with it being a new moon. Climbing up that cliff with no light at all could be treacherous. We should take advantage of whatever light we have now." Ma'tao then says, "I hear you. Let's start moving!"

With such quickness, they descend the banyan tree and make their way towards the cliff's base. They blend in so well and move with such stealthiness through the jungle to avoid drawing any attention to themselves!

As they arrive at the base of the cliff, Ma'tao starts to get a profound feeling, and his intuition stops him dead in his tracks!

He then reaches out his arm and grabs Machatlu while whispering, "Get back here! Be quiet! Some people are heading our way!"

They both quickly jump behind a grove of fadang trees and conceal themselves in the underbrush along the cliff wall!

Not much sooner, a group of six Tomhom warriors crosses in front of them!

Machatlu taps Ma'tao while gesturing that they are heading up towards the men's house. Without a sound, they come out from hiding and dart further into the jungle.

They now quicken their pace along their makeshift path, up the arduous cliff line of giant trees, sharp limestone rocks, and thorny bushes! All while avoiding any signs of human contact while being mindful of the men's house's location!

They are now halfway up the cliff as nightfall descends on the island. The climb is also becoming much more treacherous! They need to move faster!

As they pick up that pace, they start to feel a specific type of change within the air and the temperature, which could only mean one thing. Rain!

A downpour ensues! It drenches them from head to toe. With this onslaught of heavy wind and rain, their climb becomes so much more difficult!

To make matters worse, they cannot pinpoint the men's house's exact location because the smoke from their fires is no longer visible.

Yet with one foot and hand over the other, both men are still very persistent! Come hell or high water, and with their strong will to move on, nothing is going to stop or slow their pursuit!

Though both men are now bloodied and bruised, they reach the top of the cliff. Ma'tao looks at Machatlu, and while catching his breath, says, "I see the path dead ahead. We should still stay clear away from it and trail alongside from within the jungle."

Machatlu agrees, then adds, "We should try and locate the men's house without getting too close. That will give me a better starting point in locating the cave entrance!"

Ma'tao replies, "If that's what it takes, then we must hurry and be extremely careful! We don't have time to waste!"

They push on as the rain finally lets up. Both men are no longer soaking wet, but they now have to be much more careful because any sound they make will now travel much further!

They are very attentive in their surroundings as they stumble across a set lat'di from an old abandoned village. Even with the night making it a challenge to see, Ma'tao realizes that this is no ordinary lat'di!

He thinks to himself; These lat'di seem oddly familiar.

As he places his hands on them and feels around, a surge of energy pulsates through him quickly!

He feels a sudden sense of understanding and ease. It is as if Atani herself quenched every ounce of worry he had in his heart!

He then asks Machatlu, "Have you ever been here before?" Machatlu replies, "No. I've never been this way before. But check out these lat'di!"

He points to these unique stones and says, "Have you ever seen lat'di that shimmer with such brilliant colors? It's as if they have precious gemstones embedded in them!"

Ma'tao places his hands on the stones, and feeling around them, says, "There is only one other place that I've seen lat'di very similar to these! And that was in Fu'a!"

He then, with a puzzled looked turns to Machatlu and asks, "There has to be some sort of connection with Fu'a! Any idea when and why this village was abandoned?"

Machatlu looks around and just as puzzled shrugs his shoulder while saying, "I have no answer to your question. I've never seen this place before!" "But I do!" A voice calls out from behind one of those precious stones!

Both men, now startled, position themselves into a battle stance as Ma'tao calls out, "Who's there?! Show yourself! Don't make me come after you!"

Just then, slowly peeking from behind the lat'-di, they see some braids and a set of eyes. A young girl around the age of thirteen steps out timidly while asking, "You are Ma'tao, aren't you?"

Both men look at one another with surprise, then turn back to her as Ma'tao responds, "Why is it you ask? Who is it that wants to know?"

She then makes her way towards Ma'tao, looking cautiously around her. Ma'tao then asks again, "Who is it that wants to know? Who are you?"

She then says, "My grandfather has spoken so much about you! I recognized you from that special Ka'lang I Man Metgot. He also spoke about and the Maga'lahi who could lead all our people towards a better future. You need to meet him! You need to follow me now!"

Both men look at each other and unsure of what to make of this. But Ma'tao turns to the girl and says, "I am Ma'tao!" At those words, Machatlu shakes his head in disagreement, but Ma'tao continues saying, "Who is your grandfather, and where is he now?"

Machatlu grabs Ma'tao and asks, "Really?! Why are we even bothering with this? We could be walking into an ambush!"

The girl then looks to Machatlu, shakes her head, then back to Ma'tao, and says very adamantly, "My grandfather is an honorable man!"

She then turns back to Machatlu and says, "You! You are from Chochogo'. Am I right? If that were the case, we would have ambushed you already!"

Ma'tao then says, "She has a point!" He turns to the girl asking, "We are in a hurry! Is your grandfather nearby?"

She then turns and points behind her and replies, "He's with the rest of the warriors in the men's house!"

Machatlu, now even more appalled that Ma'tao is even considering this, responds, "Are you serious right now! So you're thinking of going to meet him?! You should rethink this through Ma'-tao!"

Ma'tao turns to Machatlu, saying, "As hard as it may seem to trust me on this, I feel we must do it!"

Machatlu then reminds him, saying, "Remember what I told you earlier! It hasn't been that long since my village…" He pauses for a moment, looks at the girl, then back to Ma'tao, and continues, "Our village has been at war with

Tomhom! And I don't think the bad blood has had enough time to subside!"

The girl looks at Machatlu then back to Ma'tao and with much sincerity says, "I know it may be hard to believe for both of you, but since the last battle between both our villages, greater threats have befallen us all. And yes, greater than even Chochogo'!"

Ma'tao then turns to Machatlu, saying, "Believe me, I know we need to hurry. But I know from within my heart, what she speaks the truth! Whatever it is we need to hear or do, our success comes through this village, and it's people!"

Machatlu stares deep into the eyes of Ma'tao and replies, "I sure hope you know what you're doing? But it sure would be funny, especially that we just braved that crazy climb."

Ma'tao nods while he places his hand on his shoulder and says, "You already followed me this far. I'm not going to place us in harm's way!"

Machatlu smirks while saying, "I hope not!" Ma'tao then turns to the girl and says, "We must hurry. Lead the way!"

The wind blows a cold chill through their bodies in this pitch-black night. She leads them through the old abandoned village into a ravine outlined with ifit and fadang trees.

They carefully, with a quick pace, negotiate while navigating through the jagged limestone path. And within a dense grove of lemmai (breadfruit) trees overlooking the cliff line, they arrive at the men's house!

No one is outside guarding it. And from so far, what Ma'tao and Machatlu could see is that it also looks abandoned and dilapidated.

Ma'tao then asks the girl, "Don't think I'm rude, and I've should've asked sooner. What is your name, and where is your grandfather?"

The girl looks around then back to Ma'tao, whispering, "My name is Ke'taka, and my grandfather's name is Ke'amot. He is our village kakhana! This place isn't abandoned, and they're here. Follow me."

She leads them to the backside of the men's house. In between the last two set lat'di stones, she bushes aside old lemmai leaves to expose a bamboo door. She points to it while Ma'tao and Machatlu each grab ahold of the door and lift it open. Underneath is a path that heads down into the earth!

Machatlu looks at Ma'tao in earnest, saying, "C'mon, you expect us to go down in there!"

Ignoring his question, Ke'taka bypasses him and steps down onto the underground path. Ma'tao just nods and follows after her. The tunnel they are now in is barely enough for them to fit through with their bodies. But the warmth that it provides is so much more welcoming than the cold ocean breeze that was chilling them to their core along the cliff line.

Just when it seems that they have come to a place where they will be stuck and no longer able to move, another bamboo door appears. Ke'taka knocks on it. Dead silence. No answer.

She knocks again as the silence becomes more awkward to the point they just hear each other's breathing. Nothing!

Ke'taka knocks once again. Again no answer! Ma'tao does not want to admit it, but for some reason, he is now starting to become annoyed!

He tries hard to compose himself, yet still no answer! She knocks once more as she pushes on the door, but it does not budge. Someone or something seems to be blocking the other side.

Suddenly they hear something moving behind the door! "Who or what could be waiting for them on the other side?"

Ma'tao quickly thinks. But just as fast as it pops into his mind, he rapidly releases that thought. To be fully prepared to take action and without giving fear a chance to take hold!

Ma'tao then moves Ke'taka aside as he forces his way through the door! He busts in! And with Machatlu right behind him, he shouts, "We don't have any time for this fun and games! Who here is Ke'amot?!"

"Calm down, young man!" A voice calls out from the shadows in the corner of the room. Ma'tao notices a man walking towards him with three other men seated on the ground on a guafak mat.

The room is cramped and dimly lit with coconut oil torches on each corner within this small space. Though Ma'tao cannot make out who this man is, his voice is very familiar!

Ma'tao thinks to himself, *That voice sounds like, but why would he be here? Could it be?*

The man moves forward out of the shadows and into the light! And as he comes close into view. It only confirms the suspicions of Ma'tao! It is Pulonon!

They immediately, without any hesitation, hug and greet one another! Ma'tao, so excited to see Pulonon says, "This is such a blessing to see you standing in front of me!"

Pulonon, just as excited, says, "I couldn't stay away from you all too long, especially since I know everything that's at stake! More unrest has taken ahold of the northern islands! Anatahan and Sarigan have some bad blood brewing up towards the surface again. My warriors and others have been seeing Itak much more frequently, while it brings about more fear and strife following its wake! Maga'lahi Olanok appointed me along with my Anatahan warriors to locate its whereabouts, and we tracked it back here to Guahan!"

Just then, a man older than Pulonon, six years his senior, joins and stands up off the guafak mat. He walks towards them, saying, "So this is the Ma'tao we've heard so much about. Is it true that you're from Chochogo'?"

As he asks that question, Machatlu taps Ma'-tao. The man noticing it turns to Machatlu, and with a slight smirk, says, "I surely know who you are. I could instantly smell Chochogo' flowing out of you!"

Pulonon then slaps the man on his shoulder and says, "That's enough! We spoke about this already."

Pulonon turns back to Ma'tao, saying, "This is Kakhana Ke'amot! The kakhana of Tomhom. We have been lifelong friends, and Tomhom has been a great asset to Anatahan. I feel we could be helpful to one another!"

Ma'tao, curiously then says, "Our paths in lives must be meant to cross. Atdao and Atani need us now more than ever!"

Pulonon looks places both arms on his shoulders, looks into his eyes, and sincerely replies, "On my way over, I had some visions that I didn't want to believe to be true. But seeing and hearing from you now, I can no longer ignore them! You already know whatever we need to do. You have mine, and my warriors support!"

Pulonon then looks to Ke'amot, who says, "Yes, these are some very trying times for all our people!"

Ke'amot, in turn, looks to the guafak mat and towards the two other men in the shadows sitting on it. There is dead silence for the moment, then one of them speaks, saying, "So much devastation has come to my village and my people! More than years past. If you are who the prophecy speaks of, let me ask you this!"

Ma'tao looks at this person with much intent as he tries to see this person. The man continues asking, "If you are to truly the prophesied Maga-'lahi I Mantatkilu. What makes you think that you'll be able to succeed where Gadao failed?"

Machatlu looks at this man, then back to Ma'-tao with a sarcastic smirk, scoffs, then says, "Tomhom people! I tried to warn you."

Ma'tao, staying put and standing his ground, looks back to Pulonon, who whispers, "Just answer him."

Ma'tao nods, looks back towards the man, and replies, "I mean no disrespect Saina. But we are in a hurry. I'm only willing to entertain your question out of respect for Pulonon."

He pauses for a moment as the man stands up, folds his arms, and awaits what Ma'tao has to say.

Ma'tao then continues, "First of all, let's get one thing straight. I never asked for all of this in the first place. I first thought to accept it as a means to an end, a way to be together with the only person in this world who makes me a better person. I never once stated that I could ever surpass Gadao or complete what he didn't! My concern right now, at this very moment, is bringing back Atani! And if it means taking out Itak, then that's what I'll do! So you're either going to help us or stand in our way! Which one is it?!"

An awkward quietness now fills the room. That mysterious man makes his way out of the shadows and into the light. He steps towards Ma'tao.

Pulonon takes a step back as he says, "Ma'tao, this is Maga'lahi Mata'pang. The Maga'lahi of Tomhom!"

Maga'lahi Mata'pang stops inches from Ma'tao. Both men now face to face with one another. Even though Maga'lahi Mata'pang is thirty years his senior, the others instantly could feel the power that he and Ma'tao are both exuding at that moment!

Each man quickly feels that it in one another as well. While each Maga'lahi also senses that the other will do whatever is necessary to protect their precious village along with the ones that they love!

Maga'lahi Mata'pang looks Ma'tao up and down. Then with a slight smile and nod says, "Maga'lahi Dadau and I, along with our villages, go back a long way. He speaks very highly of you. I was a bit skeptical about this alliance when he and Ke'amot first mentioned it. What's strange is that after finally meeting you, something tells me that you share the same vision of a better life for all our people and islands. Something that he had mentioned. Are you someone my people and I can trust?"

Ma'tao stares deep back into the eyes of Maga-'lahi Mata'pang, then adamantly replies, "That's up to you to decide! But I promise you this if you are willing to stand by me in locating and defeating Itak! You would have made your first friend from Chochogo'!"

Maga'lahi Mata'pang, with a slight smile, looks around at all within the room and chuckles. But upon hearing that looks back to Ma'tao and with much sincerity says, "Though I never thought I'd say this in my lifetime, but Ma'tao of Chochogo'. You now have the support from Tomhom!"

He then places his hands on Ma'tao and continues saying, "I personally will assist you in the hunt for Itak!"

Pulonon turns to both men and adds, "You also have the support from my men and me as well."

Machatlu, now showing his discontent, blurts out, "Why now?"

They all turn to him and could see that he now totally disagrees as he continues saying, "The people of Chochogo' along with our Maga'lahi tried to work with you in the past! Maga'lahi Kiighi also sent gifts and requested for peace talk negotiations. But you, Maga'lahi Mata'pang, always declined! Why now, after all-out war for so many years? Why now should we even trust you?!"

Ma'tao, in utter shock at Machatlu's accusations, turns to him and asks, "You alright? Just calm down!"

Machatlu now more enraged, thrusts himself forward towards the direction of Maga'lahi Mata'pang!

Ma'tao grabs and restrains him as Machatlu shouts, "Ask him! Ask him, Ma'tao! Ask him, their so-called Maga'lahi, why did he ignore all of Maga'lahi Kiighi's request for peace?"

Ma'tao, with Machatlu in hand, grabs onto him tighter and slightly pushes him to the side, saying, "I apologize for you feeling this way. Maybe I should've thought this through."

Machatlu calms down while taking some deep breaths. He looks back at Ma'tao then says, "I know we can't be wasting any time and gambling with lives. But I thought you should hear it straight from the mouth of the man. The man whose actions, ignited the war between Chochogo' and Tomhom!"

Ma'tao, seeing how distraught Machatlu is feeling, holds him while turning towards Maga'lahi Mata'pang and asks, "Are you someone I can trust? Does he speak the truth? Why did Cho-chogo' war with Tomhom in the first place?"

Maga'lahi Mata'pang looks down, refusing to answer. Pulonon interjects, saying, "I for one know how war and hatred could come between men. And all of us here have experienced loss. Loss of loved ones, villages, or even islands! I am not saying this to sound condescending. I am saying this because if all of us here are willing to take a step forward. That step will be the first step which will also lead us into a better future."

Ma'tao looks at Pulonon and acknowledges what he said. He then looks towards Maga'lahi Mata'pang, who still has his head down. He then turns back to Machatlu, who has calmed down now, and says, "He's right! That hatred will only grow if we decide to let it!"

Machatlu sarcastically replies, "I made a promise to my Maga'lahi and my village, so I'll take it and work with them! But Ma'tao. Let's see you if you'll still feel the same when you do find out!" Ma'tao contemplates what he just heard but finds the strength to divert his focus by thinking of his love.

He then looks back to Maga'lahi Mata'pang and says, "This is bigger than all of us! People that we love are in danger with their lives at stake! We must hurry! Who is going to lead us to the entrance to those caverns?!"

Maga'lahi Mata'pang then picks his head up. He turns to Ma'tao, and as if trying to make up for his silence earlier, he confidently says, "I will! If that'll be alright with you." Ma'tao nods while looking at Machatlu.

Pulonon then points towards the guafak mat and says, "There's something else you need to hear from someone who joined my men and me."

Just then, the other man on the guafak mat stands up. Ma'tao releases hold of Machatlu. He sets his focus on that person who is now making his way towards him as well.

As the man gets closer and more transparent, Ma'tao pauses to recollect if he has ever seen him before.

He did not seem familiar initially, but the closer the man gets, it starts to dawn on him. It is Guafi!

Chapter 16

"Into The Lair!"

Guafi, the warrior who was Sui'hans right-hand man! Ma'tao, surprised, exclaims, "Guafi, right?!"

While approaching Ma'tao, Guafi replies, "Yes! First of all, I want to thank you and your warriors for defeating and taking out Sui'han From Asuli's plans. Pulonon was kind enough to bring me along. Especially with everything that has transpired."

Pulonon interjects, saying, "He's just modest. You're going to want to hear who he is and what he has to say."

Machatlu sarcastically adds, "Yes, as if this isn't crazy enough already!"

Ma'tao ignores Machatlu's remarks and asks, "So you know where to locate these caverns and Itak?!"

Guafi looks with earnest into the eyes of Ma'-tao, then down towards the ground sadly, saying, "My mother often spoke of its whereabouts to me. I would, at times, think she was just a little superstitious. Then one day unintentionally, when we were gathering some medicinal herbs, we stumbled onto it!"

Ma'tao curiously asks, "So your mother, whom Asuli has taken hostage with your son? Is she from Tomhom?!" Guafi confirms the question by nodding his head as Maga'lahi Mata'pang jumps in and answers with a resounding, "Yes! Matangis is my sister."

Ma'tao then asks, "Guafi, were you ever able to retrieve her and your son?" Guafi looks back to Ma'tao, and with great sadness in his eyes, without even saying a word, Ma'tao already knew his answer. The pain that they had in common of being separated from loved ones!

Guafi softly replies, "Not yet. But I'm not losing hope. With the help of Maga'lahi Olanok and Pulonon, we organized a rescue party. But when we arrived at the hut they were keeping them, Asuli already took them and left."

As a tear rolls down his cheek, Maga'lahi Mata'pang says, "Don't you worry. We will get them both back. I swear this to you with the village of Tomhom behind me!"

Ma'tao looks around the room at all who are present while saying, "We have laid eyes on this Itak. Asuli has full control of the beast and uses that monster to help him achieve his sinister plans. More people are going to get hurt and possibly die if we don't band together to stop them now!"

He turns back to Guafi and asks, "Could you lead us there now?" Machatlu scowls and says, upon hearing that, "I was already going to lead us there before we decided to take this detour!"

Guafi shakes his head, acknowledging Machatlu's claim, then adds, "You may get to the general vicinity, but that doesn't mean you'll be able to enter into Itak's lair. When my mother and I first stumbled into that area, it seemed so ordinary. You'll be able to see a cavern entrance, but to discover the true entrance. One must look deeper! Pass this physical realm. One reason why

Asuli took my mother captive was because of her innate ability to do just that!"

Maga'lahi Mata'pang then says, "Matangis, who is my eldest sister, is also very gifted. She always knew when trouble was present or heading our way. She had great foresight in preventing trouble from happening to Tomhom or my family."

Ma'tao tilts his head while pondering this, then says, "Even more of a reason for Asuli to take her. With her not around, she wouldn't be able to warn anyone on Itak's presence or where it will be next."

Machatlu jumps in and says, "Well, whatever it is you do, we all need to get going now! Nothing is going to get solved if we all are standing around here twiddling our thumbs!"

Ma'tao turns to Machatlu with a slight smile, says, "Thanks for understanding. Working together through this will be beneficial for us."

Machatlu scoffs and replies, "Don't thank me just yet. But you're right. The is so much more at stake here."

Machatlu then turns to head out of the secret room. Ma'tao, at that moment, senses that there is so much more that he wanted to say, but he does not press the situation.

Maga'lahi Mata'pang then looks to Ke'taka and says, "You did great! But your path with us ends here. I need you to stay and help protect Tomhom." Ke'taka nods in agreement and heads out of the room and back to the village. He then looks to Ma'tao, and while signaling that they are ready, says, "Let's head to its lair!"

Ma'tao acknowledges what he said. And while looking back at them, he resoundingly says in the voice of a warrior chieftain, "Guafi! Lead the way!"

It is still eerily dark outside as they get back up onto the cliff line and out from under the hut. The ice-cold wind sends that chill deep into their bones once again as Ma'tao with Machatlu keeps up the pace following Guafi. Pulonon, along with the others, follows from behind.

They all move with much swiftness through the thick, dense jungle while crossing majestic ancient trees along with thorny bushes. The thick thorns brush up against each of them, cutting and scraping into their flesh. But they are so focused that they are not even bothered by any of it.

Ma'tao, with his eyes latched to every movement Guafi is making, calls to Machatlu and asks, "Any of this look familiar to you?" Machatlu, with just as much attentiveness, replies, "It's still a bit dark, but yes! We should be coming up to—" Before he finishes his sentence, Guafi shouts out, "We're here! The entrance to its nest. The entrance to Itak's lair!"

They all come to a sudden stop. The soft orange glow of the torches draws their attention to stones that are glistening in the dark. "What is this place?!" Ma'tao asks. Guafi shouts, "Be careful! Just stay where you are!"

The stones they come across are also from another ancient village. Ma'tao, befuddled, says, "This lat'di looks just like the stones Machatlu and I came across earlier and are very reminiscent of the lat'di at Fu'a."

Guafi points to the right of the stone struc-
tures, saying, "Watch out! Be careful where you
step!"

Ma'tao brings the torch above where Guafi
points. He now sees what caused all the commotion. Right smack in the middle of this ancient
lat'di set, the dim light from the torches reveal a
grand deep dark entrance to a cavern!

They all take a step and back off from the
edge while admiring the vastness of this subter-
ranean grotto!

Machatlu takes his torch and bends down to
one knee. He examines the area from where he

could and says, "Yes! It's the exact place where Itak came up from."

He then turns to Guafi and asks, "It is the place. Is it not?!"

Maga'lahi Mata'pang overhearing says, "Before Itak inhabited this area, my ancestors protected this entrance. It's is an extraordinary place! These lat'di were part of an ancient village that emitted energy that helped keep the balance within god, nature, and man! Tomhom and I are where we are today because of all they have sacrificed. I vowed to one day bring that splendor back!"

Ma'tao curiously asks, "What is their connection to Fu'a? I've seen these type of stones before."

Maga'lahi Mata'pang places his palms on one of the stones while he says, "It was told to me that before the balance shift, all the Chamoru's once lived in peace with one another in accordance with our gods. On Guahan, that perfect harmony and balance were entrusted to three villages! Tomhom from the north, Fu'a from the south, and Chochogo' in the center. When the forces of darkness, led by Asuli, who some say is being led by Chaifi himself. The atrocities he brought about in the physical realm tipped that balance! Great wars and famine throughout all the islands broke out! It is prophesied that the Maga'lahi I Mantatkilu will set things right once again. Even though I personally never believed in it, my mother always had faith and spoke of that day! It's in her memory why that little bit of hope never left my mind."

There is a brief pause at that moment, and all is quiet. Guafi breaks the silence saying, "This cavern may look like the entrance, but move back a couple of steps, then stand completely still."

At first, they are all dumbfounded. But curiosity from Guafi's instructions gets the best of them, and they do just that.

Machatlu stares into the dark cavern while asking, "Where is it? Where's the entrance?"Ma'tao turns to Guafi while saying, "Go ahead! Proceed."

Pulonon then places his hands on Guafi then says, "Steady your focus and remember your mother and son. We are one step closer to getting them back!"

Guafi closes his eyes and kneels while raising both arms towards the heavens. He then starts to chant some words that no one can make out since he utters them under his breath.

Ma'tao looks to Pulonon, who has his eyes closed as well and meditating on the moment. He then turns to Machatlu, who, with such sarcasm, shrugs his shoulders.

Then without any warning, Guafi shouts out, chanting from the top of his lungs! He is calling out and chanting!

Ma'tao starts thinking to himself, *What is he saying? What is this language he speaks?*

Whatever Guafi is chanting at first sounds like a bunch of gibberish. Yet as he continues speaking, Ma'tao could make out that he is chanting something in Chamoru, but backward! And whatever he is saying is causing a sudden change around them!

What was once complete darkness starts to change! Now the heavens begin to move. Grayish orange hazy light starts to shine through the thick billowing clouds! The clouds themselves are moving at a quick pace as if they are traveling through time and space! The wind blows hard all around them with typhoon strength winds, but Ma'tao, along with everyone else, are still securely planted where they stand! Guafi brings his arms back down and opens his eyes. Ma'tao looks around and notices that they are still in Tomhom, yet something is entirely differ-

ent!

Chapter 17

"Itak!"

Unsure where he is at, Ma'tao thinks to himself, *What is this place? Where did Guafi take us to?*

He investigates his surroundings. While he instantly gets an odd feeling like he has been here before. It is like he is in a dream state. Everything around him seems hazy and blurry. The colors that present themselves are all drab, black, white, and grays.

He looks at his hands then back to his surroundings, and this seems all too familiar! He turns to look back at Guafi and realizes that he separate from them all!

He then spots, Pulonon, Machatlu, Maga'lahi Mata'pang, and Guafi! They are standing together. He calls and tries to signal them, but they do not hear or see him for some odd reason! He moves towards their direction, but the more he moves towards them, the further they get!

Then he hears it! That same blood-curdling scream he heard in the swampland!

He thinks to himself, *Am I dreaming? It's like I've been here before! That awful scream!*

Then he sees it! It is Itak! But he is on the other side, across the cavern entrance, diving down towards the group! Its eyes are burning bright with orange-reddish flames!

But they do not see or sense it coming! Ma'tao, sensing the danger they are in by the chill running down his spine, leaps towards their direction.

Boom! He hits something hard! Something that he does not see! It is an invisible force field. He leaps again while this time is forcing his way forward! He is stopped once more, dead in his tracks! His attempts to save them completely halted!

He calls out to them yet again from the top of his lungs. But they still cannot hear him, and this time it is too late!

Itak swoops down with lightning flash speed and grabs Guafi along with Maga'lahi Mata'pang within its talons! He carries them both off into the dark abyss of its cavernous lair!

Upon seeing that, Ma'tao yells out a deafening, "No!" As he punches the invisible force field! The anger within him, coupled with his Ka'lang I Man Metgot, brings about his supernatural strength!

He punctures a hole while ripping the fabric of the force field! In seeing what he did, he grabs the Higam I Saina, and with another loud shout, screams, "Ginen I Minetgot Puntan Yan I Na'liheng Fu'una!"

He jams with all his might the adze deep into the tear he made. As the adze strikes the force field, an electrical blast pulsates through it and instantly dissipates the energy while ripping a hole big enough for Ma'tao to get through!

He rushes towards Pulonon and Machatlu, who are both now kneeling over that deep dark chasm! Both men are yelling hysterically, "Guafi! Maga'lahi Mata'pang!"

Ma'tao reaches for Machatlu, who is unaware. Machatlu, caught by surprise, turns, and with all his might, takes a swing at Ma'tao!

Ma'tao then yells, "Hold on, it's me! Relax!" Machatlu, in seeing Ma'tao, immediately gets himself under control and asks, "Where did you come from?! I thought we lost you to Itak!"

Pulonon, just as surprised, asks, "Did you see what just happened? We need to get down there and save them!"

Without saying another word, Ma'tao starts making his way down into the bottomless, dark pit towards the center of the earth. Both men make haste and follow every step he takes.

Pulonon catches up to Ma'tao and intriguingly says, "This is one odd place! It's like we're on Guahan, but not on Guahan. I'm not quite sure how to explain it."

Ma'tao quickens his paces, keeps focus ahead, and replies, "No need to explain. I know just what you mean." Pulonon then adds, "Judging by the way you're moving down this cave, it's like you been here before! Have you?"

Ma'tao, still moving fast but keeping a keen eye ahead, replies, "It seems all so familiar! I felt it when we first were transported here, and while separated from you all!"

Machatlu catches up to them, and curiously asks, "Have you?"

Ma'tao, still pushing forward, replies, "Have I what?" Machatlu continues, "What Pulonon asked! Been here before?"

Ma'tao, still peering dead ahead with much focus, responds, "Yes! It's the cross world! It's the realm between the physical and spiritual realms."

Ma'tao then comes to a sudden stop and turns to both men and with hurried importance says, "Believe it or not, I've been before, and there's not much time for explanation. But right this very moment, we are all are practically dead! Since Itak resides in this realm, we need to hurry and locate its nest! And since Itak has seen you both already, it and Asuli will be expecting you two!"

Pulonon surprisingly realizes and blurts out, "But Itak didn't see you!" Ma'tao nods his head, and confidently replies, "Exactly! And we're going to use that to our advantage."

Machatlu then adds, "Yes, we need to use that!" Ma'tao then continues saying, "We need to draw him out long enough! Long enough for me to launch that sling stone deep into the heart of that beast!"

He then looks back to both men and deep into their eyes while seriously saying, "Listen to me carefully! Be on the constant lookout. Things aren't always as they seem! The last time I entered this realm, a dark entity tried taking me out. But unlike Itak, I couldn't see it. Keep your senses sharp! And since it's only us three left, we need to keep an eye out for each other."

Just then, a voice calls out to Ma'tao, shouting, "What do you mean it's only you three?" They all stop moving forward and ready themselves for battle as Ma'tao yells, "Whoever you are, show yourself!"

No sooner than he said that, a figure jumps towards them from the cliff face above! They see a shadowy figure of a man crouched down on one knee. He is face down as he pauses from the landing in between them. He is also holding something that draws the attention of Ma'tao and Pulonon. A paddle! A certain paddle!

Ma'tao, Machatlu, and Pulonon are surprised as he slowly stands while making eye contact with Ma'tao!

As the man gets closer to their torchlight, Pulonon shouts out, "Atdao! Is it really you?!"

Atdao looks at Pulonon and smugly replies, "Why? Who else did you think it was?"Pulonon just ignores what he said and hugs him tight while saying, "It's great to see you. We came to help!"

Ma'tao relieved that it is Atdao, grabs him, and asks, "Where is everyone else?! How far is Itak's nest from here?"

Atdao just smiles as he replies, "What's the rush, Ma'tao? I thought you'd be glad to see me?"

Ma'tao, with a hurried look on his face, replies, "I'm glad you're safe, but we need to hurry for Atani's sake!" Atdao looks down then replies, "Now getting there becomes much more important to you?"

Ma'tao, now bewildered by his questions and remarks, responds, "It's always been important.

We left Atani in very critical condition. And right now, we are her only chance of saving her life!"

Atdao, with a devilish smirk, replies, "You thought you'll take me by surprise? I have something to tell you. It's already too late for her! And I'm just getting started!"

Ma'tao looks deep into Atdao's eyes and backs up slowly. While discreetly gesturing for Machatlu and Pulonon to get behind him to do the same. He then points to Atdao, who is now getting into a fighting stance, and calmly says, "She's your sister. Why are you acting this way? What exactly are you hoping to gain from all of this?"

Pulonon, shocked by what is going on, says, "I have a weird feeling about this. I don't think that is Atdao!"

Machatlu, pointing his spear in Atdao's direction, adds, "That's what I was thinking!" Atdao, with an evil grin, does not respond. And without any intentions to reason with them, advances in their direction.

Ma'tao, still slowly moving back, asks yet again, "What are you hoping to gain?"

This time Atdao responds in a very sinister voice, "What am I looking to gain out of this?" He then smirks while pulling his hair away from his face and replies, "Everything! Everything we always wanted before you and all your friends got in our way! Mark my words Ma'tao! Humatak and Ati are going to war! They are going into a war like no other! Their hatred towards each other is going to involve many other villages and islands! Many of your loved ones will die and perish in the onslaught! Ati and your people have seen their last days!"

At that very moment, he swings as he leaps towards Ma'tao. With such precision, strength, and timing, he delivers a mighty kick to the chest of Ma'tao!

The decisive blow catches Ma'tao by surprise as he flies back onto the bodies of both men behind him! Atdao runs up to him before he could gather himself. He does not wait for Ma'-tao to stand as he delivers another kick to the side of his face!

He delivers the kick with so much ferocity while shouting, "You enter here without an invitation and try to catch me by surprise! This pain I'm going to inflict on you is something that you never felt!"

Ma'tao gets up slowly as he recomposes himself. Still, in a daze and utter shock, he thinks, *If that is Atdao, he is so much stronger than when we last went up against each other.*

He then gets back to his feet, and with a smile, he says out loud, "First of all, you hit like a girl! And second, you should know better! I've kicked your butt before, so prepare to get it handed to you again!"

Ma'tao then leaps so powerfully through the air towards Atadao. He times it with so much strength and quickness that he delivers a jaw shattering kick to Atdao's face! The strike with his leg is so powerful it launches Atdao off his feet and slams him up against the cave wall!

Pulonon, still confused with what he is witnessing, rushes up to check on Atdao. Ma'tao and Machatlu also approach, but with extreme caution.

Atdao is still facedown on the ground with Pulonon haunched over his body. As they move in closer with torchlight brightening the area, they notice something extremely odd!

Ma'tao, from behind, approaches Pulonon and places his hand on his back. Pulonon turns around to face Ma'tao with a look of confusion.

Ma'tao looks down at the lifeless body, but it is not Atdao! So he is now just as confused because the person lying in front of them is Ina!

Ma'tao jumps back and exclaims, "What the ...?! Where's Atdao?! What is Ina doing here?! Is she alright?"

Before Pulonon could even answer, she opens her bloodied, bruised eyes and very slowly sits up. She is so grief-stricken and sobbing. She then asks in a panicked voice, "Where am I? How did I get here?"

Pulonon just looks back at her and replies, "Ina, it's Pulonon. Do you remember us?"

Ina looks up, and while trembling, points to Ma'tao. And with tears filling her eyes, she softly asks, "What did I do to Ma'tao that he is trying to kill me?"

Ma'tao, confused about what he sees, shouts, "What's going on here?! What happened to Atdao?! Where did you come from?!"

Machatlu grabs Ma'tao and quickly says, "They're not who they appear to be! Like you said earlier, this place is not what it seems to be!"

Ina then looks up at the three of them. Then while getting onto her feet, she puts on the same wicked look that Atdao previously had on his face. And in the same sinister voice looks straight at Ma'tao, saying, "Is this the person said to be the next Maga'lahi I Mantatkilu?! He who hits women?"

The three men then start to feel like they are becoming hypnotized while a strange feeling overcomes their entire being! They get this odd sensation deep inside as if something evil is deeply rooting itself within them!

Ina then smirks. And while slowly walking around the three of them, she wickedly utters, "There is no way that you can resist what you are feeling now. I know you all feel it. So don't try and fight it! I could even smell that sweet smell of fear seeping through your pores! I bet you didn't know how much of it you have in you!"

Ma'tao looks at Pulonon then to Machatlu. He feels his body freezing up as he says, "Are you both able to move?" Both men start to stiffen up also where they stand.

Machatlu whimpers, "I can't move!" Pulonon tries to respond, but at this moment, whatever evil spell Ina placed on them starts to take hold! He cannot even utter a single word!

Ma'tao starts feeling something sinister and evil growing from within his body, as his body tightens up from the outside. He is in such excruciating pain! He tries to focus on his breathing because now his heart is racing very fast! Whatever she is doing to them has now really instilled that sense of fear in him! Something that he has battled so much to repress. As much as he tries to block it out, the faster it appears at the forefront of his mind!

Tighter and tighter, he starts to feel that squeeze! And faster and faster, those thoughts flood his mind! He starts yelling within his mind, *What's going on?! Why is this happening?! Why are Atdao and Ina, people I vowed to protect against me now?! What do I need to do?!*

He hears nothing! Nothing but dead silence! Ma'tao could only open his eyes by now. He then turns to look at Pulonon and Machatlu. Both men are now utterly motionless with both their eyes close.

He sees Ina moving closer! Then with a sense of confidence and sarcasm, she says, "You brought this all upon yourself, Maga'lahi."

She starts up with that wicked laugh as something extraordinary happens yet again! Right before his very eyes and continuing the laughter, she looks down. She laughs even louder as she looks up. Ma'tao cannot believe his eyes. The person before him, who was once Ina, is now Magogui!

Even though the person and the voice have now changed, the wicked intentions and sinister laughter remain!

Ma'tao, now feeling the fear within getting much more significant. He somehow finds the strength and faintly asks, "Magogui? Why are you doing this?"

Magogui ignores him, and out of nowhere, throws a powerful punch! He hits Ma'tao solid square in the jaw!. Not able to defend himself or his friends, those thoughts and voices get louder in his mind! The fear is completely enveloping his sense of self and has such a firm grip on Ma'tao!

He is so overwhelmed that, Ma'tao blacks out! He is now drifting in and out of consciousness, while his life is now flashing before his very eyes!

He sees Atani's lifeless body with his warriors surrounding her. As he starts to approach her, he finds himself suddenly in Ati, where he observes his grandfather Maga'lahi Sinahi sitting with elders around a fire. It looks as if they are planning and preparing for a battle! He steadily walks towards the group but is whisked away yet again before he gets up close! He not only feels that fear, that fear of losing loved ones and his home. He is also witnessing it before his very eyes! Within this realm, the world between worlds. He sees all the different villages of his beloved Guahan and all the other islands. And with every village he peers into, every one of them is preparing for this great war!

He then hears that voice within his mind. That dark, sinister voice also has him gripped deep in his fear and trancelike state. Deep from the recesses of his mind, the voice screams then utters, "You see all this Ma'tao?! You are the reason that your loved ones and your beloved islands are in such peril! Though you caused all this pain and suffering, I'm willing to undo everything you've done. All these dire situations and events could go back to as if they never existed, but that all depends upon you!"

Ma'tao, now so drained and drenched in fear, looks at all the chaos going on around him. He then whispers, "What? What do I need to do?"

The voice even now more sinister with its sly, slow, wicked, maniacal tone says, "It's effortless, and like I said, up to you Ma'tao! You can easily restore all the things in your life that you love! All you have to do is hand over your Ka'lang I Man Metgot and the Diyuk Paton Chaifi! Hand them over willingly and renounce your claim as the Maga'lahi I Mantatkilu! Do that, and all this pain will seize to exist."

Ma'tao, engulfed in so much fear that his body is rendered useless! His thoughts seem to be his only connection to his very existence. And just like that, those seem to give way as Itak floods his mind!

Ma'tao, being forced to view all of the atrocities that Itak has caused all humankind throughout the generations! All the suffering and bloodshed takes its toll and becomes too much for him to bear!

Itak's evil power is strangling his life essence. Ma'tao, barely able to speak, utters a very painful, "Never." At those words, Itak squeezes him harder and releases its full power of dark energy into Ma'tao.

His body is now practically lifeless! In a state of delirium and with this fear gripping him tighter while setting in deeper. Ma'tao tries with all his might and every last ounce of strength to focus, but nothing seems to work. He starts to feel himself slipping away. He is slipping away into what he senses as a deep dark nothingness!

He asks himself one last question, as he fades towards that deep dark abyss. *Is this what my life amounted to? Does it all end here?*

Every breath he takes after that is weaker than the one before. As he slips further. Deep. Dark. Nothingness!

Then out of nowhere. A loud thunderous clap! The roar of it is so immense that it affects everything around him! It is so loud and practically deafening! It was also thundering enough to jolt and keep his existence intact.

A loud painful scream from that devil of a bird! A call from a woman's voice follows after. A voice that he has heard before! But this time, she follows it up by calling his name, "Ma'tao!"

He looks around to see who it is. He is still dazed but then feels someone grab onto his arm.

Ma'tao, barely even conscious at this point, opens up his eyes and sees her! He thinks to himself, Who is she?

As beautiful as she is, she does not seem familiar to him. He could only liken her to a dream. She appears to be an ally!

But here in this realm, things are not really what they seem to be! *Who is she?* He thinks again.

She pulls him by the arm, and with much haste, says, "You must get it together! Itak took your friends and will be back for you! Hurry! We need to go. And we need to go now!"

She leads the way while dragging him by the arm in tow. Ma'tao stumbling as he places one foot in front of the other. Something strange starts to happen! He instantly notices that the further away they get, the less Itak's stronghold of fear is within him!

But he is not out of the woods yet. She leads them out of the main cave path that they are on into a crevice between the rocks!

He now feels his senses coming back. Without a second to spare, he anxiously demands, "I've seen you before. Who are you?"

She looks deep into his eyes, then smiles and looks away. Then with a loving, concerned voice says, "That's not important now. How are you feeling?"

Ma'tao, now more composed, replies, "Much better. What happened back there?"

She looks around and peers out of the aperture. She hurriedly turns back to Ma'tao, saying, "Itak is so much more powerful than before! I've seen its power grow exponentially throughout all the years I've been its prisoner. The spell that monstrosity cast upon you and your friends place doubts along with terror within its host! It brings to the forefront the greatest fear within the person's mind!"

Ma'tao notices a certain sense of calmness come over himself around this woman's presence. It is as if he and she are connected somehow.

He stares with more intent as he asks, "How did you manage to free me from it?"

She looks back into his eyes with the same intensity and replies, "We can't ever succumb to fear! That's Itak's greatest strength. The power to overcome that fear with faith and love has always been within you. Itak didn't account for that! All I did was help draw it out of you."

While trying to make sense of all that is happening, Ma'tao asks, "How do we get to its nest?"

She steps away out of the crevice once more, then turns back around, saying, "We're already here. I may have bought us a little time, but Itak will be onto us soon!"

He raises one hand to feel if his Ka'lang is still on his neck. With a deep breath, he displays a sigh of relief while feeling it unharmed. And with the other, he reaches for the sling and the adze around his waist.

He briefly smiles and thinks, *Yes, they're still with me.*

But his joy lasts only seconds as he notices something's missing!

Ma'tao, now more worried, thinks, *My pouch of stones! The stone! I don't have it!*

He looks around frantically, but it is nowhere in sight! He turns to rush out of their hiding place as the woman launches at him and grabs his arm tight, asking, "Is this what you're looking for?"

He stops in his tracks and is about to relax, but places that reaction on hold as he responds, "Yes!"

She hands him the pouch as he opens it without haste. Now he could breathe another sigh of relief as he finds the Diyuk Paton Chaifi among the other stones!

She smiles at him, and with a longing voice, says, "It's hard to believe That you're in front of me now. It's been long-awaited." She pauses as she collects herself.

Then with tears running down the side of her face. She falls to her knees and continues softly, saying, "That stone, along with that Ka'lang in the hands of a true son of Guahan. Here to finally set things right. I never really thought I'd live to see that day."

With those words she utters, he immediately feels a deep connection to her grief and longing.

Then with his back facing the entrance, he bends down to help her up.

He then asks again, "Who are you?" She looks back, and with a more profound gaze into his eyes, replies, "Ma'tao, I'm—" But before she could even finish her sentence, A loud devilish scream emanates from behind them!

Suddenly he feels a strong gust of wind from behind him; it instantly fills the area! Skin piercing talons grab Ma'tao on both shoulders as he screams in horrific pain!

He is then brutally whisked away out of the aperture and up within the deep cavernous space!

As this beastly black monster takes him higher. Ma'tao hears that malicious voice of Itak within his mind saying, "You're in my world now! To escape is hopeless!" He knows that he needs to react quickly! He cannot afford to let Itak regain that type of control over him, mentally and physically!

He grabs his adze with a viselike grip while ignoring the talons' unbearable pain penetrating his skin. It is also hard for him to maintain his equilibrium as Itak swings him with so much savagery while maintaining that deathly grip!

Ma'tao grunts in pain while being slammed up against the jagged limestone rocks! The evil beast starts pecking deep and hard into his legs! But despite all the brutality, Ma'tao endures!

He could also see that he is very high up from the ground and to fall from this height could quickly kill him! So he clutches both feet together as he twists and turns to avoid those deadly blows from Itak's beak!

He then crunches his body together tightly. Then with such precision and timing, he sees Itak positioning to come in for another death peck.

As Itak's beak is about to break more skin, Ma'tao launches a powerful, deadly blow of his own to the bottom of this feathered black monster's neck!

Sounds of Itak's bones cracking and dislocating could be heard throughout the entire space! The black feathery beast caws in pain as it releases its death grip!

Ma'tao starts to fall hard and fast, towards the rugged cave floor below! He sees a bunch of jagged limestone rocks directly under him! They will easily cause some severe damage or possible death from the height he is falling!

Within that moment, as he is plummeting towards his death, that absolute peace he felt earlier comes stronger from deep within and envelopes him completely!

A thought flashes so brightly at the forefront of his mind, and he knows. Not just some inkling, he full-on knows! He knows that he will be alright!

It is then, at that exact moment, as he is about to hit those pointed sharp rocks that new powers are released! Other gifts from the gods!

Within just a few inches of becoming shredded flesh, Ma'tao comes to a dead stop and starts to hover! He manipulates his weight in space and becomes light as a feather!

He very gently softens his landing as he kneels on a clear area on the cave floor. His body has also taken on that yellowish golden glow, which transforms his skin into hard, impenetrable stone!

He receives these two new powers from the Ka'lang I Man Metgot coming together synergistically with the Diyuk Paton Chaifi and released through him!

No other Maga'lahi has ever been able to unleash that type of power before. Ma'tao is now in a state of oneness never before seen! It is also that level of physicality, spirituality, and consciousness that he needs to become one with, to save all he loves. He is now one step closer to fulfilling his destiny!

But first things first. Ma'tao then takes a deep breath and slowly opens his warrior chieftain eyes. He exhales at a slow pace as he focuses on that black evil abomination diving from above towards him.

The massive typhoon like wind Itak creates by every flap of its monstrous feathery appendages draws up dirt and debris as it zeroes in on Ma'-tao!

Unfazed and in such a state of zen, Ma'tao unwraps the sling and positions himself. He is ready for the encounter as Itak inches closer by the second.

He places the Diyuk Paton Chaifi within the Atupat Aniti and centers himself much deeper!

He hears that god awful scream in front of him but still keeps such poise!

This ancient demonic monster is now entirely focused on clawing Ma'tao and crushing him to death! But Ma'tao is pure calmness and strength while steady throughout his entire being!

He stands firm welcoming this epic collision, especially with his new rock-solid glowing body armor! It is a battle of wills as Itak draws closer.

Ma'tao slows and controls his breathing as he becomes one with his thoughts, saying, *You have caused so much pain and suffering to my island and my people for far too long, you evil beast! But more importantly, my love Atani! Your reign of terror ends now!*

With the sling locked and loaded, he lets it hang off to his side. He accurately judges the distance between them both! Now staring deep into Itak's eyes as he watches and calculates every movement. And with the precise balance of strength and control. He brings the Atupat Aniti from down on his side to up overhead. He creates that perfect revolution with this ultimate sling!

Complete and utter silence. Ma'tao then takes one deep breath. He then exhales and shouts, "Ginen I Minetgot Puntan Yan I Na'liheng Fu'una!" While he releases with all his might, the Diyuk Paton Chaifi from the sling!

A thunderous crash follows as it separates from the Atupat Aniti! It travels at lightning flash speed, racing effortlessly towards Itak! The vile black beast is so full of rage that it solely focuses on ripping Ma'tao! Itak completely ignores the deadly sling stone rushing towards him!

The demon black bird's eyes are now blazing fiery red as it lets out another devilish yell while darting even faster towards its target!

Ma'tao now knows it is only a matter of time. He did all he could do and now braces for the impact as he stands firmly in place, glowing much brighter while standing steady and strong!

The Diyuk Paton Chaifi is now in Itak's line of sight, closing the gap ever so quickly! Itak now sees the stone! Knowing the power it possesses, it tries to maneuver out of the way, but it is already too late!

The Diyuk Paton Chaifi clashes with Itak with such tremendous power! Hitting its mark, Itak's chest, dead center! The stone burns and blasts through the monster's thick black leathery feathers as it buries itself like butter deep into its grotesque flesh!

Itak is completely stunned! Having never felt anything like it ever before, it releases the loudest, horrific, nightmarish scream!

The sling stone rips more flesh driving itself inward towards Itak's black heart!

The earth starts shaking so violently as Itak continues its trajectory towards Ma'tao!

The wound within the beast starts spewing out thick, dark blood like it was rain! While the smell of burning flesh and feathers fill the air!

Itak's rage and hatred for all life now embody the beast! It opens up its talons wide to take out and end Ma'tao. The impact is inevitable!

Boom! Another thunderous explosion, followed by immense white light! The collision is otherworldly as it rocks everything around them! Both Ma'tao and Itak disappear within the blinding light!

Chapter 18

"The Reveal!"

Slowly, everything starts to dissipate. The bright light starts to dim as dust, ash, and feathers trickle-down gently from the fallout. It covers the whole cavern and also Ma'tao, who slowly begins to appear once the dust settles. The smell of burnt flesh and feathers permeates the air.

Now coughing and with a splitting headache. Ma'tao thinks to himself, What just happened? Am I still alive?

He becomes more aware and recollects what has happened. He immediately remembers that great collision with Itak.

He opens his eyes while slowly stumbling to get to his feet. He could barely even see three feet in front of him due to the dirt and debris from the fallout. He then says aloud, "How am I still alive? That collision. Itak!"

Just then, he hears someone coughing and calling out for help. There! Up ahead in the distance. It sounds like a woman. And her voice sounds very familiar.

He composes himself as he makes his way towards her. Clearing away the dirt and ashes in the air, he now sees the woman coming into view as she utters in pain, "Over here."

She begins sobbing while saying, "I'm glad you found me. I thought I was all alone."

Ma'tao approaches cautiously. He rubs the ash away from his face as she starts coming closer into view. He sees her. *Could it be? But how?* He asks himself.

Ma'tao then shouts as he hurries to get to her, "Atani! Atani! But how?" Before he could say anything else. She sees and reaches out to him and cries, "Ma'tao! Help me, Ma'tao! Hurry!"

He instantly notices that she has a big wound on her abdomen and is bleeding profusely!

Ma'tao rushes to her side, drops to his knees, and pulls Atani close to him. He then, in a panic-stricken voice, says, "What happened to you? Just breathe. I'm here now. I've got you."

Atani looks at her wound and makes a desperate attempt to try and stop the bleeding. With her blood-covered hand and in excruciating pain, she grabs onto his arm!

She clings to him tighter, signaling to him to bring his face closer to hers. With tears running down both their eyes, all is silent around them.

She uses every last ounce of energy to bring her shaking lips up towards his ear. With slight coughs and shallow breathing, she painfully utters, "We don't have much time. There's only one way to stop this. You have the power to save me."

Ma'tao, who had just gained his consciousness and awareness, starts feeling paralyzed. In seeing Atani in this state, all his doubts start creeping back into his mind.

He then painfully says back to her, "This can't be. I started all of this for us. You can't leave my side, my love. What do I need to do to stop this?"

Atani looks at Ma'tao then closes her eyes. With shallow breaths, she coughs. She continues softly yet painfully whispering, "Your Ka'lang."

She pauses to catch her breath as Ma'tao is now losing himself, as panic is now setting in deeper. Because Atani, his love is slipping away.

The situation is dire as the darkness starts closing in on Ma'tao and Atani's bodies. With tears rolling down his cheeks, his voice slightly cracks from crying as he utters, "How Atani? How could my Ka'lang stop this? Tell me, please. What do I need to do?"

She then softly says while still wincing in pain, "You need to take it off and hand it to me. It will heal me and return everything to the way it was."

Ma'tao, now overshadowed with darkness, grief, fear, and regret. He moves his hands to his neck. Reaching for the Ka'lang I Man Metgot, the pendant that initiated all this. He was not about to let his love, slip away. Not if he could do anything about it.

He is about to unclasp it from the back of his neck when he hears her yell to him, "Ma'tao! No, Ma'tao!"

He stops! It is her. The voice from his calling! Ma'tao looks in her direction. She is frantically running towards him, shouting, "Don't do it, my son! She is not who you think she is!"

Again she shows up when all hope seems futile! He thinks to himself. Then at that moment, Ma'tao recalls what Maga'lahi Hineti said to him, "When the darkness seems to have overtaken you, that's when the light comes bursting in!"

Ma'tao now starts coming to grips with everything he now truly knows, and by piecing it together, as he utters the word, "Mother?"

As she darts towards his direction, he looks down again at Atani. But this time, she is no longer in his arms!

In her place is a vile half human half beast covered in flames and ash! This horrific creature is Itak! Itak's lower body is badly mangled and useless with both legs broken! But this monster is still alive and breathing!

Ma'tao, upon noticing that, immediately pushes the beast off of him as he jumps to his feet! Itak reaches for him as it nearly got its hands around the Ka'lang!

Ma'tao then kicks the demonic creature so hard that it flies thirty feet across the cave, hitting the jagged cave walls! It is down, but not out!

Itak picks itself up with its arms at it crawls towards Ma'tao in a hurried pace, in a disjointed demonic fashion!

Lumu'ina, still running towards him, yells, "Here, Ma'tao! Take this!" Ma'tao notices that she has the Higam I Saina in hand, and he reaches out to catch it as she throws it to him!

He grabs it mid-air as she again yells to him, saying, "You need to rip out its heart from its body and destroy it!"

Ma'tao then turns around to face Itak as it is now charging towards him at a quicker pace, followed by horrific screams!

Itak's eyes are still burning fiery red as it now is so enraged! And with its razor-like claws on each of its hands, along with saliva dripping off its sharp bloodied fangs. Ma'tao could now see the true essence of this demonic creature that wants to eliminate him!

Itak then grabs onto his leg! And while gripping so tight, it slices it before Ma'tao could get away! The pain is excruciating!

Ma'tao bites his lip as he ignores the pain. He then focuses all his power and energy as he grips the adze even tighter! He then brings it up over his head and hacks it down with such brute force through Itak's shoulder blade!

With the adze embedded within its bloodied back, Ma'tao grabs the arm that has his leg! He pulls out the adze with so much savagery that it completely severs Itak's arm from its body! Again the demonic creature screams in agony!

After ripping off its arm, Ma'tao could now see Itak's still beating black heart. And lodged next to it is the Diyuk Paton Chaifi!

He does not even hesitate as he reaches in deep! His hands penetrate deep into the demonic creature's rib cage!

He grabs ahold of Itak's black heart along with the sling stone and savagely rips them out in such brutal fashion! The beast releases another horrific scream as Ma'tao, now bloodied and bruised, kneels in front of the still-beating black heart!

With the remnants of this demonic creature flailing in front of him, Ma'tao grasps the mighty sling stone within both his hands and brings it above his head. And with an all-powerful yell, he shouts,

"Ginen I Minetgot Puntan Yan I Na'liheng Fu'una!"

He then jams the stone, hard dead center into the demonic creature's life source! Itak gives one last dreadful cry as its black heart bursts into flames!

Both Itak's corpse and its heart turn to ash then disintegrate into purplish-black smoke as it disappears! Itak is now dead and defeated.

Lumu'ina runs up to her son, who is still pounding on the very ground where the heart once was. She holds him, saying, "There there now. I got you."

Ma'tao slams the area a couple more times as he drops the stone. With tears still in his eyes, he turns to Lumu'ina and softy asks, "Atani, Atdao, Ina, and Magogui. Where are they?"

She lifts his chin as she looks him in the eyes, saying, "First of all, are you alright?" Ma'tao cannot bring himself to look her straight in the eyes and turns his face as he asks her, "Are they safe?"

She turns his face towards her as she replies, "I'll take you to them."

He then, with nervousness in his voice, softly asks, "Is it really you? Are you my mother?"

With tears rolling down her eyes and while barely able to reply, she softly says, "Yes, Ma'tao. You finally found and saved me."

Ma'tao, now staring into her tear-filled eyes, asks, "So you have been here all these years?"

Now, all choked up and trying to regain her composure. She bravely replies, "Yes. I've been here. Holding onto that hope that your path will lead you here, back to me."

Ma'tao is still trying to let everything he just heard, along with what they just went through, settle in. He looks back into her eyes as he says, "I'm so sorry, I should've been there for you."

She holds both his hands as she guides him to stand. She then hugs him so tight, not wanting ever to let go.

He wipes the tears from her eyes away. And while choked up himself, he hugs her back while saying, "Thank you for holding on. I've got you now. We have so much to catch up on."

Lumu'ina takes another in-depth look into her son's eyes just to let it all soak in, as she says,

"Yes, we do, and we will. But first things first. Let's get your friends!"

Ma'tao gathers himself as he looks again into his mother's eyes and gently says, "Lead the way. Now that we found each other, I ain't letting you out of my sight." She takes her son's hand and leads him back to the aperture within the cave.

As they stand in the middle, she turns to face him, saying, "This area is a portal. It's an entrance to another dimension in which Itak used to imprison us all. It is where I've been all these years."

She then grabs her necklace, and while showing it to Ma'tao, says, "This pendant was a gift from my father. I didn't know of its significance until a couple of weeks ago. It's like it came alive! It must have been around the same time you acquired your Ka'lang I Man Metgot, because that's when I started dreaming of you!"

She then reaches out and holds the Ka'lang I Man Metgot as Ma'tao places his hands on her pendant. Immediately both pendants light up a beautiful yellowish gold! The energy then flows and envelopes both of them. Suddenly the thin veil of the dimension they were in vanishes, exposing another dimension. They are now standing in the cave that served as Itak's prison!

As the yellowish gold energy dissipates from around them, Ma'tao looks around and notices torches along the cliff walls giving just a hint of light to this dark and dreary supernatural place.

In between each torch, he notices human-sized slits embedded within the cave walls. Lumu'ina points towards that area and sadly says, "Here my son is where I've been a prisoner all these years. Every person confined here is someone that Itak can take the form of and deceive the living in the physical realm. This dimension we're in is just one of many. Your friends are over there."

She then takes Ma'tao by the hand and leads him while saying, "Your Ka'lang combined with who you are have freed me from that deep dark sleep."

She then points towards the walls as Ma'tao runs up to them excitedly. For in them, he finds Atdao, Ina, and Magogui!

Lumu'ina then yells, "Your other two friends are here!" As she moved further down and points to Pulonon and Machatlu!

They are each separated upright within their dark, dreary limestone sarcophagus! They are not awake, but he notices they are breathing.

Ma'tao also notices that they are so still and practically lifeless. Their eyes are also glazed over with a milky gloss sheen, while their skin is also a very pale white.

Ma'tao anxiously asks, "What's wrong with them? Are they alright?!" She then says, "Don't worry, my son. They are all fine."

As she says that, the Ka'lang I Man Metgot glows brighter. She then says to Ma'tao, "The Ka'lang I Manganiti controls the necklaces they are wearing. You are the only one of can sever its control over them. The Ka'lang I Man Metgot saved me and will save them as well!"

Ma'tao, now hearing what he needed. He does not even hesitate and rips it off of them so quickly while destroying each pendant with his bare hands! He waits. But not for long, as they all cough while taking in that very precious breath of life! Their eyes regain their natural colors as their beautiful brown tone returns to their skin.

Ma'tao grabs Atdao, and while looking deep into his eyes, says, "My brother, can you hear me? Are you alright?"

Atdao, along with the others, starts to regain their consciousness. He then says with a look of confusion, "Ma'tao? Yeah, I think I am. Where are we? The last place I remember being in the Sesonyan Pribidu."

He then starts looking around hurriedly as he shouts, "Ina! Have you seen her?" He then feels a tap from behind as he hears a voice say, "Hey, lower your voice. No need to shout. I have a splitting headache."

He turns around with so much joy because it is Ina who instantly grabs him! They embrace ever so tightly, both with tears in their eyes as Atdao softly says, "I thought I lost you! Are you alright?"

She utters, "Yes. I'm fine now." As he hugs her tighter, another voice calls out to them, saying,

"I don't think I'll ever leave you again considering all that has just happened."

They turn around to see Pulonon heading towards them with a big smile on his face. Atdao smiles at Ina while they release their embrace. He then greets Pulonon by placing his forehead up against his, followed by a long-awaited hug.

Pigan, leader of the Chochogo' band of Taotao Man Nanu, is among them along with Machatlu, Guafi, and Maga'lahi Mata'pang.

The group acknowledges that they are all alive and well, as Ma'tao anxiously visits each of the limestone prison cells. To release anyone else who Itak placed under that soulless spell of a trance. All the while thinking to himself, *Where is she? Hanumta stated I need to defeat Itak! And I did! She must be here!* He frantically looks around with the hope of locating Atani's life essence to bring her out of suspended animation.

Atdao takes notice, asking, "Ma'tao, it seems like everyone is already here. Shouldn't we hurry and get out of this hell hole and meet up with Atani?"

Lumu'ina holds her son's hand as she whispers, "She's who you are searching for, right?" Ma'tao, still looking around, turns to her and anxiously asks, "Yes. I need to locate her life essence! I need to save her."

Atdao grabs Ma'tao, and now more worried, asks, "Where's Atani Ma'tao? Did something happen to my sister? Tell me now!"

Ina grabs Atdao, saying, "Calm down. We all just went through a traumatic event and are all still alive! Give Ma'tao some space to let him explain."

Ma'tao, now looking more distraught, looks at Ina, nods, then faces Atdao saying, "She is still alive. If it weren't for her, we wouldn't be talking with each other right now. Her physical body, which is in suspended animation, is being looked over and protected by our warriors. Her life essence, which Itak stole, needs to be reunited with her to break the spell. I will locate it to bring her back! Mark my word!"

Lumu'ina then pulls her son close then says, "That woman you speak of, Atani. Her life essence was here, but Asuli took that pendant with him as he fled this area! She must be someone of great significance to you. Am I right?"

Ma'tao looks back at her and replies, "Not only to me but to our island and people! Do you have any idea where he fled to?"

Pulonon then interjects, saying, "Ma'tao, while I was under Itak's spell, I was able to get a glimpse of who is really behind all of this! Asuli, just like Su'ihan, is just a pawn."

Pigan then adds, "They're right. I feel while we were all under, we all shared the same visions to an extent. There is a greater evil force behind all this!"

Lumu'ina then says, "Yes, there is! As your Ka'lang was breaking the spell of Itak's trance over me while you were getting closer. I overheard Asuli. He was so enraged that he started lashing out, saying. That because you now have in your possession your Ka'lang and that sling stone. The balance between the forces of good and evil is once again shifting. And by you defeating Itak. You Ma'tao, have come closer than anyone in restoring that balance!"

Upon hearing that, Pulonon then states, "That's why they took Atani's life essence! Keeping that part of Atani under their control is their way of trying to control you."

Pigan then says, "Don't lose hope, Ma'tao. You have displayed the true spirit of the Maga'lahi I Mantatkilu. Stay strong. My people and I are with you!"

Despite all the encouragement, Ma'tao is still hurting. And with more profound pain within his heart. Along with tears in his eyes, he asks, "Who is behind this? What's his name, and where can I find him!"

Just then, all space and time come to a complete standstill! Everyone around them has become frozen in time within their last movements and standing completely still. Suddenly the ground within this dimension starts shaking under his feet while splitting in two right in front of him!

Fire and lava start spewing out from what Ma'tao could now perceive as the depths of hell! As the strong, pungent smell of sulfur fills the air!

Ma'tao then focuses the power within himself and his Ka'lang to create a force field around all present. To protect them from the lava and fire rushing towards them at great speed!

He covers them all with the power of the Ka'lang I Man Metgot just in time!

Then he notices something: something or someone coming out from within the deep dark depths. A shadowy figure starts to appear! It is the same sinister, shadowy figure that appeared when Pigan was within the Liyang Taifinakpo'!

The dark, ominous figure rises profoundly from the hellish depths below as it floats to-wards Ma'tao so effortlessly. Ma'tao tries to make out what this shadowy creature is as it lands standing directly in front of him!

Electrical sparks of gold and purple start to emit around them as both energies come into close contact with one another. A figure begins to appear out of the evil black haze of shadows!

As it comes closer into view and reveals himself, Ma'tao is in utter shock! Because who he is now looking at really confuses him. He finally composes himself as he dubiously says, "Saina? Puntan? But how? Or why?"

The evil entity just demonically laughs as he sarcastically says, "Oh, how he wishes he could be me. For if he were, he wouldn't be such a drag!"

Ma'tao, after hearing him speak, instantly knew that this evil force is not Puntan! It is just someone or something that looks like him, and in a demanding voice, says, "Who are you? Where is Atani's life force?"

This evil force paces in front of Ma'tao but cannot reach him due to the force field from the Ka'lang I Man Metgot.

So from where he stands, he maniacally says, "It finally seems that my brother has finally found himself a worthy champion! No one has ever taken out Itak! And by using my personalized Diyuk Patu in the process, for that matter. I've got to hand it to you and your loyal followers, Ma'tao. That was very ingenious! Especially you for having the gall to try and even face me!"

Ma'tao then curiously asks, "So you're Puntan's twin brother? And if you created that sling stone, you must be Chaifi? No offense, but you mustn't be that important because he didn't mention you were brothers!" As he finishes off with a sarcastic laugh himself.

Chaifi laughs it off, saying, "None taken. After eons of disagreements, I'm not surprised. Tell you what, Ma'tao. I'm going to make this short and sweet since you managed to take it this far. But don't get too cocky just yet."

He very slowly paces back and forth in front of Ma'tao as he says, "So far, you have proven to be a formidable opponent."

Ma'tao stops him there as he shouts, "Do you think that this is all some sort of game?! Where is Atani?!"

While smiling and in a very maniacal demeanor, Chaifi says, "Funny, you should say, because it is. It's always been a game! Because for you humans, our creations to even think you have the innate ability to put a stop to my plans! Well, first of all, that pisses the hell out of me, no pun intended. And second, your Atani seems to be a worthy prize. A way for me to up the ante in our current predicament."

Ma'tao is now burning with so much rage that he takes deeper breaths to control his breathing.

He then recollects what Atani said about not fighting more evil with evil. He then centers himself, focuses, and calmly says, "What is it that you want? If it's me, take me instead!"

Chaifi then hellishly shouts, "Take you! I could have very easily taken you!" Then just quick as he shows his flaming hot temper, he brings it back down to ice cool and continues saying, "But this game's number one player is going to get a shot! A chance to win back his love. If that's what you want? It is what you want, is it not?"

Ma'tao, now looking straight at Chaifi and angrily replies, "If it's Asuli you want me to beat!

Please bring him here to me now! And I promise I won't disappoint you!"

Knowing that Ma'tao already bested Asuli once, Chaifi chuckles and says, "I like your spirit. Don't let go of that. You'll meet up with him again soon, I can assure you! But what I have in store for you, Ma'tao, I think you'll enjoy. Because I know I will!"

Chaifi, now just inches away from the force field between them. He decides to get now up close and personal. Their eyes are now completely deadlocked. And non of them flinch as Chaifi chuckles again, saying, "Stare hard Ma'tao and really look deep, because I want you to meet my champion! But just like everything else so far, you Ma'tao are going to have to earn the right to face him!"

Ma'tao, while staring back deeper into Chaifi's soulless eyes, starts to see glimpses of all the suffering that Chaifi himself was responsible for unleashing throughout the whole world, including his islands and his people!

He even revisits what he saw earlier with all the villages of his beloved islands preparing for the great war!

Ma'tao then feels that very uneasy feeling of fear starting to creep back into his entire being. He then sees an unclear silhouette image of a great humanlike giant of a man-beast! In these images that Chaifi is projecting hard into his mind, this demonic creature is wreaking havoc and ripping apart human bodies while enjoying every moment of it! This monster is leaving bloodshed everywhere he stands!

Chaifi, in knowing he is starting to infect the mind of Ma'tao once again psychotically laughs while saying, "Now come towards your so-called destiny Ma'tao if you dare! Consider this as my personal invitation to you, if you have the guts! Then show up! The game starts when you find the entrance of my transdimensional cave."

While still slowly pacing back and forth, trying to intimidate Ma'tao. He continues saying, "I'm feeling competitive today, so I'll give you a hint. You can locate it somewhere around Sasalaguan. But I'm not going to spoil all the fun as to what it'll take you through! I can guarantee this, though, if you have what it takes, and with all the faith that my brother and sister placed in you. You might have a chance! But don't get too ahead of yourself. That's just cockiness, and how I really despise your cockiness! But pass what I have in store for you. And I promise not to disappoint you! You then just might have the esteemed pleasure to meet my champion!"

Chaifi now senses the energy of the force field starting to wane. So he pushes harder within his mind to infect Ma'tao as he sadistically says, "He was one of the first-ever to step foot on your beloved Guahan the first man! My Taotao Mona! My champion, Anufat! He had done my bidding before you human beings were even a thought!"

Chaifi, now more boastful and unleashing more anger, says, "How petty for you humans to even think you could step up to us immortals! Also, to be so disrespectful by stealing fire from me! And to not even be grateful by giving me, one of your creators, the very soul who stole it! I will make you! All of you feel my wrath!"

Ma'tao could now really feel the intense negative energy starting to overpower him! But he needs to hold on. Because of the fire and lava, he is protecting his people from, now creeps in, threatening to harm them!

Ma'tao digs deeper as his Ka'lang grows brighter! Then as the intensity of Chaifi's power increases, a loud majestic yell calls out from beyond, "Enough! Enough Chaifi!"

Following right after, a beautiful bright blue flash of energy synergistically melds with Ma'tao and his life force and pushes back against Chaifi!

Instantly Chaifi lets down his power and non-chalantly paces back and forth once again. He then very humorously says, "Hineti! Oh, Hineti. I was wondering when you would show. What my brother or sister can't face me themselves?"

Ma'tao is so thrilled that Maga'lahi Hineti is now there by his side! To meet with Chaifi was not something Ma'tao had prepared for, let alone intended.

Hineti quickly checks to see if his great-great-grandson is alright, which he acknowledges he is with a slight nod and a sigh of relief. Hineti, now infuriated, turns to Chaifi and shouts, "Why?! So all of you could battle it out and destroying what you all work so hard together to create in the process?! Your brother and sister both have a much better sense of reasoning than that!"

Chaifi just smirks as he replies, "So just like always. They send Hineti to pick up after themselves. It would be best if you thought about coming to work for me. I promise to make it worth your while!" Hineti just ignores Chaifi and stands firm by the side of Ma'tao.

Chaifi looks them all over one last time as he scoffs while looking at Ma'tao, saying, "I'd really like to stay and chat, but my schedule is pretty tight! You know, places to blow! People to eat!"

He then snickers sadistically, saying, "Think about it, Ma'tao! So much is riding on that choice. Especially in Atani's life! Hope to see you soon!"

Then just as quick as he appeared, Chaifi vanishes back down to his hellish underworld! Along with the fire, lava, and all his other infernal elements!

Ma'tao then breathes as everyone else around them reanimate from their time frozen state. And instantly, they are all shocked to see Maga-'lahi Hineti standing by his side!

Lumu'ina runs to Ma'tao with Magogui trailing behind as everyone else gathers around them.

They are in awe of the presence of Maga'lahi Hineti, along with the aura he is projecting!

Atdao, in astonishment, asks, "Ma'tao isn't he —" Before Atdao could finish his sentence, Ma'-tao says, "Yes, he's Maga'lahi Hineti. My great-great-grandfather!"

Ma'tao then turns back to Hineti and asks, "How's it that they could see you now, but not before? Wait, is it because we're in the spiritual realm?"

Hineti then looks around at everyone saying, "Exactly. And this is just one of its many dimensions, but this is my first time in this one. Chaifi kept this location well hidden. To be used as

Itak's prison. For if it weren't for the connection that our pendants maintain with one another, I probably wouldn't have ever located you!"

He then turns to look at Lumu'ina, and while gently touching her hand, he says, "We finally found you." With a slight look of confusion, she asks, "Aren't you, my great grandfather?"

Hineti responds, "Yes. The time is now upon us all, and it's time they both know. From this moment on, the bonds of our roots will be strengthening!" He says that while looking into the eyes of Lumu'ina, Ma'tao, and Magogui! Lumu'ina looks into her great grandfather's eyes and nods while acknowledging what he said.

Ma'tao looks at Hineti then to his mother as if there is something that he needs to know. But he places that thought aside for the moment and addresses the group saying, "Itak is no longer a threat! And though we are a step closer, we still have ways to go! A great war is brewing, and we all need to work together and fast! We need to prevent our villages and islands from going down that path! A greater evil force which presented itself has made known of his true intentions and hatred for the human race! And he will spare no one!"

He then looks to Atdao and sadly states, "If we don't put a stop to this. The two villages that will set that war into motion on Guahan are Ati and Humatak. But that's only the beginning! The northern islands are gathering their forces and creating alliances. They are planning to capitalize on the bloodshed of what the Southern Islands will start! As to who are now friends or foes, we all need to hurry in making that distinction! We will all need to cooperate and stop these embers from igniting into an all-out hell-storm!"

Maga'lahi Hineti then says, "You have all heard what Maga'lahi Ma'tao of Chochogo' has just spoken. The Chamoru people's fate and all their islands have the opportunity to be set on a different path. By the choices that each one of you makes here! Work together as one, and there is no enemy you can't defeat!"

In that instant bright blue energy fills the space within this dimension. It is so blinding that it forces everyone around to close their eyes while shielding their face. Not even a second later, they all open them and find themselves back in Tomhom within the ancient lat'di ruins!

The sun is just rising as Ma'tao looks around at everyone, but Maga'lahi Hineti is nowhere in sight. He just snickers while saying, "That guy. He knows how to make an entrance. And his exits are just as surprising."

Atdao approaches Ma'tao and humbly says, "That does have a nice ring to it, Maga'lahi Ma'tao! Please forgive me, brother, for my actions back there. And thanks for freeing us from that prison."

Both men embrace and place their foreheads together and continue moving forward. Ma'tao then says, "I appreciate it, but there's nothing to forgive. We will save Atani and prevent this war! But that will only be possible with your support."

Maga'lahi Mata'pang says, "Maga'lahi Ma'tao, whatever you need! Tomhom is at your disposal." Ma'tao replies, "The alliance with

Tomhom and Chochogo' is a great starting point to show that anything possible. With that peace and alliance, we will set the precedence."

Both chiefs embrace and place their foreheads against one another. A great show of respect. Along with the gesture that this alliance is starting to build traction with both villages!

Ma'tao then says to Mata'pang, "There is so much good that will come from this. I need to get back to my warriors. I need to get back to Chochogo'"

Pigan then says, "Find us the nearest banyan tree, and we're good as there!" Maga'lahi Mata'-pang then says, "Follow me!" They all fall in behind him as he leads them around a jungle path to a large tree on the cliff line overlooking beautiful Tomhom bay.

As they gather around the tree, Ma'tao turns to thank Maga'lahi Mata'pang once more and says, "Please hold peace talks with your ally villages. We are facing a new dawn, and we'll meet up again soon! Thank you for everything, Maga'lahi."

Ma'tapang, very adamantly replies, "I've been thinking and considering how I, the Maga'lahi of Tomhom, had a hand in the atrocities that both our villages suffered. I want your blessings and the opportunity to escort you back to your village as a show of faith, to set things right. Once and for all."

Ma'tao, caught off guard by his request, replies, "That is entirely unexpected, but it could be a great asset to us. But would that be wise?"

Mata'pang responds, "If this will benefit Tomhom and generations to come. I will undoubtedly do my part to make sure that you, Maga'lahi Ma'tao, achieve your destiny in becoming the prophesied Maga'lahi I Mantatkilu!"

So Ma'tao and Mata'pang head into the banyan tree. They are followed by Atdao, Ina, Lumu'ina, Magogui, Pulonon, and Machatlu as they are lead by Pigan back to Liyang Taifinakpo'!

Pigan guides them down a path with a couple of twists and turns, and before they know it, an opening suddenly appears. Pigan exits, and they all follow.

As soon they all are out of the banyan, shouts of joy and excitement immediately greet them! It is Tiani, along with her and Pigan's warriors, who have been guarding the banyan tree on their end.

Both Ma'tao and Machatlu are ecstatic because they arrived back at the same tree. Ma'tao makes his greetings brief as he rushes off to see Atani and the rest of his warriors.

While rushing into the cave where he last left her, Aligao runs up to him, shouting with excitement, saying, "Ma'tao! You're back."

Ma'tao, just as excited to see his best bud, grabs Aligao and hugs him, saying, "I may be late, but you know me."

He now, with a very concerned look, asks, "Has she improved?" Aligao goes from excited to somber replying, "She looks the same as when you left. But she is still breathing, though."

Ma'tao, let's go of Aligao, pats him on the shoulder, and heads over to kneel beside the body of his love. He acknowledges Da'on, who is standing vigilant by her side. By a touch to the side of his arm as a gesture of thanks. He also gives a smile of appreciation to Hanumta, who has not left Atani's side and has been sharp-eyed herself.

With tears rolling down his cheek and a choked-up throat, he bends over slowly, picks up her head, and places it on his lap. He then gives a soft kiss to her forehead as he caresses her hand within his. He could also sense her breathing, but her body feels cold to the touch.

He moves his face towards her ear, and with pain in his heart, whispers saying, "It looks like it might take just a little longer than we expected, my love. But remember, I'm never going to leave your side. It's just you and me."

He could barely finish that sentence with that excruciating internal pain from within. Ma'tao feels a hand touch him on the back, which gives him instant peace. He turns slowly to see Lumu'ina along with the rest of his warriors.

He wipes his tears as Hanumta takes Atani's head from him and places her slowly back down. He stands up as Lumu'ina hugs her son, and with an encouraging voice, says, "I held on for all these years, my son. From what I heard and now have seen. Atani is doing the same. If there is one thing I could say, cherish that love you both have for one another! Because that in itself will be what brings you both back together."

She hugs her son tightly as Ma'tao embraces her back in return. He then says, "Now that you and I found each other. I don't want to lose Atani. I can't lose her!"

Atdao nows sees Atani. And though he has his pain to deal with, he keeps calm. And with Ina by his side, she provides that needed strength he needs as he kneels next to his sister.

He, too, kisses her forehead while saying, "Whatever we need to do to save and bring my sister back, we'll make it happen!"

Ma'tao then turns to face his warriors while majestically saying, "Who else is with us? Who will stand with Atdao and me? To put an end to all this fear and hatred that has existed for far too long?" A resounding, "We are!" Is heard ringing throughout the cavern!

Ma'tao, with so much more magnificence and passion, continues saying, "What was once considered quests have now become my sole mission! For my real adversary has finally revealed himself! To save our loved ones, our villages, and our islands. I now know who I have to defeat! Follow me, my warriors, as we all rise! Rise as one to face this evil tyrant! For I, Maga'lahi Ma'-

tao will put an end to his reign of terror! Off to

Sasalaguan, we go!

Acknowledgments

I want to acknowledge everyone who made this second book in my Ma'tao series possible.

First of all, I would like to thank my family for all your love and support. Without you, I could have never reached my current level of success.

Secondly, to all my friends and readers for the inspiration in keeping the creativity flowing. Like I previously stated, keep it coming, and I'll keep going!

Contacts:

MykSteel.com
Myk.Steel@yahoo.com
Redulitaopublishing.com
redulitaopublishing@yahoo.com

www.ingramcontent.com/pod-product-compliance
Lightning Source LLC
Chambersburg PA
CBHW020905110726
47900CB00001B/21